Cops and Robbers

Donald E. Westlake
Cops and Robbers

Published by M. Evans and Company, Inc., New York
and distributed in association with
J. B. Lippincott Company, Philadelphia and New York

For Sandy

Cops and Robbers

· Prologue ·

I LEFT the car on Amsterdam Avenue and walked around
the corner onto West 72nd Street. With the heat the way
it was, I was glad the Police Department let its people wear
a short-sleeved shirt in the summer, open at the neck, but
I could have done without all that weight around my middle. Pistol, holster, gunbelt, flashlight, one thing after another, all dragging down on my pants and giving me an
uncomfortable bunched-up feeling around the waist. What
I would have liked most of all right then would have been
to take all my clothes off and just stand there in the street

and scratch. But in a way that would have been more against the rules than what I had in mind.

At the corner of Amsterdam and 72nd is the Lucerne Hotel, one of the spots where the bar-flies live who hang out along Broadway. Broadway between 72nd and 79th streets is lined with those narrow little bars, and every one of them is the same; the same loud jukebox, the same formica-and-plastic fixtures, the same fake Spanish decorations, the same big-breasted Puerto Rican girl behind the bar. All the losers from the single-occupancy hotels in the neighborhood spend their nights with their elbows on those bars, mooning at the barmaids, and then at closing time going back alone to their rooms to dream great seduction scenes before going to sleep. Or, if they have the money, which they usually don't, they take home with them one of the fourth-rate hookers who walk up and down Broadway waiting to substitute for the barmaids, who have lives of their own.

Along the block from the Lucerne to Broadway are a bunch of old buildings with small businesses on the ground floor and old-line tenants in the apartments upstairs; school-teachers' widows, retired grocers, aging garment workers. The small businesses include a couple of bars, a delicatessen, a dry cleaner, a liquor store; the usual collection, each with its piece of red neon in the window. *Schlitz. Hebrew National. Shirts Cleaned.* It was ten-thirty at night, so most of them were closed now with just the neon and their night lights glowing. Except the bars and the liquor store, of course, and they weren't very lively either, not on a hot midweek night in June.

Very few people were out tonight. A few kids ran around on the sidewalks, and cruising cabs ricocheted by at forty miles an hour, the drivers cooling their left elbows; everybody else was at home, in front of a fan.

The liquor store was midway to Broadway. When I

2

reached it, one look through the window past the animated snowman display told me there were no customers in there; just the Puerto Rican clerk, reading one of those illustrated paperbacks in Spanish, and a pair of winos stocking shelves in the back. I unsnapped my holster flap and went in.

All three of them glanced at me when I pushed open the door. The winos went right back to work, but the clerk kept watching me, his face empty, like everybody when they look at a cop.

The place was air-conditioned. Sweat cooled on my back, where I'd been sitting in the car. I walked over to the counter.

The PR was as neutral as gray paint. "Yes, officer?"

I took out the pistol and pointed it generally at his stomach. I said, "Give me all you got in the drawer."

I watched his face. For the first second or two, it was just shock, pure and simple. Then he made the switch of identities in his head—I was not a cop, I was a robber—and he clicked over to the new right response. "Yes, sir," he said, very fast, and turned toward the cash register. He just worked here, it wasn't his money.

In the back, the winos had stopped. They were standing there like a couple of part-melted wax statues, each of them holding two bottles of sweet vermouth. They were facing mostly toward each other, giving me their profiles, but they weren't looking at anything in particular. They definitely weren't looking toward me.

The PR was pulling stacks of bills out of the cash register and putting them on the counter; ones, then fives, then tens, then twenties. I grabbed the first stack left-handed and shoved it into my pants pocket, then switched the pistol to my left hand and did the rest with my right. Fives in my other pants pocket, tens and twenties inside my shirt.

3

The PR left the cash register open, and stood there with his hands at his sides, showing me he didn't have any immediate plans. I switched the pistol back to my right hand and put it away, but left the flap open. Then I turned around and walked to the door.

I could see them reflected in the windows in front of me. The PR didn't move a muscle. The winos were staring at me now. One of them made some sort of unfocused arm movement, gesturing with the vermouth bottle. The other one shook his head and the bottles in both his hands, and the movement died.

I left the store, and turned back toward Amsterdam. On the way, I closed the holster flap. Around the corner, I got back into the car and drove away.

• 1 •

THEY WERE on day shift then, which meant they had to face all that morning traffic on the Long Island Expressway. That was the only bad thing about living out on the Island, bucking that rush-hour traffic whenever they had day shift.

One of them was Joe Loomis; thirty-two years of age, he was a uniformed patrolman assigned to a squad-car beat with a partner named Paul Goldberg. The other was Tom Garrity; thirty-four years old, he was a detective third-

5

grade usually partnered with a guy named Ed Dantino. They were both stationed at the 15th Precinct on the West Side of Manhattan, and lived next door to one another on Mary Ellen Drive in Monequois, Long Island, twenty-seven miles from the Midtown Tunnel.

They drove into town together like this whenever their schedules worked that way, taking turns at whose car they'd use. This morning they were in Joe's Plymouth, with Joe at the wheel, dressed in uniform. Except for the hat, which he'd tossed on the back seat. Tom was in the passenger seat in his usual work clothes; a brown suit, white shirt, thin yellow tie.

Physically, they were more or less the same type, though there wouldn't be any trouble telling them apart. They were both just about six feet tall, and both a little overweight; Tom maybe twenty pounds, Joe maybe fifteen. In Tom, the weight concentrated mostly in his stomach and behind, while in Joe it spread out all over him, like baby fat. Neither of them liked to admit to themselves that they'd gained weight. Without saying anything to anybody, both of them had tried to go on diets a couple of times, but the diets never seemed to work.

Joe's hair was black, and very thick, and worn a little longer than it used to be; not so much because he wanted to be stylish with the new trends, as because it was always a boring pain in the ass to get a haircut, and these days it was possible to get pretty shaggy before anybody noticed or commented. So Joe ran longer between haircuts than he used to.

Tom's hair was brown, and thinning badly. He'd read a few years ago that taking a lot of showers sometimes caused baldness, so he'd been secretly using his wife's shower cap ever since, but the hair was still coming out. The top of his head was very thin now, with long roads of scalp showing where there used to be only a forest of hair.

6

Joe had the quicker personality of the two, rough and pragmatic, while Tom was more thoughtful and more imaginative. Joe was the one likely to get into brawls, and Tom was the one likely to calm everybody down again. And while Tom could sit almost anywhere and keep company with his thoughts, Joe needed action and movement or he'd get bored, he'd start to fidget.

As he was fidgeting now. They'd been sitting in this one spot in stalled traffic for almost five minutes, and now Joe was craning his head this way and that, trying to stare past the cars in front of him to see what was causing the tie-up. But there wasn't anything special to see; just three lanes of nobody moving. Finally, out of anger and frustration, he leaned on the horn.

The sound went through Tom's head like a blunt nail. "Don't," he said, waving one hand. "Forget it, Joe." He was too weary to be bugged by stalled traffic.

"Bastards," Joe said, and looked to his right. Over there, past Tom, he saw the car in the next lane; a pale blue brand new Cadillac Eldorado. The windows were all rolled up, and the driver was sitting in there in his air-conditioned comfort as neat and unruffled as a banker turning down a second mortgage. "Look at that son of a bitch," Joe said, and pointed with his jaw at the Caddy and the man in it.

Tom glanced over. "Yeah, I know," he said.

They both looked at him for a few seconds, envying him. He looked to be in his forties, very neatly dressed, and he faced front looking calm and untroubled; he didn't care if there was a traffic jam or not. And the way his one finger was tapping lightly on the steering wheel, he had a radio in there that worked. Probably even his dashboard clock worked.

Joe rested his left forearm on the steering wheel and glared at his watch. He said, "If we stay here without moving another sixty seconds by my watch, I'm going over there and study that Caddy and find a violation and give that son of a bitch a ticket."

Tom grinned. "Sure, sure," he said.

Joe kept frowning at his watch, but gradually his expression changed and he started to grin instead, remembering something he still couldn't get over. Still looking at the watch, but not really counting any more, he said, "Tom?"

"Yeah?"

"You remember that liquor store a couple of weeks ago, the guy that held it up disguised as a cop?"

"Sure."

Joe turned his head and looked at Tom. He was grinning very broadly now. "That was me," he said.

Tom laughed. "Sure it was," he said.

Joe moved his arm down from the steering wheel. He'd forgotten all about his watch. "No, I mean it," he said. "I had to tell somebody, you know? And who else but you?"

Tom didn't know whether he was supposed to believe it or not. Squinting at Joe as though that would help him see better, he said, "You putting me on?"

"I swear to God." Joe shrugged. "You know Grace lost her job."

"Sure."

"And Jackie's supposed to have swimming lessons this summer. Dinero, you know?" He rubbed his thumb and finger together, in the gesture that means money.

Tom was beginning to think it might be the truth. "Yeah?" he said. "So?"

"So I was thinking about it. The whole thing, the payments and the problems and the whole mess, and I just walked in and did it."

Meaning it as a question, but phrasing it like a statement, Tom said, "On the level."

8

"On a stack of Bibles. I got two hundred thirty-three bucks."

Tom started to grin. "You really did it," he said.

"Damn right."

A horn honked behind them. Joe looked front, and the traffic had moved maybe three car lengths. He shifted into drive, caught up, and shifted back into park.

Tom said, in a bemused kind of way, "Two hundred thirty-three dollars."

"That's right." Joe was feeling great, having the chance to talk about it. He said, "And you know what really amazed me?"

"No."

"Well, two things. That I'd even do it at all. The whole time, I couldn't believe it. I'm pointing a gun at this guy, I just can't believe it."

Tom nodded, encouraging him. "Yeah, yeah . . ."

"But the thing that really got me is how easy it was. You know? No resistance, no trouble, no sweat. Walk in, take it, walk out."

Tom said, "What about the guy in the store?"

Joe shrugged. "He works there. I'm pointing a gun at him. He's gonna get a medal saving the boss's dough?"

Tom shook his head. He was grinning from ear to ear, as though he'd just been told his daughter was head of her class. "I can't get over it," he said. "You really did it, you just walked in and did it."

"It was so *easy*," Joe said. "You know? To this day I can't believe how easy it was."

The traffic moved a little again. They were both quiet for a minute, but they were still both thinking about Joe's robbery. Finally Tom looked over at him, his expression serious, and said, "Joe? What do you do now?"

Joe frowned at him, not understanding the question. "What?"

9

Tom shrugged, not knowing any other way to say it. "What do you *do?* I mean, is that it?"

Joe made a barking kind of laugh. "I'm not giving it back, if that's what you mean. I spent it."

"No, I don't mean . . ." Tom shook his head, trying to find what he meant. Then he said, "Will you do it again?"

Joe started to shake his head, but then stopped and frowned, thinking it over. "Christ alone knows," he said.

• Tom •

MY FIRST squeal of the day was a robbery with assault, in an apartment over on Central Park West. Actually it was my partner, Ed Dantino, that took the call. Ed is a couple inches shorter than me and maybe ten pounds heavier, but he still has all his hair. Maybe he started using his wife's shower cap earlier than I did.

Finishing the call, Ed hung up the phone and said, "Okay, Tom. We're going for a ride."

"In this heat?" I was feeling a little queasy today, from

the beer last night. Usually a feeling like that goes away toward midmorning, but the heat and the humidity were keeping me from shaking it today. I'd been looking forward to a couple hours of relaxation in the squadroom until I felt better.

The squadroom isn't all that great. It's a big square room with plaster walls painted a really sickening green, and big globe lights hanging down from the ceiling. The room is full of desks, all of them old, no two of them alike, and a general smell of old cigars and used socks. But it's up on the second floor of the precinct house, and there's a big fan in the corner near the windows, and on hot humid days there's a little breath of air that passes through from time to time, giving a promise that life may be possible after all, if we just hang in there.

But Ed said, "It's on Central Park West, Tom."

"Oh," I said. With rich people, we make house calls. So I got to my feet and followed Ed downstairs. When we got to our car, an unmarked green Ford, he volunteered to drive and I didn't argue with him.

Going across town, I started thinking again about what Joe had told me this morning in the car. I still thought sometimes he was pulling my leg, but then I'd remember the way he'd talked about it, and I'd know for sure he'd been telling the truth.

What a crazy thing to do! Thinking of it was the only thing to make me forget my stomach. I'd be sitting there, trying to burp and not being able to, and the first thing you know I'd be grinning instead, thinking about Joe and the liquor store.

I almost told Ed, in the car, while we drove over, but finally decided not to. Actually it hadn't been very smart of Joe even to tell *me,* and God knows I wasn't going to turn him in. But the more people that know a thing, the more chance that the wrong people can find it out. Like, if I told Ed, I could be sure he wouldn't report it, but he just might tell somebody else. Who would tell somebody else, who would tell somebody else, and who knew where it would end?

But I could understand why Joe hadn't been able to stop himself from telling at least one other person about it, and I was kind of flattered I'd been the one he'd picked. I mean, we'd been friends for years, we lived next door to each other, we worked out of the same precinct, but when a guy trusts you with a secret that could put him away for maybe twenty years you *know* you've got a friend.

And a pretty wild-ass friend at that. Imagine going into a liquor store, *in uniform,* and pulling out a gun and just taking everything in the cash register! And he had to get away with it because who would believe a robber in a policeman's uniform was really a policeman?

While I meditated about Joe's Great Liquor Store Robbery, Ed drove directly over to Central Park West and turned south toward the address we wanted. He didn't have the siren on; where we were going, the crime had already been committed and the criminals had already gotten away, so there wasn't any sense of urgency. They were reporting the robbery because their insurance required it, and we were making a house call because they were rich.

I love Central Park West. On the one side there's the park, green and rolling, and on the other side the apartment buildings full of rich people, rolling in green. The East Side has become more fashionable in the last few years, as the slums of Harlem have crowded down from the north and the Puerto Rican slum of Amsterdam and Columbus Avenues has crowded over from the west, but there's still plenty of wealth to be found on Central Park West, particularly toward the southern end.

We parked in front of the address. It had a canopy and

13

a doorman, both of which I liked. We went inside, and going up in the elevator I said, "You do the talking, okay?"

I'd already told Ed I was under the weather, so he just said, "Sure."

It was a very expensive apartment we were headed for, on a high floor. The woman herself let us in, opening the door as though she weren't used to that kind of manual labor. She was about forty-five, and holding time away with every pill and diet and exercise she could find. She looked expensive but old, like her apartment.

She took us into the living room, but didn't suggest we sit down. It was a beautiful room, all golden and brown, with high windows overlooking the park. An air-conditioner hummed, and the sun shone through the windows, and you could almost hear the buzz of lazy insects. You get the idea; everything sun-dappled and rich and comfortable and beautiful and easy. It was just a great room to be in.

Ed did the talking for both of us, while I wandered around the room, digging how good it felt to be there. She had knickknacks and whatnots all over the place, in marble and onyx and different kinds of wood, and some in chrome or glass or green stone, and every one of them was just a pleasure to be with.

Over by the window, Ed and the woman were talking, their voices seeming to be muffled by the sunlight, muted and indistinct, like voices in another room when you're sick in bed in the daytime. From time to time I'd tune in on what they were saying, but I just couldn't build up any interest. It was the room I cared about, I didn't give a shit about the two spades that had busted in here.

At one point, I heard Ed say, "And they came in through the service entrance?"

"Yes," she said. She had a voice like a prune, very offensive. "They struck my maid," she said. "They cut the inside

14

of her mouth, I sent her downstairs to my doctor. I could have her sent back up if you need a statement."

"Maybe later," Ed said.

"I can't think why they struck her," she said. "She is black, after all."

Ed said, "Then they came in here, is that it?"

"No," she said, "they never came in here at all, thank goodness. I have some rather valuable things in here. They went from the kitchen into the bedroom."

"Where were you?"

On a glass coffee table was an ornate lacquered Oriental wooden box. I picked it up and opened it, and it had half a dozen cigarettes inside. Virginia Slims. The wood inside the box was a warm golden color, like imported beer.

The woman was saying, "I was in my office. It connects with the bedroom. I heard them rummaging around, and went to the door. As soon as I saw them, of course, I realized what they were doing."

"Can you give me a description?"

"I honestly didn't—"

I said, "How much would a thing like this cost?"

The woman looked at me, baffled. "I beg your pardon?"

I showed her the Oriental box. "This thing," I said. "How much would it go for?"

She talked down her nose at me. "I believe that was thirty-seven hundred dollars. Under four thousand."

What a great thing! Four thousand dollars for this little box. "To hold cigarettes in," I said, mainly to myself, and turned away again to put it back on the coffee table.

Behind me, the woman was being a little miffed, saying to Ed, "Where were we?"

I looked at the things on the coffee table. It made me happy to be with them. I couldn't help smiling.

15

• Joe •

I DON'T know why, for some reason I'd been pissed off all day. It had started right from the time I got out of bed this morning. If Grace hadn't avoided me, we would have had us a good old-fashioned fight, because I was really in the mood for it.

Then the car, and the traffic, none of that helped. And the heat. It felt good telling Tom about the liquor store, a thing I'd been bottling up inside me for a couple weeks, but a little while after I told him and we'd stopped talking about it I was in a rotten mood again. Only now I had something to hook onto, because I just kept thinking about that comfortable bastard in his air-conditioned Cadillac out there on the Long Island Expressway this morning. I was sorry I hadn't ticketed him for something; anything. I hated the idea that somebody was better off than me.

For me, the best way to work off a mad is to drive. Not in that stop-and-go traffic like on the Expressway this morning; that just makes things worse. But in ordinary traffic, where I can move, use my skills. I get behind the wheel, I push it a little hard, win some contests, and pretty soon I feel better. So I volunteered to drive today, and my partner, Paul Goldberg, just shrugged and said it was fine with him. Which I knew he would; he has no feeling for cars, Paul. He'd rather I drove all the time, so he could sit beside me and chew gum. I never saw anybody in my life who could chew so much gum. He went through Chiclets like kids through Kleenex.

He's a couple years younger than me, Paul is, and slender and wiry, with more strength than he looks. His name is Goldberg, but he looks Italian. He has that curly kind of black hair, and an olive complexion, and those big brown doe eyes the chicks love so much. He's a bachelor, and I guess he makes out pretty good with the women. He ought to, given his looks and potential. I don't know for sure; I hinted around a couple of times, but he never talked about his personal life while we were on patrol together. Which was only fair, since I never talked about mine either.

On the other hand, what kind of personal life does a married man with kids have to talk about?

We did a little driving around the neighborhoods to begin with today, but it wasn't the kind of movement I needed to unload the irritable feeling in my chest. It was also too hot for mooching along down side streets; what

17

we needed was to be where we could move fast enough to create a breeze for ourselves, keep ourselves a little cooled off. Me, especially, keep me cooled off.

So I headed us west over 79th Street and got on the Henry Hudson Parkway northbound. Way up ahead you could see the George Washington Bridge. On our left was the Hudson River, looking better than it really is, and across on the other side New Jersey. There were little puffs of white cloud in the blue sky, boats of different sizes were on the river, and even the city, off to our right, looked clean in the sunlight. For looking at, it was a really nice day. Of course, you can't see humidity, or a temperature in the high eighties.

I got off the Parkway at 96th Street and hit the neighborhoods again for a while. Now I was having second thoughts about telling Tom about the liquor store. Could I really trust him? What if he told somebody else, what if the word got around? Sooner or later it would reach the Captain, once it got started, and if that ever happened I was finished. The 15th Precinct had a couple of very hairy Captains for a while, guys who were in on the take, guys you could have bought off on a baby rape with a bottle of Scotch, but the boom got lowered all of a sudden, on the Captain we had at the time and also the one who'd been there before him and was assigned some place else and about to retire, and they both got their heads handed to them. Now we had a Captain who was out to make King of the Angels; spit on the sidewalk off duty and he'd write you up. Think what he'd do to a patrolman who held up a liquor store while driving his beat.

But Tom wouldn't say anything, he'd have more sense than that. I could trust him; that's why I'd told him. And face it, I'd had to tell somebody, I couldn't keep it tied up inside me much longer. Sooner or later I'd have told somebody like Grace, for God's sake, and Grace would never

18

in a million *years* understand. With Tom, no matter what else he might think, I knew he'd understand.

And keep his mouth shut. Right?

Christ, I hoped so.

I was really feeling bugged. Frustrated and irritable and about ready to punch somebody in the mouth. I'd been having days like this every once in a while for the last few months, and I didn't know what to do about them, how to deal with them. Except wait them out, wait for it all to go away, which sooner or later it always did.

Down on 72nd Street, I went over to the Parkway again. Paul had tried starting a couple of conversations, but I didn't feel like talking. I'd come close, a few times in the last week, to telling Paul about the liquor store, but I didn't really know Paul as well as I knew Tom, I didn't have that same sense of closeness with him. And now that I'd told Tom, I didn't want to tell anyone else at all. Or talk to anyone else at all. In fact, part of me was sorry I'd talked to Tom.

We got back up on the Parkway, and rolled along. The air was a little better over the river, and the motion of the car made a breeze that at least blew the stink off. My mood was picking up.

Then I spotted the white Cadillac Eldorado up ahead, moving right along. It was the same model as the one this morning, but a different color. I saw him up there, looking so cute and arrogant and rich, and all the bile came right back into me again, stronger than ever.

I eased up on him and saw he had New York plates. Good. If I gave him a ticket he couldn't be a scofflaw, fade away into some other state and thumb his nose at me. He'd have to pay up or have a mess on his hands when it came time to renew his license.

I clocked him a mile, and he was doing fifty-four. Good enough.

19

"I'm taking the Caddy," I said.

I guess Paul had been half-asleep, sitting there in the silence next to me. He sat up straighter and looked ahead and said, "The what?"

"That white Caddy."

Paul studied the Cad, and raised his eyebrows at me. "How come?"

"I feel like it. He's doing fifty-four."

I hit the dome light, but not the siren. He could see me, he wouldn't need a lot of noise. He slowed right away, and I crowded him off onto the shoulder.

Paul said, "You cut him a little close there."

"He should of braked harder." I looked at Paul, waiting for him to say something else, but all he did was shrug, as though to say he didn't care, it wasn't his business—which it wasn't—so I got out of the car and went back to talk to the driver of the Cad.

He was about forty, with those pop-eyes called thyroid. He was wearing a suit and a tie, and when I went back to talk to him he opened his window by pushing a button. I asked to see his license and registration, and stood there a long time reading them, waiting for him to start a conversation. His name was Daniel Mossman, and he leased the Cad from a company in Tarrytown. And he didn't have anything to say for himself at all. I said, "You know the speed limit along this stretch, Dan?"

"Fifty," he said.

"You know what speed I clocked you at, Dan?"

"I believe I was doing about fifty-five." There was no expression in his voice, nothing in his face, and those pop-eyes just looked at me like a fish.

I said, "What do you do for a living, Dan?"

"I'm an attorney," he said.

An attorney. He couldn't even say lawyer. I was twice as irritable as before. I went back to the patrol car and

20

got behind the wheel, holding Mossman's license and registration.

Paul looked over at me, and rubbed his thumb and finger together. "Anything?"

I shook my head. "No," I said. "I'm giving the bastard a ticket."

· 2 ·

THEY CO-HOSTED a barbecue for some friends in the neighborhood. The grill was in Tom's backyard, so that's where the party was, but they both pitched in for the food and drink, and both wives worked on the salads and the desserts and in setting things up. The first humid hot spell of the summer had broken the day before with one of those real drenching summer downpours, but by the morning of the barbecue the yard was almost completely dry. Also, the humidity was way down, and the temperature had dropped into the high seventies. Perfect weather for a party in the backyard.

There were four other couples invited, all from the same block, plus their kids. None of them were on the force, and in fact only one of them even worked in the city; Tom and Joe liked them all mostly because they could forget their own jobs while with them.

Before the party, they'd brought all the kitchen chairs and folding chairs out of both houses and scattered them around Tom's yard, and set up a bar on a card table back by the grill. They had gin and vodka and scotch, plus soft drinks for the kids. Mary had put a sheet over the card table instead of a tablecloth, one of those printed sheets with a flower design all over it, and it really looked nice there.

Before dinner, Tom and Joe took turns being bartender, one serving the drinks while the other wandered around the yard playing host. But Tom was the official chef, like it said on his apron, so while he was doing the chicken quarters and the hamburgers on the outdoor grill Joe became the bartender full time. Then, after everybody had eaten, Tom became bartender again and Joe just stood around or occasionally went to one kitchen or the other for more ice. They both had ice-makers in their refrigerators, but with fifteen or twenty people all drinking iced drinks at once—and the kids mostly spilling theirs out on the grass—you can use ice faster than any refrigerator on earth can make it. It was a good thing to have two.

It was a good party, as that kind of party goes. That is, there weren't any long uncomfortable silences, and there weren't any fist-fights. In fact, nobody got falling down drunk, which was kind of unusual. The people on the block, mostly the men, tended to be pretty two-fisted drinkers, and the way the summertime parties usually went, the survivors carried the others home. Maybe it was be-

23

cause it was so early in the season, and the group wasn't into the swing of things yet. Or maybe it was simply the nice weather after the long stretch of humidity; everybody was feeling so pleasant and comfortable that nobody wanted to spoil it with a hangover.

It was getting toward evening when Joe wandered over to the bar again and said, "How's the ice holding out?"

"We need some."

"No sooner said," Joe told him, and went over to his own kitchen, and brought back a glass pitcher full of the little half-moon cubes. He worked his way through the guests to the card table, where Tom was standing with his chef's apron still on. He didn't have any customers right at that moment. Joe put the pitcher down and said, "There you go."

Tom began to switch the ice cubes to his Colonial ice-bucket. Joe rooted around among all the dirty glasses on the card table, and finally said, "What did I do with my drink?"

"I'll make you another."

"Thanks."

Joe was drinking scotch and soda. Tom knew that wasn't considered a summertime drink, but he'd never said anything; it was what Joe liked all year 'round, so why pester him?

Tom started making the drink, and Joe turned to look at the freeloaders all over the lawn in the gloom of twilight. The men were talking with men, the women were talking with women, the kids were running around the adults like motorcycles around traffic stanchions. It occurred to Joe that of all the women currently in the backyard the only one he really wanted to ball was Mary, who was Tom's wife. Then she turned, and he realized in the half-light he'd made a mistake and it was Grace he'd been staring at, his own wife. He grinned and shook his head,

24

and almost turned to tell Tom what he'd just done when he realized that wouldn't be a good idea.

He looked around some more, and at last saw Mary way over by the house. Both women were wearing slacks with stripes, and fuzzy sweaters; Mary's pink, Grace's white. Because of the party they'd both gone off to the beauty parlor this morning and had come back with hairdos that sat up on top of their heads like Venusian helmets, hair styles that had absolutely nothing to do with who they really were. But that was women for you, they did that sort of thing.

Tom said, "Joe?"

Joe turned. "Yeah?"

"You remember that— Here." Tom handed over the fresh drink.

"Thanks."

"You remember," Tom said, "that thing you told me the other day about the liquor store?"

Joe pulled at his drink, and grinned. "Sure."

Tom hesitated, biting his lower lip, looking worriedly at the people at the other end of the yard. Finally, all in a rush, he said, "Have you done it again?"

Joe frowned, not sure what he was getting at. "No. Why?"

"You thought about it?"

With a little shrug, Joe looked away. "A couple times, I guess. I didn't want to push my luck."

Tom nodded. "Yeah, I guess so."

One of the guests came up then, stopping the conversation for a while. He was named George Hendricks, and he ran a supermarket over in the five towns. He was a little drunk now, not terrible, and he came up with a loose grin on his face and said, "Time for a refill."

"You're a screwdriver," Tom said, and took his glass.

"You're goddam right I am," George said. He was about

25

thirty pounds overweight, and always hinting about what a sex maniac he was. Now he said, mostly to Joe, since Tom was busy making his drink, "You two both still work in the city, huh?"

Joe nodded. "Yeah, we do."

"Not me," George said. "I'm out of that rat-race for good." Up till a few years ago, he'd managed a Finast in Queens.

Drunks always irritated Joe, even when he was off duty. Skeptical, a little bored, he said to George, "It's that different out here?"

"Hell, yes. You know that yourself, you moved out here."

"Grace and the kids are out here," Joe said. "I'm still in the city."

Tom held George's fresh drink out to him: "Here."

"Thanks." George took the glass, but didn't drink yet. He was still involved in his conversation with Joe. He said, "I don't see how you guys stand it. The city is nothing but wall-to-wall crooks. Everybody out to chisel a dollar."

Joe merely shrugged, but Tom said, "It's the way of the world, George."

"Not out here," George said. He made it one of those definite, don't-argue-with-me statements.

"Out here," Tom said, "just like any place else. It's all the same."

"You guys," George said, and shook his head. "You think everybody's crooked in the whole world. It's being in the city gives you that idea." He gave a knowing grin, and rubbed his thumb and finger together. "Being in on it a little."

Joe, who'd been looking at the women again, trying without success to develop an interest in George's wife, turned his head and gave George a flat stare. "Is that right?"

"One hundred per cent," George said. "I know about New York City cops."

26

"That's the same everywhere, too," Tom said. He wasn't offended; he'd given up being sore about slurs like that years ago. He said, "You think the guys in the precinct out here could make it on their salaries?"

George laughed and pointed his drink at Tom. "See what I mean? The city corrupts your mind, you think everybody in the world is a crook."

Suddenly irritated, Joe said, "George, you come home every night with a sack of groceries. You don't do that on any employee discount, you just pack up those groceries and walk out of the store."

George was outraged. He stood up straighter, and got drunker. "I work for them!" he said, his voice loud enough to carry to the far end of the yard. "If the chain paid a man a decent salary—"

"You'd do the same thing," Joe said.

Smoothly, Tom said, "Not necessarily, Joe." He was a natural host, he eased groups through the rough spots. He said to Joe, but for George's benefit, "Everybody hustles, but nobody wants to. I don't want Mary to work, you don't want Grace to work, George doesn't want Phyllis to work, but what are you gonna do?"

George probably embarrassed at having gotten mad, made a heavy attempt at humor. "Lose the house to the bank," he said.

Tom said, "The way I see it, the problem is really very simple. There's so and so much money, and there's so and so many people. And there isn't quite enough money to go around. So you do the only thing that's left; you steal to make up the difference."

Joe gave Tom a warning look, but Tom hadn't been thinking about the liquor store just then, and in any case didn't notice him.

George, still trying to make up for his bad temper, said, "Okay. I can go along with that. You got to make up the difference, and you do a little of this and that. Like me with the groceries." Then, with a smirk, and another heavy attempt at humor, he added, "And you guys with whatever you can get."

"Don't kid yourself," Joe said. He was still serious. He said, "In our position, we could get whatever we wanted. We restrain ourselves, that's all."

George laughed, and Tom gave Joe a thoughtful look. But Joe was moodily glaring at George; he was thinking he'd like to give him a ticket.

· Tom ·

THE WAY to take somebody out of a place full of his friends is to do it fast. This was a coffee shop on Macdougal Street in Greenwich Village, a hangout of several different kinds of freaks, and at one o'clock on a Saturday night it was full; college students, tourists, local citizens, hippies passing through town, a general cross-section of people who don't like cops.

Ed waited outside on the sidewalk. If worse came to worst, I'd push Lambeth into running and he'd run straight into Ed's arms.

He was at a table midway along on the right, just as the finger had said. He was with four other people, two male and two female, and he had a bunched-up handkerchief in his left hand and kept patting his nose with it. Either he had a cold or he was on something; most of them sooner or later try a free sample of what they sell.

I stopped behind his chair, and leaned over him slightly. "Lambeth?"

When he looked up over his shoulder, I saw that his eyes were watery and red-lined. It was still maybe a cold, but it was still more likely heroin. He said, "Yeah?"

Despite what they say in the movies, a plainclothes detective is not instantly recognizable as a cop. "Police," I said, low enough so he'd be the only one to hear the word clearly. "Come on along with me."

He had a loose kind of grin. "I don't think so, man," he said, and faced around to his friends again.

He was wearing a fringed deerskin vest. I reached over his shoulders and yanked the vest back around his arms, pinning him like a straitjacket. At the same time, I lifted him and kicked the chair out from under him.

Nobody thinks faster than his body. If he'd just let himself drop to the floor then, he would have gotten away from me. Maybe long enough for his friends and some busybody bystanders to louse me up. But his body reacted automatically, getting his feet under him, helping him to stand, and the instant he had his balance I turned him toward the front and ran him full speed at the door.

He yelled, and tried to squirm to the side, but I had him pinned and moving. The door was closed, but would open with a push; I pushed it with his head. We'd gone through so fast there hadn't been time for anybody to react along the way.

Lambeth was still struggling when we hit the street. Ed was standing there, and our Ford was parked right in front.

I didn't slow down, but kept running across the sidewalk and slammed Lambeth into the side of the car. I wanted the wind and the fight out of him. I pulled him back a foot or two, and bounced him off the car again, and this time he sagged and quit fighting.

Ed was beside me with the cuffs. I let go of the vest, slid my hands down Lambeth's arms, and lifted his arms up behind him like pump handles, bending him over the trunk of the car. Ed clicked the cuffs on, and opened the Ford's rear door.

I was shifting Lambeth over into position to shove him into the car when somebody tapped me on the upper arm, and a female voice said, "Officer?"

I looked around at a middle-aged tourist woman in a red-and-white flowered dress and a straw purse. She looked angry, but as though she was making a great effort to be reasonable. She said, "Are you absolutely sure that much violence was necessary?"

Lambeth's friends would be coming out any second. "I don't know, lady," I said. "It's how much I used." Then I turned away from her again and kicked Lambeth into the car and followed him in. Ed shut the door behind me, got behind the wheel, and we pulled away from there as the coffee-shop door opened and people began to pile out into the street.

Lambeth was crumpled up on the right side of the rear seat like a dead dog. I adjusted him around into a sitting position. He looked dazed, and he mumbled something, but I couldn't tell what.

Up front, Ed said, "Tom?"

"Yeah?"

"Looks like you're gonna get another letter in your file."

I looked at him, and he was checking the rear-view mirror, looking at the situation behind us. "Is that right," I said.

31

"She's taking down the license number," he said.

"I'll blame you," I said.

Ed chuckled, and we turned a corner, and headed uptown.

After a couple of blocks, Lambeth suddenly said, "My arms hurt, man."

I looked at him. He was wide awake, and apparently rational. You don't switch off a cold that easily. I said, "Don't stick needles in them."

"With these cuffs on, man," he said. "I'm all twisted around."

"Sorry," I said.

"Will you take them off?"

"At the station."

"If I give you my word of honor, I won't try—"

I laughed at him. "Forget it," I said.

He gave me a level look, and then a sad kind of smile. "That's right," he said. "Nobody's got any honor around here, do they?"

"Not the last time I looked."

He wriggled around for thirty seconds or so, and apparently finally got himself into a more comfortable position, because he stopped moving, and sighed, and settled down to watch the city go by.

I settled down, too, but not that much. We were traveling without siren or flashing light, in an unmarked green car, which meant we were going with the general flow of the traffic. Unless there's a specific reason to make a fuss, it's better not to. But the result was, we were from time to time being stopped by red lights, and from time to time crawling along in very slow traffic, and I didn't want Lambeth to suddenly decide to jump out of the car and make a run for it with Ed's cuffs. The door was locked, and he seemed quiet, but I nevertheless kept my eye on him.

After three or four minutes of watching the world outside the window, Lambeth sighed and looked at me, and said, "I'm ready to get out of this city, man."

I had to laugh again. "You'll get your wish," I told him. "It'll probably be ten years before you see New York again."

He nodded, grinning at himself. He seemed less freaky, more human, than he'd been back in the coffee shop. "I dig," he said. Then he gave me a serious look, and said, "Tell me something, man. Give me your opinion on a question I have in my mind."

"If I can."

"What do you say; is it the bigger punishment to get sent out of this city, or to stay here?"

"You tell me," I said. "Why'd you stay here long enough to get yourself into a bind like this?"

He shrugged. "Why do you stay, man?"

"I'm not dealing," I said.

"Sure you are," he said. "You're dealing in machismo, man, just like I'm dealing in scat."

Ever since drugs got tied in with the cultural revolution, the junkies have had a richer line of horseshit. "Anything you say," I said, and turned away to look out my own window.

"None of us started out this way, man," he said. "We all started out as babies, innocent and pure."

I looked at him again. "One time," I said, "a guy a lot like you, full of talk, he showed me a picture of his mother. And while I was looking at it he made a grab at my hip for my gun."

He gave a big broad grin; he was delighted. "You stay in this town, man," he said. "You're gonna like what it does to you."

• Joe •

THE WOMAN was all right coming down the stairs. She was bleeding from a long cut on her right arm, and she had blood all over her face and hands and clothes, some of it her own and some of it her husband's and I guess she was still dazed by it all. But when we went out the front door and she looked down the tenement steps and saw the crowd of people standing around gaping at her, she flipped her lid. She started screaming and struggling and carrying on, and it was hell to get her down the steps to the sidewalk,

34

particularly because all the blood made her slippery and tough to hold onto.

I didn't like that situation at all. Two uniformed white cops dragging a bloody black woman down the steps into a crowd in Harlem. I didn't like any part of it, and from the expression on Paul's face he didn't like it either.

The woman was yelling, "Let me go! Let me go! He cut me first, let me go! I got a right, I got a right, let me go!" And finally, as we neared the bottom of the stoop, I could hear over her yelling the sound of a siren coming. It was an ambulance, and I was glad to see it.

We got to the sidewalk just as the ambulance came to a stop at the curb. The crowd was keeping out of it so far, giving us a big open space on the sidewalk, moving out of the way of the ambulance. All I wanted was to get this over with and go away somewhere for a while. The woman was wriggling and squirming like an eel, a long black eel covered with blood and screaming with a voice like a fingernail on a blackboard.

It was one of those high-sided ambulances, a boxy van, and it carried four attendants, two in front and two in the back, all dressed in white. But not for long. The four of them climbed out and came running over to us and got hold of the woman. One of them said, "All right, we've got her."

"About time you got here," I said. I knew they'd been as fast as could be expected, but the situation had me scared, and when I'm scared I get mad, and when I'm mad I sound off.

They didn't pay any attention to me, which was the right thing to do. One of them said to the woman, "Come on, honey, let's fix the old arm."

Their being dressed in white had made a connection with the woman, because now she started to yell, "I want my own doctor. You take me to my own doctor!"

The four attendants hustled the woman to the ambu-

35

lance, having as much trouble with her as we'd had, and a second ambulance arrived, pulling in behind the first. Two guys came out of this one, both also dressed in white, and came over to us. One of them said, "Where's the stiff?"

I couldn't say anything; I was having trouble breathing. I just pointed at the building, and Paul said, "Third floor rear. In the kitchen. She really cut him to pieces."

Two more had come out of the back of the second ambulance, carrying a rolled-up stretcher. The four of them went up the stoop and into the building. At the same time, the first four were getting the woman into the first ambulance, with some trouble. So much movement, so many flashing red lights, kept the crowd from deciding to join in; they'd just be spectators this time.

Paul and I were finished with this one, for right now. We still had to call in, and later on there'd be forms to do at the station, but for the next couple minutes the action had moved away from us. And it hadn't happened any too soon.

Excitement carries you through the tense parts. It had been that way from the beginning, from the first time I was around at a violent situation, which was a ten-year-old kid hit by a cab on Central Park West. He was still alive, the kid, and when you looked at him you wished he wasn't. But the excitement and noise and movement had carried me through the whole scene, and it wasn't until we were driving away from it that I had Jerry, an older cop who was my first partner, pull the car over to the curb and stop so I could get out and up-chuck.

That's never changed, from that day to this. I don't up-chuck any more, but the run of emotions is still the same; the excitement carries me through the tense part or the ugly part or the violent part, and then there's a sick queasy letdown that comes after it.

The patrol car was across the street where we'd left it,

with its engine off and its flasher on. The two of us went over there, pushing our way through the crowd, ignoring the questions they were asking us and ignoring what was going on behind us. When we got to the car, we stood beside it a minute, not talking or moving or doing anything. I don't know what Paul was looking at; I was looking at the car roof.

A siren started again. I looked around, and the first ambulance was leaving, taking the woman to Bellevue. I turned to look at Paul, and he had blood smeared all over his shirt-front, and dotted on his face and arms like measles. "You got blood on you," I said.

"You, too," he said.

I looked down at myself. When we'd come down from the third floor, I'd been on the side of the woman where her cut arm was, and I had even more blood on me than Paul did. My bare arms, from elbow to wrist, were soaked in blood, the hair all matted, like a cat that's been run over. Now that I was looking at myself, with the sun beating down on me, I could feel the blood drying against my skin, shrinking up into a thin wrinkled layer of scab.

"Christ," I said. I turned away from Paul and leaned my left side against the car and stretched my left arm away from me across the white car roof, where the flashing light kept changing the color of it. I couldn't think about getting clean, I couldn't think about what I was supposed to do next, all I could think was, *I've got to get out of this. I've got to get out of this.*

37

• 3 •

THEY WERE both on the four-to-midnight shift that time, so they got to drive home pretty late at night, after most of the traffic had thinned out. That was the advantage of the four-to-twelve; they got to drive into town in the middle of the afternoon, before the rush hour, and in any case in the opposite direction from most of the traffic, and then at the other end of the shift they could drive home along practically empty roads.

The disadvantage of the four-to-midnight was that it

38

was the busiest shift of all. They weren't driving during the rush hour, but they were *working* during it, and then on into the evening, the high-crime period of the day. Muggings hit their peak between six and eight, when people are coming home from work. Around the same time, the husbands and wives start fighting with each other, and a little later the drunks join in. And store robberies—like the one Joe had pulled—occur most frequently in that period between sundown and ten o'clock, when most of the stores finally close. So when they were on the four-to-midnight shift they tended to spend most of their time working, and very little of it sitting down.

But then midnight would come around at last, and this shift too would come to an end, and they would get to sail home along practically deserted highways once they'd left Manhattan, all by themselves, thinking their thoughts. Which is what they were doing now.

Tom was driving his Chevrolet tonight; six years old, bought used, a gas burner and an oil heater, with bad springs and a loose clutch. He kept talking about trading it in on something a little newer, but he couldn't bring himself to take it to a used-car dealer and try to get a price on it. He knew too well what this car was worth.

They were riding along without any conversation between them, both tired from the long day, both remembering things that had happened earlier in the week. Tom was going over in his head the conversation with the hippie junk dealer, trying to find better answers to the things the guy had said, and also trying to figure out why he couldn't seem to get that conversation out of his mind. And Joe was remembering the blood drying on his arm in the sun, stretched out across the roof of the patrol car, looking like something from a monster movie and not anything that could ever have been a part of himself at all. He didn't particularly want to remember that scene, but it just seemed to stay in his head, no matter what.

Gradually, as they left the city behind them, Tom's thoughts shifted away from the hippie, roamed around, touched on this and that, and settled on a new subject. It wasn't exactly Joe's liquor store, though the liquor store was behind what he was thinking about now. All at once he broke the silence, saying, "Joe?"

Joe blinked. It was like coming out of sleep, or a dentist's anesthetic. He looked at Tom's profile and said, "Yeah?"

"Let me ask you a question."

"Sure."

Tom kept looking straight ahead through the windshield. "What would you do," he said, "if you had a million dollars?"

Joe's answer was immediate, as if he'd been ready for this question all of his life. "Go to Montana with Chet Huntley," he said.

Tom frowned slightly and shook his head. "No," he said. "I mean really."

"So do I."

Tom turned his head and studied Joe's face—they both had very serious expressions—and then he looked out the windshield again and said, "Not me. I'd go to the Caribbean."

Joe watched him. "You would, huh?"

"That's right." Tom grinned a little, thinking about it. "One of those islands down there. Trinidad." He stretched the word out, pronouncing it as though saying it was tasting something sweet.

Joe nodded, and looked around at the glove compartment. "But here we are instead," he said.

Tom glanced at him again, then faced front. He felt very cautious now, like a man with a bag of groceries walking on ice. He said, "Remember what you told George last week?"

40

"Big mouth? No, what did I tell him?"

"That we could get anything we want," Tom said, "only we restrain ourselves."

Joe grinned. "I remember. I thought you were gonna tell him about my liquor store."

Tom wasn't going to get distracted by side issues now; he'd started moving, and he was going to keep moving. Ignoring the liquor-store remark, he said, "Well, what the hell, why don't we?"

Joe didn't get it. "Why don't we what?"

"*Do* it!" Tom said. He'd been bottling this up for days, his voice was vibrating with it. "Get everything we want," he said, "just like you said."

Skeptical, Joe said, "Like how? Liquor stores?"

Tom took one hand off the wheel to wave that away, impatient with it. "That's nothing, Joe," he said, "that's crap! That stinking city back there is full of money, and in our position by God we really *can* get anything we want. A million dollars apiece, in one job."

Joe didn't believe it yet, but he was interested. "What job?"

Tom shrugged. "We've got our choice. Anything we want to work out. Some big jewelry company. A bank. Whatever we want."

Suddenly Joe saw it, and he started to laugh. "Disguised as cops!"

"That's right!" Tom said. He was laughing, too. "Disguised as cops!"

The two of them sat in the car and just laughed.

41

• Joe •

THE SUBWAY had fucked up again. Paul and I were positioned at a manhole on Broadway, where the people were coming up. They'd been down there for over an hour, and there'd been some smoke, and now they'd had to walk single file in the tunnel for a ways, and come up a metal ladder, and at last out onto the street. It was nine-thirty at night, traffic was being detoured around us, and we had our patrol car between the manhole and the street, flasher going.

Most of the people coming up were just stunned, all they wanted was to get the hell away from there. A few were grateful and said thank you to Paul or me for helping them up the last few steps. And a few were pissed off and wanted to take it out on a representative of the municipal government, which at the moment was Paul and me. These last few we ignored; they'd make an angry remark or two, and then they'd stomp off, and that would be the end of it.

Except this one guy. He stood around on the other side of us, away from the manhole, and yammered at us. He was about fifty, dressed in a suit, carrying an attaché case. He was like a manager or supervisor type, and all he wanted to do was stand there and yell, while Paul and I helped the rest of the people up out of the manhole.

He went on like this: "This city is a disgrace! It's a disgrace! You aren't safe here! And who cares? Does anybody care? Everything breaks down, and nobody gives a God damn! Everybody's in the *union!* Teachers on strike, subways on strike, cops on strike, sanitation on strike. Money money money, and when they work do they *do* anything? Do they teach? Don't make me laugh! The subways are a menace, they're a menace! Sanitation? Look at the streets! Big raises, big pay, and look at the streets! And you *cops!* Gimme gimme gimme, and where are you? Your apartment gets robbed, and where *are* you? Some dope addict attacks your wife in the street, and where's the *cops?*"

Up till then we ignored him, the both of us; like he was a regular part of the city noise. Which in a way he was. But then he made a mistake, he overstepped himself. He reached out and tugged at my elbow, and he yelled, "Are you listening to me?"

They're not going to start grabbing me. I turned around and looked at him, and he was so amazed he went back a step. The city had finally noticed him. I said to him, "I'm

43

coming to the conclusion you fell coming up those stairs and broke your nose."

It took him a second to work it out, and then he back-pedaled some more, and yelled, "You mustn't care much about keeping that badge of yours."

I was about to tell him what he could do with the badge, pin first, but he was still backing away, and the hell with him. I turned back and helped Paul with a fat old lady who was having trouble climbing because of bad ankles. But I kept thinking about what the guy had said.

· 4 ·

IT WAS a hot sunny day, and they were both in Joe's back-yard. Where the barbecue was in Tom's backyard, Joe had put in a pool; one of those above-the-ground pools, four foot high and ten foot across. They were both drinking beer, Joe was in a bathing suit and Tom was in slacks and shirt, and Joe was trying to fix the pool filter. The damn thing was always getting screwed up one way or another, it was about the most delicate machine ever made. It sometimes seemed as though Joe spent his entire summers fixing the pool filter.

They'd lived next door to one another for nine years now. Tom had bought his house first, eleven years ago, and when Joe wanted to move out of the city after Jackie was born it happened the house next door to Tom was just going on the market. Back then, they'd both been in uniform, and sometimes even partnered. They'd known each other for years, liked one another, it seemed they ought to make good neighbors. And they did.

The houses weren't the greatest in the world, but they were livable. They were in a development put up right after the war, back when the notion of curving streets was still new. They had three bedrooms, all on one floor, and a smallish attic that a lot of the guys in the neighborhood had converted to a fourth bedroom. Fortunately, neither Tom nor Joe had families big enough to need that, and neither intended to have families any bigger than they already had, so they could keep their attics as attics, and fill them with all that junk everybody gradually collects through life, that nobody has any use for any more, but that nobody wants to throw away.

The houses weren't bad. They were old enough to have been built before plastics were really big, which meant they were constructed fairly well, mostly of wood. They had clapboard siding that had to be painted every few years, they had half-basements for the utilities, the backyards were a pretty good size, and there was a detached one-car garage at the rear of each and every property. Gravel driveways separated the houses and defined the property lines, and every house in three or four blocks in all directions looked exactly the same, except for color of paint job or any special additions or changes that anybody might have made. Neither Tom nor Joe had made any special changes, so they both had the original basic house, just the way it had come from the architect's drawing board; only a little older.

Most people put up fences along the sides of their back-yards, mostly to keep little kids inside, but Tom and Joe hadn't done that. Between Tom and his neighbor on the right there was a basket-weave wooden fence put up by the neighbor, and between Joe and his neighbor on the left there was a chain-link fence covered with vines put up by that neighbor, but between their own two yards there was nothing but the remains of a hedge planted by some previous owner of one of their houses. The hedge had big gaps in it where they walked back and forth all the time, and they could never agree who was supposed to keep it trimmed, so nobody did, and it was gradually dying. And taking years to do it.

In every single house in the development that either of them had ever heard of, the kitchen linoleum was all cracked and buckled. In a lot of houses, including both of theirs, the basement leaked.

They hadn't done any more talking about the robbery idea since that one time in the car, but they'd both been thinking about it. Not that it was real, not that they thought they would actually commit a major robbery somewhere, but just that it was nice to daydream about a possible way of getting themselves out of this grind.

Joe wasn't thinking about the robbery idea at the moment, mostly because his mind was taken up with the problem of the pool filter, but Tom's mind was ticking along on the subject, and all at once he said, "Hey."

Joe was sitting cross-legged on the ground, surrounded by hoses and washers and nuts. He put a double handful of parts down, wiped his face with his hand, drank beer, looked over at Tom, and said, "What?"

"What do you think the Russians would pay for him," Tom said, "if we kidnapped their ambassador?"

Joe squinted at him in the sunlight. "You serious?"

"Why not? Profitable and patriotic both."

47

Joe thought about it for a couple of seconds, and then he looked all around the backyard and said, "Where the hell are we going to keep the Russian ambassador?"

Tom looked off toward his own yard next door. "Yeah," he said. "That's a problem."

Joe shook his head and went back to the pool filter. Tom drank some more beer. They both thought their thoughts.

• Tom •

THE SQUEAL was at a junior high school; they'd found a missing teacher, dead.

It was about eleven in the morning, a cloudy day that promised rain for later on. Ed and I drove over in the Ford and parked in the school zone out front. It was one of the old gray stone school buildings, three stories high, looking more like a fortress than a place for kids. A concrete-covered play yard was on the right, surrounded by eight-foot-high chain link fence. Nobody was in it.

A recent fad among the kids has been to write nicknames on walls and subways and all over the damn place in either spray paint or felt-tip pen, both of which are very tough to get rid of, particularly from a porous surface like stone. The fad is for a kid to write his name or his nickname or some magic name he's worked out for himself, and then under it write the number of the street he lives on. "JUAN 135," for instance, or "BOSS ZOOM 92," that kind of thing.

The fad had hit the school building. As high as a child's arm could reach, the names and numbers were scrawled everywhere on the walls, in black and red and blue and green and yellow. Some of the signatures were like little paintings, carefully and lovingly done, and some of them were just splashed and scrawled on, with runlets of paint dripping down from the bottoms of the letters, but most of them were simply reports of name and number, without flair or imagination: "Andy 87," "Beth 81," "Moro 103."

At first, all of that paintwork looked like vandalism and nothing more. But as I got used to it, to seeing it around, I realized it gave a brightly colored hem to the gray stone skirt of a building like this, that it had a very sunny Latin American flavor to it, and that once you got past the prejudice against marking up public property it wasn't that bad at all. Of course, I never said this to anybody.

Inside, we went to the principal's office, and he said he'd show us where the body was. Walking down the corridor with us, he said, "The room *was* a girl's lavatory, but all of the plumbing is out of it now. That's as far as they got with the modernizing plan." He was balding, about forty, with a moustache and horn-rim glasses and a slightly prissy manner, as though he were more sinned against than sinning.

We got curious stares from the teen-agers we passed, so apparently the news wasn't general yet about the discovery of the teacher's body.

Ed said, "Why didn't you report her missing?"

"So many of these younger teachers," the principal said,

"they're apt to take two or three days off without warning, we didn't think a thing of it. Another teacher noticed the smell this morning, that's why she happened to look."

I said, "We'll want to talk to her. The other teacher."

"Of course," he said. "She's in the building at the moment. With Miss Evans, what we think happened, a group of them must have decided to rape her, and took her in there. At some point she must have fought back. I don't think they brought her in there with the intention of killing her."

Intentions didn't matter, if she was dead. None of us said any more, until the principal stopped and pointed at a door and said, "She's in there."

I went to the door as Ed said to the principal, "What about her family? You try calling her at home?"

I opened the door and took a step in, and the smell hit me in the face. Then, in the dim light through the dirty translucent windows, I saw her lying on the floor over against the green wall. Plaster showed white where they'd pulled the sinks out. She'd been there for a week, and there were rats in the building. "God," I said, and backed out, and slammed the door.

The principal was answering Ed's question, saying, "She lived alone in—" Then he noticed, and said, "Oh, I'm terribly sorry! I should have warned you, I suppose."

Ed took a step toward me, looking worried. "You okay, Tom?"

I waved my hand at him, to keep back away from the room. "Leave it for the ambulance." I could feel the blood draining out of my head, a sensation of coldness in my arms and feet.

The principal, still prissy but bewildered, said, "I'm really very sorry. I took it for granted you were hardened to that sort of thing."

I pushed past the two of them, needing to get outdoors. Hardened to that sort of thing. Jesus H. Christ!

• 5 •

THEY HAD the midnight-to-eight shift that week. It's the
quietest of the three shifts, but at eight o'clock in the morning, driving home eastward into the rising sun, a man's
eyes feel covered with sand and he thinks his stomach will
never be comfortable again.

Joe left the station first and got the Plymouth out of the
lot and drove down the block to double-park across the
street from the precinct house. He had to wait ten minutes
before Tom came out, looking disgusted, and slid into the
passenger seat.

Joe said, "What's the problem?"

"Little talk from the Lieutenant," Tom said. "Some damn thing about narcotics."

"What about it?"

Tom yawned, fighting it, and gave an angry shrug. "Anything you pick up, be sure you turn it in. The usual noise."

Joe put the Plymouth in gear and started through the maze crosstown and downtown to the Midtown Tunnel. "I wonder who they caught," he said.

"Nobody from this house," Tom said. He yawned again, giving in to it this time, and rubbed his face with both hands. "Boy, am I ready for sleep."

"I got me an idea," Joe said.

Tom knew at once what he meant. Looking at him, interested, he said, "You do? What?"

"Paintings from a museum."

Tom frowned. "I don't follow."

"Listen," Joe said. "They got paintings in those museums, they're worth a million dollars each. We take ten, we sell them back for four million. That's two million for each of us."

Tom's frown deepened. He scratched the side of his jaw, making a sound like sandpaper. "I don't know," he said. "Ten paintings. They'd be as tough to hide as my Russian ambassador."

"I could put them in my garage," Joe said. "Who's gonna look in a garage?"

"Your kids would wreck them in a day."

Joe didn't want to give this up; it was the only idea he'd managed to come up with. "Five paintings," he said. "One million apiece."

Tom didn't answer right away. He chewed the inside of his cheek and brooded out at the traffic and tried to figure out not only what was specifically wrong with the paintings idea, but also a general rule to live by, to guide his thinking on the subject of the robbery. It was a way of

53

taking it seriously and yet not taking it seriously at the same time. Finally he said, "We don't want something we have to give back. Nothing we have to keep around us or hide for a while. We want something with fast turnover."

Reluctantly, Joe nodded. "Yeah, I guess you're right," he said, admitting it. "We're not in a position for that kind of thing."

"That's right."

"But we don't want cash. We talked about that."

Tom nodded. "I know. Everybody keeps serial numbers."

Joe said, "So it isn't that easy."

"I never said it was."

They were both quiet for a while, thinking it over. They were practically to the tunnel when Tom spoke up again, restating the rule he'd worked out earlier; narrowing the range of it, refining it. Gazing out the windshield, he said, "What we want is something we can unload fast, for big money."

"Right," Joe said. "*And* a buyer. Some rich person with a lot of cash."

They were about to enter the tunnel. "Rich people," Tom said. He was thinking very hard. They both were.

• Joe •

THERE WERE camera crews from two of the television news programs that showed up to cover it. The way we handled that, Paul and I were the first car that reached the scene after the call came in, so Paul got interviewed by the one crew and I got interviewed by the other.

I wasn't nervous at all. I'd never been interviewed personally on television before, but of course I'd watched the news sometimes when other guys did it, at the scene of an explosion or a big water-main break or something like that.

Three times I'd seen guys I actually knew in real life being interviewed. Also, sometimes while taking a shower I'd run a fantasy kind of interview in my head, the questions and the answers and all, and how I'd hold my face. So you might say I was pretty well rehearsed.

The way they set things up for the interview, they put the camera so it was facing the building, so the building would show behind me and the interviewer while we were doing our thing. It was one of those huge office buildings being constructed there, and the hardhats kept steady working away at it all through the interview. One of their number had got himself killed, but that had only held their interest for maybe five minutes. Where money is concerned, you keep your mind on the job, you get it done.

These buildings are going up all over town, big glass and stone boxes full of office space. Practically none of them have apartments in them, because who wants to live in Manhattan? Manhattan is a place you work in, that's all.

The buildings have been going up ever since the end of the Second World War. Good times, bad times, boom, recession, it doesn't matter, they just keep going up. For the last ten years or so, most of them have been on the east side of midtown, Third Avenue and Lexington Avenue, around there. The first thing you know, they'll give Third Avenue a classier name, the way they did with Fourth Avenue when the big office buildings went up on it and it was turned into Park Avenue South.

Anyway, that's the section where most of the new buildings are concentrated, but there's others going up all over the place. The World Trade Center way downtown. Sixth Avenue across from Rockefeller Center. And a couple up in my precinct, including this one where they'd just had the death and where I was going to get myself interviewed.

A guy I was talking to in a bar a couple years ago said

it was his opinion that the main characteristic of New York is that it's going through all the phases of the phoenix at once. You remember reading about the phoenix in high school? That's what he said New York was; but all at once. New York is living, and it's on fire, and it's dying, and it's ashes, and it's being reborn, all at the same time and all the time. And boy, those buildings look it, coming up out of brick rubble where yesterday's buildings were knocked down, coming up new and clean and pretty, and every once in a while killing somebody along the way.

The interviewer was a light-colored spade, with a moustache. You could see he thought he was the hottest thing in Bigtown. He and the director and the sound man and a couple other people fussed around a while, getting everything set, and then they started the interview. Somebody had written a little lead-in paragraph for the interviewer to say, and he had it on a clipboard he held in his other hand. The hand without the microphone, I mean. He had it on the clipboard, but he'd memorized it, because once he started talking he never looked at the clipboard at all.

Here's how it went: "Tragedy struck today at the site of the new Transcontinental Airlines Building on Columbus Avenue when a worker fell thirty-seven stories within the uncompleted building to his death. Patrolman Joseph Loomis was among the first at the scene." Then he turned to me and said, "Officer Loomis, could you describe what happened?"

I said, "The decedent was a full-blooded Mohawk Indian employed in putting the steel framework of the building up. What they call working the high iron. His name was George Brook. He was forty-three years of age."

The interviewer had been looking me straight in the eye the whole time I talked, as though I was hypnotizing him. As soon as I stopped, he whipped the microphone from my mouth back to his and said, "What apparently went wrong, Officer Loomis?"

I said, "Apparently his foot slipped. He was on the fifty-second story, which is as high as they have so far reached, and he fell thirty-seven stories and landed on the concrete floor at the fifteenth. He fell through the interior of the building, and the fifteenth is the highest story that they have a floor finished and put down."

Zip, the microphone went back over to him, and he said, "He found death thirty-seven stories down." *Zip,* the microphone came back to me.

I said, "No, he was probably dead from about the fortieth story on down. He kept hitting different metal beams on the way. They knocked some parts off him."

A spade can't turn white, but he tried. His eyes looked panicky, and very fast he said, "There are many full-blooded Mohawk Indians working the high iron, aren't there, Officer Loomis?"

He wanted to change the subject? I didn't give a damn. I said, "That's right. There's a couple tribes of them live over in Brooklyn, they're all steelworkers."

Zip. "That's because they have a special affinity for heights, isn't it?" *Zip.*

I said, "I don't think so. They come down pretty often. About as often as anybody else."

You could see I'd suddenly caught his attention. He was interested in spite of himself. He said, "Then why do they do it?"

I shrugged. I said, "I suppose they have to make a living."

Not on television. His eyes filmed over, and in the furriest of brush-off voices he said, "Thank you very much, Officer Loomis," and turned away from me, ready to go into a close-out spiel.

Screw him. Just to louse up his timing, I said, "My

58

pleasure," as he was opening his mouth again. Then I turned around and walked off.

I watched it that night, and all they used was the very first part of what I'd said. The rest was something the interviewer did on his own after I'd left; he stood in the same spot, with the construction going on behind him, and told you what happened. He said, among other things, "He found death thirty-seven stories down." So much for accuracy, the bastards.

I don't know what Paul said, but he didn't get on the tube at all. He claimed afterwards it was anti-Semitism.

· Tom ·

Two BIG Mafia men had got picked up in our area the night before, and Ed and I were among the six plainclothesmen assigned to take them downtown this morning. These were really very big important Mafia people from New Jersey, and it was rare to find them actually in the city like this, where we could get hold of them. One of them was named Anthony Vigano and the other was named Louis Sambella.

Nobody knew if there was going to be any trouble or

not. It wasn't too likely anybody would try to break them loose from us, but it was just possible some enemies of theirs might take a shot at them while they weren't surrounded by their bodyguards. So a lot of precautions were taken, including transporting them in two different unmarked cars, with three officers in each car.

I was driving one of the cars. I was alone in the front seat, and Vigano was squeezed in the back seat with Ed on his left and a detective named Charles Reddy on his right. We drove downtown without any incident, and then we had to take them up to a hearing room on the fourth floor. Arrangement had been made ahead of time, so we were met by a couple of uniformed cops at the side entrance and taken to an elevator already waiting for us.

Vigano and Sambella were very similar types; heavy-set, florid, their faces fixed in that expression of contempt that people get when they've been bossing other people around for a long time. They were expensively dressed, but maybe overdressed, the stripes a little too dominant on their suits, the cufflinks a little too big and shiny. And too many rings on their fingers. They smelled of after-shave and cologne and deodorant and haircream, and they weren't fazed a bit.

Nobody had said a word all the way down in the car, but now, once we were in the elevator and headed up for the fourth floor, Charles Reddy suddenly said, "You don't seem worried, Tony."

Vigano gave him a casual glance. If it bugged him to be called by his first name he didn't show it. He said, "Worried? I could buy you and sell you, what's to worry? I'll be home with my family tonight, and four years from now when the case is over in the courts I won't lose."

Nobody said anything back. What was there to say? "I could buy you and sell you." All I could do was stand there and look at him.

61

• 6 •

THEY BOTH had the day off, and were at home. There was
a birthday party going on in the kitchen of Joe's house. It
was his daughter Jackie's ninth birthday, and the kitchen
was crammed with kids and mothers, a lot more of them
than the room could really hold. But nobody seemed to
mind. The kids seemed to enjoy being squeezed in together
like that, and the mothers were having a good time pretending to be working too hard.

Joe stood in the kitchen doorway, watching with a little

grin on his face. He got a kick out of the racket and the mess the kids were making, and he also liked looking at the mothers' bodies as they moved around trying to keep things organized. It was a hot day anyway, and the kitchen was small, and everybody was sweating, and nobody was wearing a lot of extra clothing in the heat. The women were very sexy moving around, with their hair plastered to their foreheads and their faces shiny and their dresses wet in the small of the back and their legs making brushing sounds against each other as they walked.

Joe had a little fantasy going in the back of his head, in which he would catch the eye of one of the mothers and give her a little come-here kind of head gesture, and she'd come over and say, "What is it?"

"Telephone," he'd say.

"For me?" she'd say.

"Come take it in the bedroom," he'd say. (He grinned to himself at that sentence, he really liked it.)

So they'd go into the bedroom and she'd pick up the phone and turn to him a little confused and say, "There isn't anybody here."

And he'd grin at her, and maybe wink, and say, "I know. What do you say we rest a minute?"

And she'd grin back, and give him a look, and say, "What do you have in mind, Joe?"

And he'd say, "You know what I have in mind," and he'd put her down on the bed and fuck her into the basement.

All of which was going on in the back of his mind, while mainly he was just standing there, leaning against the doorjamb, getting a kick out of watching all the kids at their birthday party.

Tom came into the house, coming in the front way for once, because he knew the birthday party was going on in the kitchen and he'd figured Joe would be staying far

63

away from it. He searched the house, and was surprised at last to find Joe practically inside the kitchen, standing there in the doorway and letting the waves of heat and noise roll over him.

Tom tugged at his elbow. Joe, enjoying the party and his fantasy, gave him an irritable look and didn't move, but Tom made a head gesture meaning come-with-me-I-want-to-talk. Joe nodded at the kitchen, meaning he wanted to stay and watch the party, but Tom jabbed his thumb urgently toward the living room and finally Joe gave up and went with him.

The two of them walked into the living room, where it was a lot quieter, and where Joe said, "Okay, what is it?"

Excited, talking in a half-whisper, Tom said, "I've got it!"

Joe was feeling very irritable. "You got what?"

Tom held up one finger and grinned. "Half," he said. "I've got our problem half-solved."

Joe displayed his irritation by humoring Tom in a heavy-handed way. "Which problem was that, Tom?" he said.

"The heist."

Suddenly Joe was frightened of being overheard. "For Christ's sake!" he said, and looked over his shoulder toward the kitchen.

"It's okay, they can't hear us with that racket."

Joe hadn't been thinking about the robbery idea, and he didn't want to think about it. To get it over with, he moved in closer to Tom and said in a low voice, "All right, what is it?"

This time, Tom held up two fingers. He said, "You remember, we decided we needed two things. Something we could turn over right away for a lot of money, and somebody with a lot of money to do the buying."

Joe nodded, listening but not really involved. His attention was still back with the party and his fantasy. Up till now, they'd both enjoyed talking about the robbery at dull times when there was nothing else to do, like while driving in to the city to go to work, but it was only a theoretical kind of thing that they said they were going to do but that neither one of them really intended to pull off. Now there'd been a change, and the robbery had grown more real to Tom. That hadn't happened yet with Joe, so he just nodded, listening with half of his attention, and said, "Yeah, I remember."

"I've got the buyer," Tom said.

Joe frowned at him, and didn't bother to hide his skepticism. "Who?"

"The Mafia."

"What?" Joe stared at him. "Are you crazy?"

"Who else has two million dollars cash? Who else buys hot goods at that volume?"

Joe looked away, gazing across the living room, starting to think about it. "Christ, Tom," he said, "they do, don't they?"

Tom said, "I told you about those cargo heists on the piers that I worked on that time. It all went straight to the Mafia. Four million a year, they figured that was worth."

Joe thought about it, looking for flaws. "But that wasn't one robbery," he said. "That's over a whole year."

"They're in the business," Tom said. "That's the point."

"All right," Joe said. "So what do we sell them?"

"Whatever they want to buy," Tom said.

• Tom •

JOE AND I had talked it over and decided together how best to approach the Mafia. We decided we didn't want to go through channels, starting with some rank and file punk on the streets. That way, either we wouldn't get to the top at all, or the word would filter out through some informer somewhere along the line, and we'd be in trouble before we even did anything. Besides, the Mafia is always talked about as though it's a business, and in any business, if you've got a problem or a proposition, you should go to the top and leave the clerks strictly alone.

So we decided the thing to do was make our pitch directly to Anthony Vigano. He was, as he'd said he would be, out on bail, so it should be possible to get to see him. We decided it would be better if just one of us approached him, and since it had been my idea in the first place I was the one who would go. Also, Joe didn't feel very much like doing it. It wasn't his kind of thing.

There were files on Vigano downtown, and because of my identification I had simple and easy access to the files. They included Vigano's address, over in Red Bank, New Jersey, plus a lot of other information about the things he'd been involved with over the years. He'd spent eight months in jail when he was twenty-two years old, for assault with a dangerous weapon. Other than that, he had more arrests than I had hairs on my head, but no convictions. He'd been a union officer a few times in his life, and he had an import-export business for a while, and he was a major stockholder in a New Jersey brewery, and he was a part-owner of a trucking company down in Trenton. The arrests had involved drugs and extortion and receiving stolen goods and bribery and just about every crime on the books except playing hookey. There had even been two attempts to get him on income-tax charges, but he'd wriggled out of both of them, too.

There had been three attempts on his life over the years, the last one nine years before, in Brooklyn. He traveled with bodyguards, one of which had been killed that time in Brooklyn, and so far he didn't have a scratch on him. And apparently there hadn't been any more internal disputes since the Brooklyn incident.

His place in Red Bank was an estate near the shore there, a full square block surrounded by a high iron fence and eight-foot-tall hedges. I got the Chevvy and drove over to New Jersey and took a spin around the place once, by day, just checking it out, and through the closed iron gates you could see the black-top road curving in through

67

crew-cut lawn with big oak trees on it, and leading over to a three-story high brick mansion with white trim and four white pillars on the front. There were two or three expensive-looking cars parked in front of the house, and a casual-looking guy dressed like a gardener was hanging around just inside the iron gates. Gardener, hell.

A part of our thinking in this situation all along had been that in our position we could get supplies for the robbery right from the force itself, from the Police Department, and now for the first time we put that idea into effect. There's a room upstairs at the precinct full of disguises, including dresses and false stomachs and all kinds of things; I went up and checked out a moustache and a wig and a set of horn-rim glasses with clear lenses. Then I turned over all my identification to Joe, and took the train down to Red Bank. The idea was, I wanted to visit Vigano without him being able to return the favor.

I took a cab from the station to Vigano's place. If the driver knew anything about the address, he gave no sign of it. I paid him, got out of the car, waited for him to drive away, and then walked over to the gate.

Somebody inside the gate suddenly flashed a light in my eyes. I put my forearm up to block it, and said, "Hey! You don't have to blind me."

A voice said, "Whadya want?" It was a gravel voice, the kind you make with pizza and cigars.

I kept my forearm up. I didn't want all that light on my face out here. I said, "Get that God damn light out of my eyes."

It took him a couple seconds longer; then he lowered the flashlight beam till it was aimed at about my belt-buckle. I still couldn't see anything past it, but at least it wasn't blinding me. And it wasn't showing my features big and clear to anybody observing.

He said, "I still want to know what you want."

I lowered my forearm. "I want to see Mister Vigano," I said. I was suddenly feeling very nervous. I was here without any of the protection I usually carry. Not so much the gun, as the status of being a police officer.

He said, "I don't recognize you."

I said, "I'm a New York City cop, with a proposition."

He said, "We don't take defectors."

"A proposition, that's all," I said. "I'm willing to go see somebody else."

Nothing happened for maybe ten seconds, and then all of a sudden the light went out. Now I couldn't see anything at all. "Wait there," the voice said, and footsteps went away.

After a minute or so my eyes adjusted to the dark again, and I could make out lights in the house inside there. I didn't know if there was anybody standing inside the gate or not.

I waited nearly five minutes. That gave me plenty of time to come to the conclusion that I was an idiot. What the hell was I doing here in the first place? This whole robbery thing was just something Joe and I talked about in the car, going into the city and going home. Sometimes we talked and thought as though we were serious about it, but were we? Was I really going to steal something and collect a million dollars and go live in Trinidad? That's just daydreams.

The reason I became a policeman is because I wanted a civil-service job. I took a couple of the state civil-service exams, and I became a clerk in an Unemployment Insurance office in Queens, and one day when I had nothing to do I read a police-recruiting poster on the billboard in the office. The idea I got from the poster was that being a policeman combined civil service with a little bit of glamour or excitement. The clerk job was too boring to put up with any more, so I switched over. And the poster didn't lie. Being a policeman is exactly that; civil service plus excitement.

But I don't know, the last few years everything seems to be going to hell. Sometimes I think it's just me getting older, but other times I look around and I notice everybody else has the same attitude. Like New York is getting crappier by the second, and money is getting tighter, and everything is just more tense and troubled and futile than it used to be.

It's been coming this way for a long time, I don't mean this is any sudden change. I mean, the reason I moved my family out to Long Island eleven years ago was because already by then New York was a place where you didn't want to bring up your children. Everybody else moved out then too. We all knew the city was getting impossible, and we all freely admitted to one another that we were moving out because of the kids.

Well, now the city *is* impossible. It isn't even a place for adults any more. I hate driving in there every workday, I don't even like to look in that direction. But what am I going to do? You get married, you have kids, you commit yourself to a mortgage on a house, payments on the car and the furniture; all of a sudden there aren't any more decisions you can make. I couldn't decide tomorrow morning to stop being a New York City cop. Give up my seniority, my civil-service status? Give up my years toward the pension? And where would I find another job at the same pay? And would it be any better?

You go along and go along, and it seems as though you're running your own life, and it never occurs to you that your life has gradually closed around you like a Venus flytrap and *it's* running you.

During this whole period of time, while the idea of the robbery was still theoretical, I found myself remembering over and over what that hippie pusher had said, about all of us having started out different from this. It's true. I'd find myself sometimes doing things, or saying things, or just thinking things, and I'd suddenly look around at myself and not believe it was me. If I could have looked ahead when I was ten years old to the man I was going to turn out to be, would I have been pleased?

And I just have this vague feeling that it isn't necessary, that this isn't who I have to be. Joe and me both, my partner Ed, all of us, we've narrowed ourselves down, we've made ourselves blunt and tough because that's the only way to survive. But what if we were in a different kind of setting? Even that hippie was a ten-year-old kid once. But we all of us get together in that city like hungry animals jammed in together in a pit, and we beat on each other because that's all we know how to do, and after a while all of us have turned ourselves into people you don't want to bring your kids up among.

So you sit in the car on the way to work, and you fantasize a million-dollar robbery, life in a Caribbean island, out and away from all this lousy stuff. They make movies about robberies, and people go to them and love them. Or watch them when they show up on television. And every once in a while somebody tries it in real life.

A flashlight was coming down the drive from the house. I tensed up, seeing it come. I could still turn around and walk away from this, let it stay in the land of fantasy. I think it was only the idea of facing Joe that kept me from doing it.

There were several people behind the flashlight, I couldn't be sure how many. The flashlight didn't point at me at all now; first it pointed at the ground, and then it pointed at the gate as it was being unlocked. A voice said, "Come in." It wasn't the gravel voice from before, but a different one, smoother, oilier.

I stepped in, and they shut the gate behind me. I was

71

frisked, fast and expert, and then hands held my arms just above the elbows and I was walked up to the house.

I didn't get to use the front entrance. They took me around the side and into an entrance with snow shovels and overcoats and overshoes in the small room inside. We went through that into an empty kitchen, and they frisked me again, more thoroughly, going through all my pockets. There were three of them, and two searched me while the other stood off a ways behind me. They were dressed in suits and ties, but they were unmistakably hoods.

When they finished with the second search, one of the friskers went out of the room. The other two and I waited. I looked around the kitchen, which was like the kind you see in a fairly small restaurant. Big chopping-block table in the middle, with copper pans hanging from racks over it. Stainless-steel ovens and grill and sinks. Apparently Mr. Vigano did a lot of entertaining.

It had occurred to me there was a possibility Mr. Vigano might decide to kill me. I couldn't think of any reason for him to do it, but I couldn't discount the possibility. I admired the kitchen rather than think about that.

The frisker came back and said to the other two, "We take him to Mr. Vigano."

"Fine," I said. I said it partly because I wanted to be sure my voice was still working.

The frisker led the way. The other two took my arms again, and we left the kitchen in a group.

It was a weird sort of stop-and-go method we had, the four of us, traveling through the house. First the frisker would go on ahead through a doorway or around a corner, and then he'd come back and nod to us, and the rest of us would move forward and catch up with him. At which point we'd stop again, and he'd go on to the next phase of the trip. It was like being a piece on a board game, something like Monopoly or Sorry, moving one square at a time. I don't know if the idea was that they didn't want me to be seen by members of Vigano's family who weren't a part of the mob operation, or if he had Mafia people staying with him that I wasn't supposed to see and maybe identify. But whatever their intention the result was that I got a slow-paced guided tour of the first floor of Vigano's house.

It was a strange house. Either Vigano had bought it furnished from the previous owner, who had been somebody with a lot of good taste, or he'd had the thing done for him by an expensive decorator. We went through rooms filled with obviously valuable antiques, graceful furniture, flocked wallpaper, crystal chandeliers, heavy draperies, all sorts of tasteful and quietly expensive things; just the kind of surroundings I'm happiest among. But then on the wall there'd be hanging some lousy painting of a crying clown, with real rhinestones sprinkled on his hat. Or a lovely marble-topped table would have one of those ashtrays on it made of a flattened gin bottle. Or a modern black parson's table would have a lamp on it composed of a fake brass statue of two lions trying to climb up the trunk of a tree and the shade would be cream-colored with purple fringe. Or a room with a beautiful wallpaper would have one of those porcelain light-switch plates in a free-form star shape. Absolutely the most amateurishly done bust of President Kennedy I've ever seen was sitting on a huge gleaming grand piano, next to a green glass vase with pussy willows in it.

And finally, at the end of the guided tour, they took me through another door and down a flight of stairs and into a bowling alley.

It was amazing. A one-lane bowling alley in the basement, a long narrow brightly lighted room like a pistol-practice range. There was the normal kind of curved leatherette settee behind the lane, and Vigano himself was

73

sitting there alone. He was wearing a gray sweatsuit and black sneakers and a white towel around his neck, and he was drinking beer from a Pilsner glass. A bottle of Michelob was on the score table.

Down at the far end of the lane, a heavy thirtyish guy in a black suit was setting up the pins. He was another hood, like the two who'd brought me in and who now stood back by the door, waiting to be called on.

I moved forward to the settee. Vigano turned his head around and gave me a heavy smile. He had heavy-lidded eyes; it was as though he only allowed the dead part of his eyes to show, the living parts were hidden away behind the lids. He looked at me for a few seconds, and then put the smile away and nodded at the settee. "Sit down," he said. It was a command, not hospitality.

I stepped through the central opening in the settee and sat on the side opposite Vigano. Down at the other end of the lane, the hood in the black suit finished setting up the pins and hoisted himself up onto a seat hidden away out of sight. Only his highly polished shoes showed, hanging down over the black valley where the ball would stop.

Vigano was studying me. "You're wearing a wig," he said.

I said, "The story is, the FBI takes movies of your visitors. I don't want to be identified."

He nodded. "The moustache phoney too?"

"Sure."

"It looks better than the wig." He drank some beer. "You're a cop, huh?"

"Detective Third Grade," I said. "Assigned in Manhattan."

He emptied the rest of the beer from the bottle into the glass. Not looking directly at me, he said, "I'm told you don't have any papers on you. Wallet, driver's license, nothing like that."

74

I said, "I don't want you to know who I am."

He nodded again. Now he did look at me. He said, "But you want to do something for me."

"I want to sell something to you."

He squinted slightly. "Sell?"

I said, "I want to sell you something for two million dollars cash."

He didn't know whether he was supposed to laugh or take me seriously. He said, "Sell me what?"

"Whatever you want to buy," I told him.

I could see him deciding to get annoyed. "What bullshit is this?"

I talked as fast as I knew how. "You buy things," I said. "I've got a friend, he's also a cop. In our position, with what we know about how things work, we can go anywhere in New York you want and get you anything you want. You just tell us what it is you'll pay two million dollars for, and we'll go get it."

Shaking his head, seeming to be talking more to himself than to me, Vigano said, "I can't believe any DA in the world would be this dumb. This is a stunt you worked out for yourself."

"Sure it is," I said. "And how can it hurt you? Your boys frisked me on the way in, I don't have a recorder on me, and if I did it's entrapment. I'm not crazy enough to just hand stuff over to you and expect two million dollars in cash right back, so we'll have to work out intermediaries, safe methods, and that means you can't possibly get picked up for fencing stolen goods."

He was studying me hard now, trying to work me out. He said, "You mean you're actually offering to go steal something, anything I want."

"That you'll pay two million for," I said. "And that we can handle; I'm not going to get you an airplane."

"I've got an airplane," he said, and turned away from

75

me to look toward the pins set up at the far end of the lane.

I could see him thinking it over. I felt I hadn't said enough, hadn't explained it right, but at the same time I knew the best thing to do right now was keep my mouth shut and let him work it out for himself.

The fact was, he had nothing to lose, and he should be smart enough to see it. If I was crazy or stupid or just a horse's ass kidding around, it still wouldn't cost Vigano anything to tell me what he'd be willing to buy from me. So long as I didn't ask for an advance payment, it was strictly to Vigano's advantage to play along with me.

I saw that understanding come into his face before he said anything. I watched him work it out, slowly and cautiously, looking for traps and mines the way somebody in his position would have to do, and I saw him come around finally to the understanding that there was nothing hidden underneath at all. I had come here asking a question, which it wouldn't hurt him to answer. And if I was telling him a straight story, it might eventually profit him to answer. So why not?

He gave a sudden decisive nod, and looked at me with his heavy-lidded eyes, and said, "Securities."

The word didn't immediately make sense to me. All I could think of was security guards in stores and banks. I said, "Securities?"

"Treasury bonds," he said. "Bearer bonds. No common stocks. Can you do it with an inside man?"

I said, "You mean Wall Street?"

"Sure Wall Street. You know anybody in a brokerage?"

I had been thinking all along it would be something in our own precinct, where we knew the territory. "No, I don't," I said. "Do I have to?"

Vigano shrugged and waved it away. His hands were surprisingly big and flat. "We'll change the numbers," he

76

said. "Just make sure you don't get me anything with a name on it."

I said, "I don't follow you."

He breathed heavily, to show me how patient he was being. "If a certificate has the owner's name on it," he said, "I don't want it. Only papers that say, 'Pay to the bearer.'"

"Did you say Treasury bonds?"

"Right," he said. "Them, or any other kind of bearer bond."

I found myself interested in this in a separate way from the question of stealing things. I'd never heard of bearer bonds. I said, "You mean they're like a different kind of money."

Vigano grunted, with a little smile. "They *are* money," he said.

I felt happy at the thought, the way I'd been happy in that rich woman's apartment on Central Park West. "Rich people's money," I said.

Vigano grinned at me. I think we were both surprised at how well we were getting along with one another. "That's right," he said. "Rich people's money."

I said, "And you'll buy them from us."

"Twenty cents on the dollar," he said.

That startled me. "A fifth?"

He shrugged. "I'm giving you a good price because you're gonna deal in volume. Usually it's ten cents on the dollar."

I'd meant the percentage was low, not high. I said, "If it's pay to bearer, why don't I sell it myself?"

"You don't know how to change the numbers," he said. "And you don't have the contacts to get the paper back into legitimate trade."

He was right, on both counts. "All right," I said. "So we'll have to take ten-million-dollars' worth to get two million from you."

"Nothing too big," he said. "No certificate over a hundred thousand."

"How big do they get?" I asked him. This whole thing was heady stuff.

"U.S. Treasury bonds go up to a million," he said. "But they're impossible to peddle."

I couldn't help it; I was awed and I had to show it. "A million dollars," I said.

"Stick to the small stuff," Vigano told me. "Hundred grand and down."

A hundred thousand dollars was small stuff. I felt my mind shifting around to that point of view, and doing it with the greatest pleasure. Years ago there was a show on Broadway called *Beyond the Fringe* and they did a bit from it on television one time that I saw. (I've never seen a Broadway show.) The bit was a monologue by an English miner, and at one point he said something like, "In my childhood I wasn't surrounded by the trappings of luxury, I was surrounded by the trappings of poverty. My problem is I had the wrong trappings." That line stayed with me over the years because it was exactly the way I felt; I was surrounded by the wrong trappings. And any time I found myself in the midst of the right trappings, it made me very happy.

Vigano was watching me. "You got the idea now?" he said.

Business; back to business. "Yes," I said. "Bearer bonds, no larger than a hundred thousand dollars."

"Right."

"Now," I said, "about payment."

"Get the stuff first," he said.

"Give me a number to call. One that isn't tapped."

Vigano said, "Give me your number."

"Not a chance," I said. "I already said I don't want you to know who I am. Besides, my wife isn't in on it."

He looked at me with a surprised grin. "Your wife isn't in on it," he said. The grin got wider, and then he laughed out loud, and then he said, "Your wife isn't in on it. All of a sudden, I believe you're on the level."

Everything had shifted. He'd made me feel like a fool, and I wasn't even sure why. Angry, but trying not to show it, I said, "I am on the level."

His grin faded away and he got serious again. Reaching over to the score table, he picked up a ballpoint pen and a small blank memo pad. He extended them to me, saying, "Here. I'll give you a number to write down."

He wouldn't put his own handwriting on even a telephone number. I took the pad and pen and waited.

He said, "It's in Manhattan. Six nine one, nine nine seven oh."

I wrote it down.

He said, "You call that number from inside Manhattan; no interborough, no long distance. You ask is Arthur there, they'll say no. You call from a phone booth, or some phone you're sure of. You leave your number, Arthur should call you back. You'll hear from me within fifteen minutes. If you don't, I'm not around, try again later."

I nodded. "All right."

"When you call," he said, "you say your name is Mister Kopp. K - O - P - P."

I grinned a little. "That's easy to remember."

"But don't call me with questions," he said. "You do it or you don't. If you take ten million in securities from Wall Street, I'll read about it in the paper. Otherwise, if I get a message from you I don't answer."

"Sure," I said. "That's okay."

"Nice talking to you," he said, and picked up his beer glass again. He hadn't offered me one.

He wanted the conversation to be finished, so I got to

my feet. "You'll be hearing from me," I said. I knew it was bravado to say it, and that it didn't make me look any better, but I went ahead and said it anyway.

He shrugged. He wasn't interested in me any more. "That's fine," he said.

• Vigano •

VIGANO WATCHED the visitor leave with his escorts. He
waited thirty seconds, brooding, sipping at his Michelob,
and then pressed the intercom button on the scoreboard.

Waiting for Marty to come in, he thought back over the
conversation. Could the guy have been on the level? It was
hard to believe, and yet anything else was even harder to
believe. What other reason could he have for pulling a
stunt like this, coming here cold with such an off-the-wall
idea? There was no profit for any law-enforcement agency

81

in it, and nothing to be gained by any potential competitor.

After all, he wouldn't ever have anything else to do with the guy unless there really was a multi-million-dollar bond theft on Wall Street. Which would get into the papers and onto the television news, no doubt about it. Anybody calling up and claiming to be Mr. Kopp and claiming to have stolen bonds would be given the brush-off right away unless there had been a robbery to match, one that Vigano knew about from his own sources.

So assume the guy was on the level. What was the likelihood he'd actually go through with a robbery and get away with it? Very very thin. And if he didn't do it, Vigano wouldn't have lost anything.

But if he did really pull it off, Vigano would stand to gain a hell of a lot.

It was a nice position to be in. Vigano toasted himself with Michelob, and Marty came in, saying, "Yes, sir, Mr. Vigano?"

Vigano turned to him. "The guy that's going out now," he said. "I want his name and address and what he does for a living."

"Yes, sir," Marty said, and left again.

It would probably come to nothing. But just in case something good did come out of it, Vigano wanted to have his homework done. It's the details, he thought, that make the difference between a winner and a punk.

He got to his feet, selected a ball, and bowled a strike.

• Joe •

WHEN TOM and I talked over the Mafia idea, one thing we agreed on right away was that if the mob found out who we were, there was no way we could go through with it. Neither of us wanted mobsters around with that kind of hold over us. Either we could contact Vigano and stay anonymous, or we'd have to give up that idea and try to think of something else.

We took it for granted, the two of us, that Vigano would have Tom followed after their conversation; if he talked to Tom at all. So the first most necessary thing was to break Tom loose from the people tailing him.

The last train to Penn Station from Red Bank pulls in to New York at twelve-forty. There aren't many people on that train, particularly on a week night, which was part of the reason we'd picked it. Also, where it came in at Penn Station there was only one staircase up to the terminal.

I was in uniform, and I got to the station fifteen minutes ahead of time. We'd rehearsed this three times, and the train had never been anywhere near this early, but we wanted to be absolutely sure. I went to the head of the stairs leading up from that platform, and stood there, waiting.

Standing there, it occurred to me this was the first time in my life I'd worn the uniform when I wasn't on duty. I've never been exactly gung ho for the force. The only reason I was in that uniform at all was because the Army didn't need any tank drivers the day in basic training when I got classified. The choices open to me were cook or military policeman or something else, I forget what. Something crappy. They were also picking orderly-room clerks and finance clerks that day, but my test profile wasn't too good in the right areas for those jobs. What I really wanted was to drive a tank, but I wound up an MP.

I was an MP for a year and a half, eleven months of it assigned to the Vogelweh dependent housing area outside Kaiserlautern, Germany. I dug it. I got a kick out of carrying a .45 around on my hip, and doing the target shooting, and driving around town in a jeep at night to keep the white troops and the black troops from beating each other's head in. I hadn't had any job at all before I was drafted, I mean nothing that I wanted to get back to, and I never had any interest in college, so when I got out of the Army the question was what would I do for a living, and the answer was plain and simple. Go on the same as before. The uniform changed from brown to blue, the side-arm changed from a .45 automatic to a .38 revolver, and you had to be a little more careful how you dealt with people, but otherwise it was pretty much the same job.

Which was nice at first, it made for a nice transition from soldier to civilian. But after a while the same job gets to be a drag and a bore and a pain in the ass, no matter what it is. Whether you're carrying a gun or not, driving around the city or not, it doesn't matter; it gets boring.

For a long time, it seemed as though there was always something else to take up the slack, keep me interested in life even when the job was dull. Getting married, for instance. Having kids. Moving out of the apartment out to Long Island. Those are like the mountains, and the valley is your dull everyday life.

It had been a long time between mountains.

For the last couple years, I'd been thinking about women, about maybe shacking up with somebody somewhere. Get me a girl in town, somewhere in my precinct. I was pretty sure a girl on the side would drain off all this stored-up boredom again, at least for a while, but somehow I never seemed to get started at it. My heart wasn't in it. I knew it was possible, I personally knew four guys in the precinct who had exactly that kind of arrangement, but it was like I didn't have the energy to make the first moves, to look around in any way more than just eyeing my friends' wives and wondering how they'd be in the sack. Maybe I was trying to keep myself from disappointment, maybe down in the bottom of my brain I had the idea a girl on the side would finally be the biggest letdown of all. With no place left to go from there.

I heard the train come in, down below; the way the brakes squealed, they could probably hear it up on 42nd Street. I stood at the head of the stairs, just to one side, looking down. The stairs were concrete, and wide enough

85

for three people abreast, and they were flanked on both sides by amber tile walls.

Tom got to the stairs first, the way he was supposed to. If I hadn't already seen him in the disguise I wouldn't have recognized him. The wig was a different hair color, and longer than his usual hair, and it seemed to change the whole shape of his head. Then he had a David Niven kind of moustache, which made his face look younger for some reason. And the horn-rim glasses changed his eyes entirely, so he looked like an accountant somewhere.

As for me, the uniform was my main disguise. People rarely look past the uniform to see the individual man. The only extra disguise I wore was a droopy moustache, like a western sheriff's, and I'd put that on more for the hell of it than because I thought I really needed it. There wouldn't be any reason for anybody to tie me up with Tom.

About a dozen other passengers came along behind Tom, the usual number for this train, and it wasn't hard at all to pick out Vigano's men from among them. Three of them, all dressed differently but all unmistakably hoods, with hard faces and hunched shoulders.

I was surprised at how hard it hit me, when I saw those three guys among the bunch of people coming up the stairs behind Tom. Up till that second, I guess I really hadn't believed it; that Tom would go through with it, or that he'd get in to see Vigano, or that Vigano would wind up listening to him and believing him. But it must have happened, or those three guys wouldn't have taken the train.

Tom was moving fast, coming up the stairs two and three at a time. The three shadows were mixed in with the pack, all of it moving more slowly; when Tom reached the head of the stairs, the nearest other passenger was still eight steps down.

Tom went by me without a look, the way he was supposed to. He went past, and I immediately stepped for-

86

ward to block the staircase. I held my arms out and said, "Hold up a minute. Hold it, there."

Momentum kept them coming up a few more steps, but then they stopped and all looked up at me. People obey the uniform. I saw two of Vigano's men pushing their way up past the other passengers toward me, and the third one going back down the stairs; probably to look for another way up. But there wasn't any, not from that platform. By the time he found another exit it would be too late, and he'd come up in the wrong place anyway.

They were all milling around on the stairs, a dozen of them packed in tight together. New Yorkers expect that kind of thing, so there wasn't any major complaint. One of Vigano's men, having shoved himself up to the front of the pack, where his head was at the level of my elbow, looked past me down the corridor, watching Tom hustle away. He made an irritated face, but tried to keep his voice neutral when he said to me, "What's the problem, officer?"

"Only be a minute," I told him.

His eyes kept flicking back and forth between the corridor and me, and I could tell by his expression when Tom turned the corner down there. But still I held them all, while I counted to thirty slowly. The third hood reappeared at the foot of the stairs and trotted up them, looking disgusted.

I stepped to the side, slow and casual. "Okay," I said. "Go ahead."

They streamed past me, Vigano's men moving at a dead run. I watched them go, and I knew they were wasting their time. We'd practiced this enough, Tom and I, so that we knew how long it would take him to get to the nearest exit and out to where his car was parked, with the special police permit showing on the sun visor. By now, he was probably already making the turn onto Ninth Avenue.

I strolled the other way.

87

· 7 ·

THERE WAS a certain amount of leeway in setting up the work schedules at the precinct, so Tom and Joe could usually adjust things around to be on duty at the same hours. They got cooperation from the precinct because it was understood they had a car pool together. If they'd both been patrolmen, or both on the detective squad, they could probably have worked it out one hundred per cent of the time, but operating out of two different offices the way they did there were bound to be times when the work schedules were in conflict, with nothing to be done about it.

Because of one of those conflicts, it was three days before they got to talk about Tom's meeting with Vigano, and when at last they did get together Joe was too worn out to pay much attention. He'd been on a double shift, sixteen hours straight, caused by some special activity over at the United Nations. In fact, it was the stuff at the United Nations, involving a couple of African countries and the Jewish Defense League and some anti-Communist Polish group and who knows what all, that had created the conflict in the work schedule in the first place.

It wasn't that Joe himself had had to go over to the UN, but a lot of uniformed men from the precinct had been sent down there for the duration of the special circumstances, and that meant the guys who were left had to double up to cover the territory.

That was one of the big differences between the patrolmen and the detective squad. The detectives were chronically short-handed, and used to it, but there was never any time when orders would come down that would strip out half the men from the squad and leave the rest to take up the slack. The patrolmen though, were under normal circumstances up pretty close to full strength, until every once in a while the phone would ring in the Lieutenant's office, a couple of buses would pull up out front to take the boys away, and the ones left would have to start scrambling. Like today.

Today, the result was that they rode back together in Tom's car that afternoon with Tom excited and ready to talk, and Joe just sitting there as though he'd been hit by a fire hydrant. In fact, having come to work eight hours before Tom, he had his own car in the city, the Plymouth, and was just leaving it there, because he didn't think he had the stamina to drive it all the way home. He'd come back in with Tom tomorrow, and drive the Plymouth home tomorrow night, if all went well.

At first, Tom didn't realize just how far out of it Joe was. They got into the car together and Tom headed for the tunnel, and as they drove he gave a quick rundown on what Vigano had said. Joe didn't make any response, mostly because he was barely listening. Tom tried to capture his attention by talking louder and faster, trying to push some of his own enthusiasm into Joe's ear. "It's simple," he said. "What are bonds? They're just pieces of paper." He glanced over at Joe. "Joe?"

Joe nodded. "Pieces of paper," he said.

"And the great thing is," Tom said, "we can actually do it." He gave Joe another look, with some annoyance in it. "Joe, you with me?"

Joe shifted around in his seat, moving his body like a sleeper who doesn't want to wake up. "For Christ's sake, Tom," he said, "I'm dead on my feet."

"You aren't on your feet."

Joe was too tired for humor; it just made him grouchy. "I *been* on my feet," he said. "Double shift."

"If you pay attention to me," Tom said, "you can say good-bye to all that."

They were just entering the Midtown Tunnel. Joe said, "You really believe in this?"

"Naturally."

Joe didn't make any answer, and Tom didn't say anything else while they were in the tunnel. Coming out the other side, Tom said, "You got change?"

Joe roused himself and patted his pockets, while Tom slowed for the toll booths. Joe didn't have any change, so he got out his wallet. "Here's a dollar," he said.

"Thanks." Tom took the dollar, gave it to the attendant, got the change back, and passed it to Joe, who sat there looking at the coins in his palm as though he didn't know what he was supposed to do with them.

Driving away from the booth, Tom said, "How'd you like a job like that?"

"I don't want any job at all," Joe said. He dropped the coins in his shirt pocket and rubbed his face with his palm.

"Just standing there all day," Tom said, "taking money in."

"They all rake off a little," Joe said.

"Yeah, and they get caught."

Joe squinted at him. "We won't?"

"No, we won't," Tom said.

Joe shrugged, and looked out the side window at the black buildings and brick smokestacks of Long Island City.

Tom said, "The big difference is, we won't do it over and over. One big job, and quit. I go to Trinidad, you go to Montana."

Joe turned his head to Tom again. "Saskatchewan," he said.

Tom, thrown off the track, frowned at the trucks he was driving among, and said, "What?"

"I thought it over," Joe told him. He was beginning to wake up despite himself, though he was still in a bad mood. He said, "What I'd really like to do is get Grace and the kids out of this country entirely. But completely out, before it goes to hell altogether."

"Where's this you want to go?"

"Saskatchewan." Joe made a vague gesture, as though pointing northward. "It's in Canada," he said. "They give you land if you want to be a farmer."

Tom gave him a grin of surprise and disbelief. "What do you know about farming?"

"A hell of a lot less than I'll know next year." They were now on that part of the Expressway lined on both sides with cemeteries, and Joe brooded out at it all. It's like

91

somebody's idea of a sick joke, all those tombstones stretching away on both sides of the Expressway just a couple miles from Manhattan; like a parody of a city, in bad taste. Neither of them had ever mentioned it to the other, but those damn cemeteries had bugged them both from time to time, over the years of driving back and forth. And the funny thing was, they bothered the both of them more in the daytime than at night. And more on sunny days than rainy days. And more in the summer than in the winter.

This was a sunny day in July.

Neither of them said any more until they were past the cemeteries. Then Joe said, "I'm really thinking about that, you know. Just pack everybody in the car and take off for Canada. Except with my luck, it'd break down before we got to the border."

"Not if you had a million dollars," Tom said.

Joe shook his head. "There are times," he said, "I almost believe we're gonna do it."

Tom frowned at him. "What's the matter with you? You're the one that's *done* it already."

"You mean the liquor store?"

"What else?"

"That was a different thing," Joe said. "That was—" He moved his hands, trying to think of the word.

"Small-time," Tom said. "I'm telling you to think big-time. You know what Vigano had?"

Small-time wasn't the word Joe had been looking for. Irritated, he said, "What did he have?"

"His own bowling alley. Right in the house."

Joe just stared. "A bowling alley?"

"Regulation bowling alley. One lane. Right in the house."

Joe grinned. That was the kind of high life he could understand. "Son of a bitch," he said.

"Go tell *him* crime doesn't pay," Tom said.

Joe nodded, thinking it over. He said, "And he told you securities, huh?"

"Bearer bonds," Tom said. "Just pieces of paper. Not heavy, no trouble, we turn them right over."

Joe was wide awake now, interested, his irritation forgotten. "Tell me the whole thing," he said. "What he said, what you said. What's his house look like?"

• Joe •

To ME, Broadway in the Seventies and Eighties is the only part of Manhattan that's worth anything at all. Paul and I cover that area in the squad car a lot, and I kind of like it. The people are maybe a little uglier-looking than the average, but at least they're human; not like the freaks in the Village or the Lower East Side. Midtown has all the pretty people, all those marching men in their suits and good-looking girl secretaries out wandering around during lunch, but that isn't where they *live*. There isn't anything human or livable in that area at all; it's just stone and glass

94

boxes that the white-collar people work in all day. On their own time, they go somewhere else.

Anyway, we're supposed to cover the cross-streets and West End Avenue and Columbus and Amsterdam and Central Park West, but whenever I'm at the wheel I tend to be on Broadway. Unless I feel like doing some fun driving or giving out some tickets, in which case I go over to Henry Hudson Parkway.

Two days after Tom and I had our talk in his car about Vigano, Paul and I were heading south on Broadway, me driving, when all of a sudden, half a block ahead of us, two people came struggling out of a hardware store onto the sidewalk. They were both male, both Caucasian. One was short, heavy-set, fiftyish, wearing gray workpants and a white shirt with the sleeves rolled up above his elbows. The other was tall, lanky, twentyish, wearing army boots and khaki pants and a green polo shirt. At first, all I could see was that they were struggling with one another, going around in a circle as though they were dancing.

Paul saw it too. "There!" he said pointing.

I accelerated, then hit the brakes as we got closer. I could see now that the tall young one had a small zippered bag in one hand and a small pistol in the other. The short guy was clinging to the tall guy's waist, holding on for dear life, and the tall guy was trying to club him with the pistol. There were a lot of pedestrians on the sidewalk, as usual, but they were falling back, giving the two men plenty of room.

Paul and I both jumped out of the car at the same time. He was closer to the curb, while I had to run around the front of the car. At the same time, the tall guy finally managed to break loose from the short one. He gave him a shove backwards, and the short guy staggered a couple of steps and then sat down hard. The tall guy had seen us coming, and he waved the pistol at us.

I yelled, "Drop it! Drop it!"

All of a sudden the son of a bitch fired two shots. Out of the corner of my eye I saw Paul go down, but I had to keep my mind on the guy with the gun. He'd turned and started to run southward along the sidewalk.

I reached the sidewalk, went down on my left knee, propped my forearm on my raised right knee; all those years of practice paid off after all. I was sighted on his back, with the green polo shirt, and then on his legs. But the sidewalks were full, there were too many faces and bodies past him, right in the line of fire. And he was smart enough not to run in a straight line but to shift back and forth as he went.

I kept the pistol aimed, in case I could get a clear shot with nobody beyond him, but it didn't happen. "Damn it," I whispered. "Damn it." And he disappeared around the corner.

I got back to my feet. Over by the storefront, the older man was also getting up. Paul was on his back on the sidewalk, but struggling to sit up, moving like a turtle on its back. I moved to him, holstering the pistol, and crouched beside him as he finished sitting up. He looked stunned, as though he didn't know where he was. I said, "Paul?"

"Jesus," he said. His voice was slurred. "Jesus."

His left trouser leg was wet, stained dark, sodden with blood, midway between the knee and the crotch. "Lie down," I said, and poked at his near shoulder. But he wasn't really conscious at all; he didn't hear me, or didn't understand me. He just went on sitting there, his mouth hanging open, his eyes blinking very slowly.

I got up again, turning toward the squad car, and the old man clutched at my arm. When I looked at him, pulling my arm away, he shouted, "The money! The money!"

I could have killed him. "Shut up about money!" I yelled, and ran to the car to call in.

• 8 •

THEY BOTH had that afternoon off. Tom was mowing his front lawn, wearing just a bathing suit in the sunshine, when Joe came around from between the houses and said, "Hey, Tom." He too was dressed in a bathing suit, and he was carrying two open cans of Budweiser beer.

Tom stopped. He was panting and sweating. "What?"

"Come take a break."

Tom pointed at the beer. "Is that for me?"

"I even opened it for you," Joe said, and handed him

97

one of the beers. "Come on, the kids are out of the pool for once."

Tom took a swig of beer, and they walked down the driveway between the houses and over into Joe's backyard. It was a really hot sunny day in July, and the pool looked great to the both of them. Cool water in a container of light blue, nothing looks better than that on a hot day. Except a beer.

Tom said, "The filter's working?"

Joe put his finger to his lips. "Easy, it'll hear you. Come on, cool off."

Joe had a short sturdy wooden ladder in an A shape over the side of the pool; you went up three steps on one side of the A, and down three steps into the water on the other side. They both climbed up and over, Joe first, and while Joe waded around the four-foot-deep water throwing out leaves and sticks and pieces of paper and dead bugs, Tom sat back on one of the steps of the ladder, so he was in water up to his neck. With his right hand he held the beer can up out of the water.

Joe looked over at him and laughed. "You look like the Statue of Liberty."

Tom grinned, saluted with the beer, and took a swig. It was tough to drink in that position, but Joe was watching, so Tom did it for the effect. Then he said, "You know what I was thinking before? When I was over there with the lawnmower?"

"What?"

"Remember I told you I used to go to City College nights?"

Joe waded over to lean against the side of the pool to Tom's left. "So?"

Tom moved up a step, so the water was only chest-high and it was easier to drink. "What I was thinking," he

98

said, "if I'd kept at it, you know where I'd be today?"

"Where?"

"Right here. I *still* wouldn't be a lawyer, not for two more years."

"Sure," Joe said. He nodded. "You put a penny away every day, at the end of the year you're still poor. It's the same principle."

Tom stared at him. "It is?"

They looked at one another, both bewildered, until Tom lost interest in the subject and changed it, saying, "Listen, what about the wives?"

Joe switched his bewilderment to the new topic. "What?"

"What do we tell the wives?"

"Oh," Joe said. "About the robbery, you mean."

"Naturally."

Joe didn't see any problem. He shrugged and said, "Nothing."

"Nothing? I don't know about you and Grace," Tom said, "but if I put Mary in Trinidad, she's going to know she's in Trinidad."

"Sure," Joe said. "Then. When we're ready to move, that's when we tell them. After it's all over."

Tom hadn't made up his own mind about that yet. There were times, particularly at night, when he very strongly wanted to tell Mary about it, talk it over with her, see what she had to say. Frowning, he said, "Not now at all?"

"In the first place," Joe said, "they'd worry. In the second place, they'd be against it, you know they would."

Tom nodded; that was what had kept him quiet up till now. "I know," he said. "Mary wouldn't approve, not ahead of time."

"They'd throw cold water on the whole idea," Joe said. "If we tell the wives, we'll *never* do it."

"You're right," Tom said. He was disappointed, but he

was also relieved that the question was resolved. "Not till it's all over," he said. "Then we tell them."

"When we're ready to take off out of here," Joe said.

"Right," Tom said. Then he said, "The thing is, you know we can't leave the country right away."

"Oh, sure," Joe said. "I know that. They'd be on our asses in five minutes."

"What we've got to agree right now," Tom said, "is that we bury the money and neither one of us goes near it until we're ready to leave."

"That's fine with me."

"The big advantage we've got," Tom said, "is that we've seen every mistake there is."

"That's right. And we know how not to make them."

Tom took a deep breath. "Two years," he said.

Joe winced. "Two years?"

"We've got to play it cool," Tom said.

Joe looked pained, as though he had an ankle cramp down underwater. He wanted to argue against it, but on the other hand he had to agree with the theory of it; so he was stuck. Reluctantly, but giving in, he said, "Yeah, I suppose. Okay, two years it is."

• Tom •

In the weeks after my visit with Vigano, I got to learn an awful lot about stocks and bonds, and about brokerages, and about Wall Street. I had to, if we were going to take ten million dollars away from there.

Wall Street itself is only about five blocks long, but the brokerages are scattered all around that whole area down there below City Hall; on Pine Street and Exchange Place, on William Street and Nassau Street and Maiden Lane.

I've heard the Wall Street district described as the only

101

part of New York that looks like London. I can't say about that, since I've never been to London, but I do know it has the narrowest and crookedest streets of any part of the city, with narrow sidewalks, and the big bank buildings crowding as close to the curb and each other as they can get. Writers all the time talk about that section in terms of "canyons," and I can see why. With the streets so narrow and the stone buildings so tall and close together, the only time the sun shines on Wall Street is high noon.

For the first time in my life I was beginning to see that breaking the law could be just as complicated as upholding it. I'd always thought of the police side of things as being tougher than the crook side, but maybe I'd been wrong; there's nothing like standing in the other guy's shoes to make you sympathize with him.

There were so many *details* to figure out. How to do the robbery, for instance; whether it should be day or night, whether we should try for a diversion, just exactly how we were going to work it. And how to be sure we were taking the right bonds; before this, neither one of us had known zip about stocks and bonds. And how to make a getaway after the robbery in those narrow crowded streets. And how to hide the loot afterward until we sold it to Vigano; which was ironic, since all along we'd been telling each other we had to steal something that didn't need to be held onto or stowed out of sight.

But there it was. And the brokerages didn't make it any easier. They were guarded like banks; no, they were tougher than banks.

Let me tell you just how tough they were. First of all, there's a special section of the Police Department with headquarters down in the Wall Street area that deals with nothing at all except stock market crime. There are cops in that section that know more about the financial world than the editor of the *Wall Street Journal,* and those cops

102

keep tabs on the brokerages all the time, talking to the personnel directors, talking to the security directors, checking up on their ways of handling things and protecting themselves, and always no more than one phone call away in case there's any kind of trouble.

And then there's the internal security departments. All the big brokerages have them; private uniformed guards, security files, closed-circuit TV, and all of it run usually by an ex-cop or an ex-FBI man. Guys that treat a stock brokerage as though it were a top-secret atomic-testing laboratory, and whose entire job is to see to it that none of the millions of pieces of paper that flow through Wall Street every day ever gets stolen.

Of course, some do. But most stock market robberies are inside jobs, and there's a good reason for it. Stocks and bonds, like dollar bills, carry serial numbers. Usually, the only way to steal securities and get something for your pains is to be an employee of a stock brokerage and alter the records so the brokerage isn't aware that anything has been stolen. With bearer bonds, it's possible for somebody like Anthony Vigano, with his expertise and his contacts, to alter the numbers and peddle the bonds back into legitimate channels, but other than that an inside job is the only kind of job possible on Wall Street.

But even if it weren't, even if there were any point in breaking into a stock brokerage and stripping the vault, they've gone out of their way to make things tough. For instance, a couple of years ago a bank down in that area closed down, and a restaurant was going to move into the space they left vacant. Before they could, though, they had to pull the vault out, and they had one hell of a time doing it. Not only was it wired with all kinds of alarms, not only did it have sixteen-inch-thick concrete walls reinforced with steel rods, but it actually had two separate walls all the way around the vault, and the area between the two walls was filled with poison gas. The workmen taking the vault walls down had to wear gas masks.

That isn't merely being tough; it's being insane.

Still, Joe and I had an edge over the normal safecracker or the normal dishonest employee. We had the facilities of the Police Department to help us, to provide us with material for the robbery and specific information—such as blueprints of alarm systems and other security measures—on whichever brokerage we finally decided to concentrate on.

There was one that looked promising, called Parker, Tobin, Eastpoole & Co. They were in a building near the corner of John and Pearl streets, and I went down there one day to check them out. The building had the typical small lobby of that area—they really don't like to waste space, those financial people—and three elevators. Parker, Tobin, Eastpoole & Co. was on the sixth and seventh and eighth floors, but I already knew it was the seventh floor I wanted, since I'd checked out the alarm-system on file at Police Headquarters downtown.

The elevator was pretty full, and three of us got off together at the seventh floor. Which was good; it gave me a chance to hang back and look at things while the other two went forward to the counter.

The elevator had opened onto a fairly large room, much wider than deep, divided the long way by a chest-high counter. The security arrangements seemed to be typical for a large brokerage. Two armed and uniformed private guards were on duty behind the counter. On the wall in back of them was a large pegboard with maybe twenty plastic ID tags hanging from it, plus room for about a hundred more. Each tag had a color photograph on it of the person it belonged to, plus a signature written underneath. Mounted on the short wall down to the right were six closed-circuit television sets, each showing a different

104

area of the brokerage, including one showing this reception area I was standing in. Above the sets was the TV camera, turning slowly back and forth like a fan. On the other short wall, the one down to my left, was a second pegboard, smaller than the first, holding about twenty-five ID tags marked in big letters: VISITOR. Doorways at both ends of the room led into the work areas.

There was a steady stream of activity around the counter. Arriving employees were picking up their ID tags, departing employees were turning them in, messengers were delivering manila envelopes. I got to stand there for maybe a full two minutes, checking things out.

The first thing I noticed was that only one of the guards dealt with the people who came to the counter. The other one stood back by the rear wall, keeping an eye on things; watching the people, looking over at the television sets, staying alert while his partner did the detail work.

Then there were the television sets. They were in black-and-white, but the pictures were crisp and clear. You could see the people moving around in different rooms, and you could make out their faces with no trouble at all. And I knew this bank of six sets would be repeated probably three or four other places on this floor; in the boss's office, in the security chief's office, in the vault anteroom, maybe one or two other places.

It was also more than likely to be going on video tape. They have video tape now that can be erased and recorded on again, the same as regular sound tape, and that's what they'd have. They might keep the tape for a week or a month or maybe even longer, so that if it turned out later that somebody had pulled a fast one, they could run the tapes through again and see who was where at what time.

"Can I help you?"

It was the guard, the one who dealt with people, looking across the counter at me. He was brusque and impatient, because of the amount of work he had to do, but he wasn't suspicious. I stepped forward to the counter, trying for the world's most innocent and stupid smile. Pointing at the television sets, I said, "Is that me?"

He gave a brief bored look at the screens. "That's you," he said. "What can I do for you?"

"I've never been on television before," I said. I looked at the screen as though I was fascinated; and to tell the truth, I was. I'd worn the moustache again, and I was amazed at what I looked like with a moustache. Totally different. I wouldn't have recognized me if I met me walking down the street.

The guard was getting impatient. He looked me over for manila envelopes and said, "You a messenger?"

I didn't want to hang around and pester him for so long that I became memorable. Besides, I'd seen all I was going to see out here, and there was no way I was going to get inside. Not today. I said, "No, I'm looking for the personnel office. I'm supposed to come to work here."

"That's on the eighth floor," the guard said, and jabbed a thumb toward the ceiling.

"Oh," I said. "Then I'm in the wrong place."

"That's right," he said.

"Thanks," I said, and went back over to the elevators and pushed the button. While waiting, I looked around some more. You sure had to admire their security. And yet, this was the likeliest prospect.

• Joe •

I DIDN'T much like visiting Paul in the hospital. I don't like hospitals anyway, but I particularly don't like them when there's a brother officer in there. I don't like that reminder.

Did you ever watch pro football on television, and notice what happens when one of the players gets hurt? He's laying there on the ground, moving his knees a little, and maybe one or two other players go over to see what the story is, but all the rest kind of walk off by themselves and pretend they have a problem with their shoes. I know exactly how they feel, I do. It isn't they're heartless or any-thing, it's just they don't like to be reminded how easy it could turn out to be one of them.

Same with me. I had plenty of chances to visit Paul, but until I was feeling really good and guilty I wouldn't go at all. Then I'd finally go and there'd be nothing to say, and we'd sit around and watch soap operas together for half an hour. It's a funny thing, we always had plenty to talk about in the car, but not in the hospital. The hospital is death on conversation.

So I was there again, going back and forth at the foot of the bed. Paul was in a semiprivate room, but the other bed was empty right now. His windows gave a good clear view of a brick wall. It you stood right next to the window and looked down you could see green grass, but if Paul could have stood next to the window he wouldn't have to be in the hospital, and from the bed what you saw was brick wall.

The television set mounted on the wall was turned on, but the sound was off. Paul was sitting up in bed, news-papers and magazines all around him, and he kept sneak-ing glances at the TV.

I was trying to think of something to say. I hate long uncomfortable silences.

Paul said, "Listen, Joe, if you want to get back out there, it's okay."

I stopped walking, and tried to look interested. "No, no, this is fine. What the hell, let Lou drive around a while." Lou was Paul's replacement in the car, a rookie.

Paul said, "How's he doing?"

"He's okay," I said. I shrugged, not much caring. Then I tried to keep the conversation alive, saying, "He's too gung ho, that's all. I'll be glad to get you back."

"Me too." He grinned and said, "Can you believe it? I *want* to go to work."

108

"A couple of times," I told him, "I would have traded places with you."

All of a sudden he started scratching his leg through the covers. "They keep telling me it won't itch any more," he said.

"I haven't seen the doctor yet," I said, "that knew his ass from his elbow." I nodded at the other bed. "At least you don't have the old geek around any more. They send him home?"

"Naw," Paul said. "He died." He was still scratching through the covers.

"That must have been fun."

"Middle of the night." He stopped scratching, and yawned. "He fell right out of bed," he said. "Woke me up. Scared the crap out of me."

"Nice little vacation for you," I said. And I thought, *Nice little conversation we're having.*

"Oh, it's great," he said.

I didn't have anything else I wanted to say about an old man falling out of bed and dropping dead, so the silence came back again for a while. I looked up at the television set, and it showed a guy in a rowboat floating around in a toilet tank. Television is fucking incredible sometimes.

Paul shifted around in the bed, kicking his legs out this way and that, and a couple of his magazines slid off onto the floor. *Like the old man,* I thought. "Boy, my ass gets to hurting," he said. He couldn't seem to decide what position he wanted to be in. "Pins and needles, you know?"

"I know," I said. I picked the magazines up and tossed them on the bed again. "You ought to roll over on your other side," I told him. "Lie on a nurse, that'll help."

"Have you seen the beasts around here?"

"I've seen them."

And so much for that conversation. I looked at the television set again, and the commercial was over—I *hope*

109

that was a commercial—and what was up there on the screen? A hospital room, one guy in the bed and one guy walking around the room, talking to him. "We're on television," I said.

Paul said, "The guy in the bed has amnesia."

I looked at him. "Where'd you get it?"

He grinned at me. "I forgot."

No place to go from there either. Christ, conversation is impossible in the hospital, it really is.

Paul glanced over at the empty bed. He had a thoughtful look on his face, and he said, "You know what used to get me about him?"

"What, the old guy?"

"He was always saying he hadn't done anything yet." Paul gave me a look, with this strange-looking kind of crooked smile on his face. He said, "He'd wasted his life, that's what he thought, he hadn't done anything with himself. He was older'n hell, but all he wanted was to get healthy and get out of here, so he could start doing something."

"Like what?"

"*He* didn't know, the poor old fart." Paul shrugged. "Just something different, I guess."

I looked at the other bed. I could almost see the old man falling out of it onto the floor. I wondered what he'd done for a living.

· 9 ·

THEY BOTH had that Saturday off, so they took the families to Jones Beach, using both cars. The beach was hot and crowded, the way it always is, but the kids liked the chance to run around in the sand sometimes instead of just jumping in and out of the pool in the backyard, and the wives liked any excuse at all that would get them out of the house. And Tom and Joe liked to look at women in bathing suits.

After a while, the two men were the only ones left on the blankets, spread out well back from the ocean. Mary

111

and Grace were both down by the water's edge with the smallest kids, and the other kids were all off running around somewhere, pestering people. Tom was sprawled on his stomach on the blanket with his chin propped on his forearms so he could look at the girls in bikinis, and Joe was sitting cross-legged on the next blanket over, reading the *News*.

The planning of the robbery had settled into a sort of hobby they had, like two guys who operate a model railroad set together. Tom had been casing the brokerages and the general Wall Street area, checking out possible getaway routes, collecting maps of the financial district and writing out long descriptions of the security arrangements at various brokerages. Joe had been raiding the Police Department files downtown for information on burglar alarms and any special police surveillance arrangements there might be in that area. The two of them had maps and charts and memos and lists enough to choke a whale, a huge growing pile of paperwork they kept locked away in the liquor closet in the game room in Tom's basement. They'd thought it over and decided that was the best place to keep it all because nobody ever went down into the game room, and Tom was the only one with a key to that closet. Mary had had a key at one time, but she'd lost it a couple of years ago and hadn't ever replaced it because she didn't have any need for it.

In a way, the planning of the robbery had by now become an end in itself. When they'd first started talking about it there hadn't been any reality in the plans at all, it had just been a funny and interesting thing to talk about on the way to work. But gradually it had become more real to both of them, and the way it had become real was that now they were really doing the preliminaries. They would go out and talk to the Mafia, they would study different brokerages, they would make lists and keep records, they would talk over various plans for the robbery; they would do everything except the robbery itself. Although they never acknowledged that to themselves, not consciously.

The thought of the robbery was never very far from either of their minds these days; it gave them an interest in life. Including while they were at the beach.

"Well, here's one thing," Joe said, tapping the newspaper. "We don't do it the seventeenth."

Idle, unalert, still looking at girls in bikinis but automatically knowing what Joe was talking about, Tom said, "How come?"

"Parade for the astronauts."

A vision came into Tom's head; narrow streets, filled with crowds and bands. "Oh, yeah," he said.

Joe folded the paper and put it down. He was feeling vaguely irritable, as though some of the sand here had gotten into his brain. He said, "When the hell *are* we gonna do it?"

Tom shrugged one shoulder, and kept on watching the bodies all around him. "When we figure out how," he said. "Look at that one with the volley ball."

"Fuck the one with the volley ball," Joe said. He didn't feel like listening to a lot of horseshit.

"Gladly," Tom said.

Joe said, "Listen, I'm serious." He said it low-voiced and tense, and held his newspaper tight in his right fist.

Tom rolled over onto his side and gave Joe a look. He was vaguely surprised, and still feeling lazy and at peace with the world. He said, "What happened to you all of a sudden?"

What had happened to Joe, he hadn't been able to get out of his mind the vision of the old man in the hospital, dying and falling out of bed. It seemed to him when he thought about it that the old man had been making one last desperate leap toward life, and had fallen, and it had

113

been all over for him; too late. Usually, Joe was more interested even than Tom in looking at girls in bikinis, but for the last few days it seemed that all he could think about was time going by.

But he couldn't very well talk about all of that, Tom would think he was crazy. Or turning into a weak sister. He shrugged, irritable and angry and frustrated, and said, "Nothing happened to me. We just keep fucking around on the fringes, that's all."

Tom frowned. Joe was talking very tough and mean, and Tom wasn't sure yet whether he wanted to take offense or not. Holding that issue in abeyance for a second, he said, "So what do you want to do?"

"The robbery," Joe said. "Or at least get moving on it." He slapped the newspaper down onto the blanket with a disgusted gesture.

"Fine," Tom said. He was beginning to get a little irritated himself. "Like how?" he said.

"You've been checking out the brokerages. What's the story?"

Tom sat up, grudgingly giving up his leisure. "The story," he said, "is that they're very tough."

"Tell me." Joe wanted action, he wanted movement, he wanted the sense that something was happening *now*.

"Well," Tom said, "half of them are no good to begin with."

"Why not?"

"In a brokerage," Tom told him, "there's two places where they have guards. I mean, in addition to the main entrance. And the two places are the cage and the vault."

"The cage?"

"That's what they call the place where they do the paperwork, where they move the stocks and bonds in and out of the company. And the vault is where they store them."

114

"So we want the vault," Joe said. Simplicity, that was what he wanted, simple questions and simple answers.

"That's right," Tom said. "We want the vault. But with half of them, the vault is down in the basement and the cage is up on some other floor, and they've got closed-circuit TV between them."

Joe made a face. "Ow," he said.

"You see the problem," Tom said. "While we're taking care of the guards down in the basement, there's some clown up on the seventh floor watching us do it. And taking pictures of it."

"Taking pictures?"

"They put it all on video tape." Tom made a sour smile, and said, "Which they can run for the jury at our trial."

"Okay," Joe said. "So the ones with the cage and the vault on different floors, they're out."

"With the rest of them," Tom said, "where the cage and the vault are both on the same floor, you've still got guards in both places, plus guards at the entrance, and you've still got closed-circuit TV."

Joe frowned. None of this was making him feel any better. He said, "They've *all* got that?"

Tom nodded. "Any outfit big enough to have what we want," he said, "has TV. The little companies don't, but we're not going to find ten million dollars in bearer bonds lying around at one of the little companies."

"Then we can't do it at all," Joe said. "It just can't be done." There was an angry sense of relief in that, in giving it up for good and for all, and knowing there wasn't any hope.

A voice behind them suddenly said, "Are you robbers?"

They both turned around, and there was a little kid standing there behind them, a little boy of maybe five or six. He had a shovel in his hand, and he was covered with sand, and he was looking at them with bright curious eyes

115

like a parrot. Tom just sat there staring at him, but Joe quickly said, "No, we're the cops. *You're* the robber."

"Okay," the kid said. He was agreeable.

"You better take off now," Joe said, "before you get arrested."

"Okay," the kid said again, and turned around, and toddled off through the sand.

They both looked after him. Their hearts were pounding like sixty, it was amazing. "Christ," Joe said.

Tom said, "We better do our talking in the car from now on."

"What talking?" Joe was bitter, and he let it show. "You already described the situation, and it can't be done."

"Maybe it can," Tom said. "As long as the cage and the vault are both on the same floor, there's a chance we can pull it off."

Joe studied his face. "You think so?"

"People commit robberies all the time. *We* should be able to."

"Maybe," Joe said.

"What bothers me most," Tom said, "is how we're going to stash the bonds after we get them. Remember, we kept saying we didn't want anything we were going to have to hold onto."

Joe shrugged. "We can only sell Vigano what he wants to buy," he said. "Besides, we can call him right away afterward, we won't have to keep the bonds very long at all."

"I suppose so."

"The time that bothers me," Joe said, looking away toward the water, "is the two years."

Tom gave him a warning look. "We agreed, Joe."

"Yeah, I know we did. But look what happened to Paul. Shot in the leg. Another eight inches, he'd be shot in the balls. A little higher, he's shot in the heart, he's dead."

Tom shrugged that off, saying, "Paul's going to be okay, you said so yourself."

"That isn't the question," Joe said. "I don't want a million dollars buried in the ground, with me buried right next to it."

"We can't do it and run, we talked that over—"

Joe interrupted, saying, "Yeah yeah yeah, I know we did. I still think that's a good idea. But not for two years, that's too long."

Tom said, "What, then?"

"One year."

"What, cut it in half?"

"A year is a long time, Tom," Joe said. "You want to live like this any longer than you absolutely have to?"

Tom frowned, looking away. He was staring at a girl in a bikini, without seeing her.

"The idea is to get out of this," Joe said. "Remember?" Tempted against all his resolves, Tom shook his head and said, "Ahhh, Christ."

"One year," Joe said.

Tom held out a few seconds longer, but finally he shrugged and said, "All right. One year."

"Good," Joe said. He grinned, a lot happier than before, and grudgingly Tom grinned back.

• Tom •

THAT WAS one of the days when our schedules didn't
match. Joe was in the city working, and I had the day off.
Naturally it was raining, so I moped around the house and
read a paperback and watched some of the game shows on
television. Mary took off in the car for the Grand Union in
the middle of the day, so when the show I was watching
came to an end I wandered back into the bedroom to take
a look at my old uniform. If we ever really did do this
robbery, that's what I'd be wearing for my disguise.

I hadn't worn the uniform in three or four years, but it was still there, hanging in the bedroom closet, pushed way down to one end, behind the raincoat liner for the raincoat I left in a restaurant two years ago. I laid it out on the bed and looked it over for a minute; no holes, no buttons missing, everything fine. I changed into it, and studied myself in the mirror on the back of the closet door.

Yeah, that was me, I remembered that guy. The years I'd worn this blue suit, hot weather and cold, rain and sun. For some damn reason I suddenly found myself feeling gloomy, really sad about something. As though I'd lost something somewhere along the line, and even though I didn't know what it was I felt its absence. I don't know how to explain it any better than that; it was a sense of loss I felt.

Well, crap, I didn't come in here to get the rainy-day blues. I came in here to check out my disguise for the big robbery. And it looked fine, it was in perfect shape, no problem.

I was still standing there, trying to forget that I was feeling sad about something I couldn't remember, when all of a sudden Mary came walking in, and looked at me with her mouth hanging open.

I'd thought she'd be at the store at least another hour. I turned and gave her a sheepish grin, and tried to figure out what the hell I was going to say to her. But I couldn't think of a thing, not a single word came into my mind to explain what I was doing here in the bedroom in my old uniform.

After her first surprise, she helped me out of my paralysis by making a joke out of it, coming farther into the bedroom and saying, "What's this? You've been demoted?"

"Uh," I said, and then finally my brain and my tongue started working again. "I just wanted to see how I looked

119

in it," I said, and turned to study myself in the mirror again. "See if it still fit."

"It doesn't," she said.

"Sure it does." I turned sideways and gave myself a good view of my profile. "Well, it's maybe a little tight," I admitted. "Not much."

Past me in the mirror I could see her smiling at me and shaking her head. She'd kept her own figure almost exactly the same, in spite of having kids and being a housewife for years, so she was in a good position to be thinner-than-thou if she wanted. And even though it was ridiculous, I felt defensive on the subject. I turned and said, "Listen, I could still wear it. If I had to, I could. It wouldn't look that bad."

"No, you're right," she said. "It isn't terrible." I couldn't tell if she meant it or if she was humoring me.

Being agreed with was just as bad as having an argument. I patted my stomach, looking at it in the mirror, and said, "I've been drinking too much beer, that's the trouble."

She made an I-wouldn't-argue-with-you face, and walked over to the dresser. I watched her in the mirror. She picked up her watch from the dresser top and headed for the door, winding it. In the doorway, she looked back at me and said, "Lunch in fifteen minutes."

I said, "I'll have iced tea today."

She laughed. "All right," she said.

After she went out, I gave myself another critical look. It wasn't that bad. A little tight, that's all. Not bad.

120

· 10 ·

THERE'S A strange sense of dislocation in leaving one's family at ten or eleven o'clock at night and going off to work. There's more of a feeling of *leaving* them, of a deep break between family life and job life. Neither Tom nor Joe had ever gotten over that atmosphere of loss, but it was another of the things they'd never discussed together.

Maybe if they'd worked the midnight-to-eight shift all the time they would have gotten used to it, and not felt any stranger about it than a guy who leaves for work at

121

eight in the morning. But constantly switching around from shift to shift the way they did, they never really got a chance to become used to the idiosyncracies of any one schedule.

Since the incident with the little kid out at Jones Beach, they'd done most of their talking about the robbery in the car on the way to or from work, and they both seemed to prefer for that the drive at eleven o'clock at night, heading in toward the city. The sense of dislocation from home and family probably helped, and so did the darkness, the interior of the car lit by nothing but the dashboard and oncoming headlights. It was as though they were isolated then, separate from everything, capable of concentrating their minds on the question of committing the robbery.

This night, they were both quiet for the first ten or fifteen minutes in the car, westbound on the Long Island Expressway. Traffic was moderate coming out of the city, but light in the direction they were going. There was plenty of leisure to think.

Joe was driving his Plymouth, his mind only very slightly on the road and the car, but mostly away, on Wall Street, in brokerage offices. Suddenly he said, "I go back to the bomb scare."

Tom's mind had been full of his own thoughts, involving burying the bonds and calling Vigano and figuring out the safest way to make the switch for the two million dollars. He blinked over toward Joe's profile in the darkness and said, "What?"

"We ought to be able to do that," Joe said. "Phone in, tell them there's a bomb in the vault, then answer the squeal ourselves."

Tom shook his head. "Won't work."

"But it gets us in, that's the beauty."

"Sure," Tom said. "And then a couple other guys come to answer the squeal before we get out again."

"There ought to be a way around that," Joe said.

"There isn't."

"Bribe a dispatcher to give the squeal to us instead of one of their own cars."

"Which dispatcher? And how much do you bribe him? We get a million and he gets a hundred? He'd turn us in within a week. Or blackmail us."

"There's got to be a way," Joe said. The bomb-scare idea appealed to him on general dramatic grounds.

"The problem isn't to get in," Tom said. "The problem is to get away afterwards with the bonds, and where we stash them, and how we make the switch with Vigano."

But Joe didn't want to listen to any of that. He insisted on the primacy of his own area of research. "We've still got to get in," he said.

"We'll get in," Tom said, and all of a sudden the idea hit him. He sat up straighter in the car, and stared straight ahead out the windshield. "Son of a bitch," he said.

Joe glanced at him. "Now what?"

"When's that parade? Remember, there was a thing in the paper about a parade for some astronauts."

Joe frowned, trying to remember. "Next week sometime." It had been on Wednesday, he remembered that. "Uhhh, the seventeenth. Why?"

"That's when we do it," Tom said. He was grinning from ear to ear.

"During the parade?"

Tom was so excited he couldn't sit still. "Joe," he said, "I am a goddam mastermind!"

Skeptical, Joe said, "You are, huh?"

"Listen to me," Tom said. "What are we going to steal?"

Joe gave him a disgusted look. "What?"

"Give me a break," Tom said. "Just tell me, what are we going to steal?"

123

Shrugging, Joe said, "Bearer bonds, like the man said."

"Money," Tom said.

Joe nodded, being weary and long-suffering. "Okay, okay, money."

"Only *not* money," Tom said. He kept grinning, as though his cheeks would stretch permanently out of shape. "You see? We still got to turn it over before it's money."

"In a minute," Joe told him, "I'm going to stop this car and punch your head."

"Listen to me, Joe. The idea is, money isn't just dollar bills. It's all kinds of things. Checking accounts. Credit cards. Stock certificates."

"Will you for Christ's sake get to the point?"

"Here's the point," Tom said. "Anything is money, if you *think* it's money. Like Vigano thinks those bearer bonds are money."

"He's right," Joe said.

"Sure, he's right. And that's what solves all our problems."

"It does?"

"Absolutely," Tom said. "It gets us in, gets us out, solves the problem of hiding the loot, solves *everything*."

"That's fucking wonderful," Joe said.

"You're damn right it is." Tom played a paradiddle on the dashboard with his fingertips. "And that," he said, "is why we're going to pull off that robbery during the parade."

• Joe •

I DROVE THE squad car down Columbus Avenue to a Puerto Rican grocery near 86th Street. I pulled in to the curb there and said to Lou, "Why don't you get us a coke?"

"Good idea," he said. He was a young guy, twenty-four years of age, his second year on the force. He wore his hair a little too long, to my way of thinking, and I almost never saw him without razor cuts all over his chin. But he was all right; he was quiet, he minded his own business, and he had no bad habits in the car. At one time or another I've had them all, the farters and the nose-pickers and the ear-benders and everything else. Lou wasn't the good friend that Paul was, but I have done a lot worse.

I'd picked a Puerto Rican store because it would take him longer in there to buy two cokes than in a regular store. The little Puerto Rican groceries all over town are filled with men and women, all of them four feet tall, most of them sitting on the freezer case, all of them yammering away at top speed in that language they claim is Spanish. Before anybody can hit a cash-register key and take your dollar and give you your change, he has to yell louder than everybody else for a minute or two, to make sure he's got his point across. Then, with your change in his hand, he thinks of the clincher argument and starts to yell again. So I was going to have all the time I needed.

I'd switched off the engine before Lou got out of the car. I watched him crossing the sidewalk in the sunlight, hitching his gunbelt, and once he was inside the store I opened my door, stepped out, went around to the front of the car, lifted the hood, and removed the distributor cap. Then I shut the hood again, and got back behind the wheel.

We had a heat wave starting. It wasn't eleven in the morning yet, and already the temperature was almost ninety. From the feeling of my shirt-collar on the back of my neck, the humidity was up over the top of the scale. A hell of a day to be at work.

Hell of a day for a parade, too. They wouldn't call it off, would they?

No. The Wall Street ticker-tape parade is a tradition, and traditions don't care about the weather. They'd have their parade.

And Tom and me, we'd get our two million.

Lou came out with the two cans of soda. He got into the car, handing me mine, and said, "They sure do like to talk."

126

"They got more energy than I do," I said. "In this heat."

We popped the tops, and the both of us drank. I was in no hurry for the next step. I scrunched down in the seat a little, putting my face over by the open window, looking for a breeze. There wasn't any.

"It's too hot for crime," Lou said. "A nice lazy day."

"It's never too hot for crime," I said.

"I'll bet you," he said. "I'll bet you there isn't one major crime in this city today. Not before, say, four o'clock this afternoon."

Talk about a sure thing. I almost took him up on it, except I didn't want him remembering the conversation afterward and starting to wonder why I'd been so eager to take his money. But talk about a lock!

What I did, I said, "What about crimes of passion? A husband and wife get mad at each other, they're irritated anyway because of the heat, and *pop,* one of them goes for the butcher knife."

"All right," he said, conceding the point. "Except for that kind of thing."

"Oh," I said, "now you're making exceptions. No major crime, except this kind and that kind and the other kind." I grinned at him, to show him I was kidding and that he shouldn't get sore.

He grinned back and said, "I notice you don't want to take the bet."

"Gambling's illegal," I told him. "Except OTB." I straightened up and took another swig of soda and said, "Time to move on. We got an hour before we're off duty."

"At least when we're moving there's a breeze," he said.

"Check."

I hit the ignition key, and of course nothing happened. "Now what?" I said.

Lou gave the key a disgusted look. "Again?" he said. Because this would be the third time in a month we'd had

127

a car break down on us; which was what had given me the idea.

I fiddled with the key. Nothing. "I told them they didn't fix it," I said.

"Well, shit," Lou said.

"Call in," I told him. "I've had it."

While he called in to the precinct, I sat there on my side of the car looking long-suffering and drinking my coke. He finished and said, "They'll send a tow truck."

"We ought to *drive* a tow truck," I said.

He looked at his watch. "You know how long they'll take to get here."

"Listen," I said. "We don't both have to hang around. Why don't you shlep on back to the station and sign us both out?"

"What, and leave you here?"

"It doesn't matter to me," I said. "No crap. There's no need us both being stuck here."

He wanted to take me up on it, but he didn't want to look too eager about it, so I had to persuade him a little more. Finally he said, "You really don't mind?"

"I got no place to go anyway."

"Well . . . Okay."

"Fine," I said. And, as he was getting out of the car, I said, "Be sure to sign me out. I won't go straight back."

"Will do," he said. He climbed out to the sidewalk, bent to look in the car at me, and said, "Thanks, Joe."

"You'll do the same for me next time."

"Yeah, and there will be a next time, won't there?"

"Count on it," I said.

He laughed, and shook his head, and shut the car door. I watched him in the rear-view mirror as he walked away; around the corner and out of sight.

I sat there almost half an hour before the tow truck showed up. They use them all the time in midtown these days, towing the tourists' cars away. But this one finally got there, and the two guys got out of it, and one of them said to me, "What's the problem?"

"It won't start, that's all."

He gave the car a squint, like he was a doctor and this was the patient. "I wonder why."

That's all I needed, an amateur mechanic. All the tow-man is supposed to do is tow the car off to where it can be fixed. I said, "Who knows? The heat maybe. Let's take the thing in and get it over with."

"Keep your shirt on," he said.

"I don't want to," I said. I looked at my watch. "I'm off-duty in fifteen minutes."

So they put the hook on the front, and I sat behind the wheel of the squad car, and they towed me over to the police garage on the West Side, over near the docks. That block is practically nothing but Police Department, with police warehouses on the north side and the garage in the middle of the block on the south side. The garage is a sprawling red-brick building, three stories high, with ramps inside so you can drive all the way up to the roof. It's an old building, with black metal window frames, and I've heard it was once used to stable police horses. I don't know if that's true or not, I was just told it one time.

Extending westward from the garage to the far corner is a fenced-in area full of patrol cars and emergency vehicles and paddywagons and even a bomb-squad truck, looking like a big red wicker basket. Most of those vehicles are junk, and are kept around simply so that the mechanics can cannibalize parts off them to keep clunkers like the car I was sitting in more or less in running order.

Extending eastward from the garage to the corner are three or four more warehouse buildings, partly owned or leased by the Department, and partly civilian. About five or six years ago somebody found a load of slot machines in one of those buildings, down in the basement. Nobody *ever* figured that one out.

The block is one-way, and runs west to east, and both curbs were lined with police vehicles, most of them not working right now. The entrance to the garage was also clogged with vehicles, and more of them were parked on the sidewalk between the front of the garage and the cars parked at the curb. This is a block that cabdrivers avoid like the Black Death, because you can get stuck in a traffic jam here forever, and which civilian driver is going to honk at a traffic jam caused by the Police Department?

Like the jam we caused right now. The tow truck came down the one open lane in the middle of the street, and stopped in front of the garage. I looked in the rear-view mirror to see if we were blocking anybody behind us, but with the front end of the car up in the air all I could see was a rectangle of blacktop directly behind me. I didn't much care anyway, one way or the other. If somebody was behind us, tough.

A mechanic came wandering out of the garage with a clipboard in his hand. He was a colored guy, short and heavy-set, wearing police trousers and a sleeveless undershirt. It was a filthy undershirt. He walked around the tow truck and came ambling down to the squad car, and said to me, "Problems, Mac?"

"Won't start," I said. "Dropped dead on me."

"Give it a try," he said.

Now, that was stupid. Did he think we would have gone through all of this, dragging this car downtown on a hot day like this, without first having given it a try? But that was what they always said, every time, and there was no point arguing with them. I gave it a try, and all it did was click. I spread my hands and said, "See?"

"Can't do anything with it today," he said.

130

"I don't care," I said. "I'm off-duty two minutes ago. My partner went on in already."

He sighed, and got his clipboard and a pencil ready. "Name?"

"Patrolman Joseph Loomis, Fifteenth Precinct."

He wrote that down, then went around to the back of the car to copy down all the appropriate numbers. I waited, knowing the routine because I'd been through it too many times already, and when he came back I already had my hands ready to take the clipboard before he started extending it to me. "John Hancock," he said, and I nodded and took the clipboard and signed my name in the line where it said *Signature*.

I handed him the clipboard back, and he turned and waved it at the driver of the tow truck. "Put it down there somewhere," he said, and waved toward the far end of the block.

The truck started forward with a jerk, and a second later so did the squad car. It snapped my head back, but not very much. I held onto the steering wheel for balance, and out of habit, and we rolled on down the block. The mechanic stood where he was until we went by, and the look he gave the car was weary and irritated.

The nose of the squad car bobbed a little as we moved, as though I was in a speedboat. The front being angled up so high gave the same idea, and all of a sudden I remembered a summer vacation when I was a kid, maybe ten or eleven, and the whole family went up in the Adirondacks somewhere for a week. We rented a cabin on a lake. I mean, near the lake; you had to walk down this dirt path between two other cabins to get to the water, and I can still remember the way those stones felt under my bare feet. And there was a rich man there that owned a house at the other end of the lake, a white house bigger than the house I lived in back home in Brooklyn, and he had a

131

speedboat. Red and white. He gave me a ride once, two other kids and me. We put on these orange life vests and sat in the back seat, and when the boat started up I was scared out of my mind. We went like a bat out of hell, and the front was up so high I couldn't see where we were going. But at the same time, it was really great; the wind and the noise and the spray, and the shore being so far away. Afterwards, remembering it while safe on dry land, it was even greater, and I spent the rest of that week wondering why we weren't rich, too. Rich was obviously a better thing to be, so why weren't we? That's the way kids think.

I hadn't remembered that for maybe twenty years.

There was a free space against the curb down near the corner. They stopped the truck and I got out of the car to watch them jockey it into place. I looked at my watch when they were finishing up, and it was ten after twelve. Plenty of time.

The driver of the tow truck said, "You want a lift back to the station?"

I almost said yes, I almost forgot the situation that much. But I caught myself in time and said, "No, I'll walk."

"Up to you."

I gave them a wave and they drove off, and I watched them go. Sometimes I amaze myself. Could it be this whole business still wasn't real to me, that I could forget it that easy? I'd damn near gotten into that truck to ride back to the station with them, just as though this was any other day and I didn't have anything else on my mind at all. Amazing. Shaking my head, I turned and walked over to Eleventh Avenue and headed south.

My role now was just to walk around for about ten minutes. One of the secondary advantages of pulling this caper in uniform is the fact that a cop is the only guy on earth who can stand around a street corner loitering and not attract any attention. It's his *job* to loiter. Anybody else, somebody's likely to say, "Who's the guy on the corner? What's he up to?" But not a cop.

I'm surprised criminals don't pull *all* their jobs wearing the blue.

After ten minutes, I headed back around to where I'd left the car. Now, who's going to look twice at a cop doing something to a patrol car? I opened the hood, put the distributor cap back on, got behind the wheel, started the car, and headed down to where I was supposed to meet Tom.

· Tom ·

THE DIFFERENCE between committing a crime and planning a crime is the difference between being in a snowstorm and looking at a picture of the blizzard of 'eighty-eight. Joe and I had spent a long time planning this robbery, organizing things, working out the details, and none of it had ever bothered me; but all of a sudden we were in the storm, and no fooling.

I slept lousy the night before. I kept waking up and being afraid there was somebody in the house. I never felt so defenseless in my life, lying there in the darkness, listening, trying to hear whoever it was that was in the next room. Then I'd drift off again and have bad dreams, and wake up once more.

I only remember one of the dreams. Or just one part. I was very small, and I was in a very big empty dark room, and the walls were falling outward. Slowly. Just falling out and back. Terrifying.

We'd picked a day that I had off and Joe was working, so I spent the morning hanging around on my own, trying not to show Mary how tense and irritable I was. Joe had already told Grace he'd be on double shift today, and Mary thought I was supposed to be working this afternoon, so we were both covered for the time of the robbery.

But how the early part of the day dragged on! Half a dozen times, I was on the verge of getting into the car and driving on into the city just to be doing something, even though it would be hours before I was supposed to meet Joe, and I'd have a tougher job killing time in New York than at home. But it was just impossible to sit still, I had to be up and around and moving. I took the Chevvy down to the local car wash and then drove around for half an hour, I spent some time cleaning out the garage, I even took a walk around the neighborhood, something I've never done in my life before. And it was weird how close to the house I became a stranger, walking past houses that looked like mine but that didn't have any more to do with my life than some shepherd's hut in Outer Mongolia. That walk did more harm than good, and I was glad when I got back to my own block, to houses I knew, and the sense of safety that comes from being where you belong.

Then, when it was finally time to go, I got very jittery and nervous, and couldn't seem to get myself organized to leave the house. I kept forgetting things and having to come back. Including the uniform. I had it packed in a

135

little canvas bag, and I damn near left without it. That would have been bright.

Did you ever have a tense situation sometime in your life, and you turn on the radio, and all the song lyrics seem to refer directly to the problem you're going through? That's what happened on the drive into the city. Every song that came on was either about somebody making a mistake that loused up his whole life, or somebody who has to give up his home and go wandering around the world, or somebody putting himself in danger even though this girl that loves him doesn't want him to do it.

I was almost sorry we hadn't told Mary and Grace what we were doing, because they really *would* have talked us out of it. That way, neither one of us would have backed down, but I still wouldn't be driving west on the Long Island Expressway this morning, with my old patrolman's uniform in a canvas bag beside me on the seat.

Don't get me wrong. I don't mean I wanted to give it up. I still wanted to do it, the reasons for doing it were still just as valid as they'd ever been, and my plans for afterward still excited me as much as when I'd first worked them out. But if the situation had been taken out of my hands one way or another, and I'd been *forced* to turn back, I admit I wouldn't have put up too much of a fight.

Well. I got to Manhattan with time to spare, drove over to the West Side, and parked in the low Forties, near Tenth Avenue. Then I walked down to the Port Authority terminal, carrying the bag with the uniform in it, and changed clothes in a pay stall in the men's room there.

Leaving, heading across the main terminal floor for the Ninth Avenue exit, I was stopped by a short old woman wearing a black coat—in weather like this—who wanted to know where to buy tickets for a Public Service bus. She irritated me at first, distracting me when I was so tense anyway, and I couldn't figure out why she was bothering

136

me with questions like that when just ahead of us there was a huge sign reading: INFORMATION; but then I remembered I was in uniform. I shifted gears, became a cop, and gave her courteous directions over to the ticket windows along the side wall. She thanked me and scurried away, pulling the coat tight around her as though she were in a high wind that nobody else could feel. Then I walked on, left the building without being asked any more questions, and headed back for the car.

Walking along, I got this sudden vision in my head of the same thing happening again, only in a more serious way than with the old woman. I could see Joe and me on our way to commit a felony and being stopped by somebody who'd just been mugged, or getting mixed up with a lost child, or being the first cops on the scene at a serious automobile accident.

And what could we do if something like that happened? We'd have to stay, we'd have to play out the policeman's role. There just wouldn't be any choice, it would be far too suspicious for us to refuse to have anything to do with whatever it might be. The next cops to come along would surely be told about it, and we didn't want the idea getting around ahead of time that there were a couple of fake cops up to something in the city.

That would be damn ironic; kept from committing a robbery by the call of duty. I grinned as I walked along, thinking I would tell Joe about it when I saw him. I could just see his face.

At the Chevvy, I opened the trunk and put the canvas bag in it, with my other clothes. The license plates and numbers were in there, in a shopping bag; they'd been there for a week, ever since we'd picked them up.

I shut the trunk, got behind the wheel, and drove over by the piers. The New York City piers have gone to hell in the last ten years or so, with most of the harbor business now being done over in Jersey, so there's plenty of places in through there, particularly under the West Side Highway, where you can have all the privacy you want. Some of the trucking companies store empty trailers there, which form walls to shield you from the sight of the occasional car or truck heading down Twelfth Avenue.

I tucked the Chevvy in by a highway stanchion, next to a parked trailer, and looked at my watch. I was still running ahead of schedule, but that was all right. And now that I was really committed to it, and I'd made the first couple of moves in the planned operation, I was actually calming down, getting less and less nervous. The build-up had made me tense, but now the tension was draining away and I felt as easy in my mind as if I was just waiting here for Ed Dantino to show up so we could go on duty. Very strange.

It was a hot day, too hot to sit in the car. I got out of it, locked it, and leaned against the fender to wait for Joe.

• 11 •

THEY COULD hear the parade before they saw it; crowd noises, march music, and drums. Mostly the drums, you could hear them from blocks and blocks away.

There's a feeling about the sound of a parade that something is about to happen, something fast and dramatic and maybe hard to deal with. It's the drums that do it, hundreds and hundreds of drums stretched away for blocks, all thumping out the same steady beat. It's a little faster than a normal heartbeat, so if you're not marching along with it you can find it making you a little tense or excited.

Of course, if you're tense or excited to begin with, because you're about to commit your first grand larceny, drums like that can just about give you a coronary.

Both of them felt that, but neither said anything about it. They were pretending with one another that they were calm and businesslike, which was probably a good way to behave, since keeping up the facade seemed to help them deal with their nervousness and not get immobilized by it.

Back when they'd met over by the piers, the fact was they really had both been calm. Each of them had successfully done the first simple step of the plan—Joe in getting the squad car, Tom in switching into uniform and finding the place to stash the Chevvy—and there was a sense they shared of having accomplished something and of being in control of the situation. Then, when they'd first met, they'd busily switched the license plates on the squad car and put the new peel-off numbers on its sides, and they'd still had that same feeling of being smart and organized and well-prepared and in control.

But as they drove downtown, and particularly when they got down into the narrow streets of the financial section, they both got to thinking about accidents and unforeseen circumstances and all the things that can go wrong with the best plan in the world. The tension started in them again, and the pounding of the drums didn't help.

Parker, Tobin, Eastpoole & Company was in a corner building, with the front facing onto the street where the parade was going by. Down the block, another building had an arcade that ran through to the next street over. It was that street they were heading for, a block away from the crowds and jam-up of the parade, but close enough so they could hear it loud and clear.

There was a fire hydrant near the arcade entrance. Joe parked the car there, and they got out and walked through the arcade, both automatically pacing themselves to the

140

sound of the drums. Ahead of them, the arched opening of the arcade framed a black mass of people facing the other way; past them and over their heads, they could see flags being carried by.

As they walked along, Joe suddenly burped. It was incredibly loud, it seemed to bounce off the windows of the shops along both sides of the arcade, it echoed like a cathedral bell. Tom gave him a look of astonishment, and Joe rubbed his front and said, "I've got a very nervous stomach."

"Don't think about it," Tom said. He meant he didn't want to think about his own nervousness.

Joe gave him a one-sided grin and said, "You give great advice."

They came to the end of the arcade and stepped out onto the sidewalk, and the parade noise was suddenly much louder, as though a radio had been turned up. A band was going by, in red and white uniforms; they could catch glimpses of it through spaces between the people on the sidewalk. Another band had just passed by and was half a block away to the left, playing a different marching song but with the beat of the drums at the same time. A third band was down to the right, coming this way, its sounds buried within those made by the first two, plus the talking and yelling and laughing of the onlookers. Police officers in uniform were placed here and there, but they were concentrating on crowd control and paid no attention to Tom and Joe; in any case, what were they but just two more cops assigned to the parade?

There was a narrow cleared strip of sidewalk along between the building fronts and the massed people watching the parade. They turned left and walked in single file along that strip, moving now in the same direction as the band on the other side of the people, but because they were striding out they were moving just a little faster. Joe went first, marching steadily along in time to the music and the drums, and watching everything at eye level; the people, the cops, the building entrances. Tom followed, moving in a more easy-going way, looking up at the people gawking out of all the windows above street level; practically every window in every building had at least one person standing in it or leaning out of it.

No one paid any attention to them. They went into the corner building and took the self-service elevator. They were alone in it, and on the way up they put on the moustaches and plain-lensed horn-rim glasses they'd been carrying in their pockets. Those were the minor parts of their disguises, the uniforms being the main part; nobody looks past a uniform. The people outside looking at the parade were watching uniforms go by, not faces, and wouldn't be able later on to identify one single musician who'd walked past.

With his glasses and moustache on, Tom said, "You do the talking when we get up there, okay?"

Joe gave him a grin. "Why? You got stage-fright?"

Tom didn't let himself be aggravated. "No," he said. "I'm just out of practice, is all."

Joe shrugged. "Sure," he said. "No problem."

At that point, the elevator stopped, the door opened, and they both stepped out. Tom had been here before, of course, and had described it all to Joe and drawn him rough sketches of what the guarded reception area looked like, but this was Joe's first actual sight of the place, and he gave it a fast once-over, orienting the reality to his previous mental picture.

There was none of the activity around the counter now that there'd been when Tom had come here the last time; that would be because everybody was watching the parade. And now there was only one guard on duty. He was leaning on the counter, looking over toward the six television screens that showed the different parts of the brokerage. On three or four of the screens windows showed, and people could be seen looking out at the parade. From the expression on the guard's face, he was wishing he could be at a window, too.

That was one of the extra advantages of pulling this job during the parade; the route to the money would be much less populated than usual. It wasn't the main reason for doing it now, but it was an extra little bonus, and they were glad to have it.

The guard looked over when they came out of the elevator, and they could see his face relax when he saw the uniforms. He'd been resting his elbows on the counter, but now he straightened up and said, "Yes, officers?"

Walking forward to the counter, Joe said, "We had a complaint about items ejected from the windows."

The guard blinked, not understanding. "You what?"

"Objectionable articles," Joe said. "Ejected from windows near the northeast corner of the building."

Tom had to admire the toneless neutrality of Joe's voice, he sounded just like a patrolman on the beat. That only came with practice, as Tom had said in the elevator.

The guard had finally figured out what Joe was talking about, but he still couldn't believe it. He said, "From *this* floor?"

"We got to check it out," Joe said.

The guard glanced at the television screens, but of course none of them showed anybody throwing objectionable articles out the windows. A little later they'd be throwing paper, confetti, ticker tape, but those aren't objectionable articles, except to the Sanitation Department. That's the trademark of a parade in the Wall Street area; a snowstorm of paper when the hero goes by that the parade is in honor of. Or this time, the heroes, in the plural; a group of astronauts who'd been on the moon.

143

The guard said, "I'll call Mr. Eastpoole."

"Go ahead," Joe said.

The phone was on a table by the rear wall, near the pegboard with the ID tags on it. The guard made his phone call with his back turned, and Tom and Joe took the opportunity to relieve the tension a little; yawning, moving their shoulders around, shifting their feet, hitching their gunbelts, scratching their necks.

He talked low-voiced, the guard did, but they could hear what he was saying. First he had to explain things to a secretary, and then he had to explain things all over again to somebody named Eastpoole. That was the third name in the company's brand-name, so Eastpoole had to be one of the major bosses, and you could tell it by how respectful and soft-pedaled the guard's voice became as he described the problem.

Finally, he hung up the phone and turned back, saying, "He'll be right out."

"We'll go in to meet him," Joe said.

The guard shook his head. He was apologetic, but firm. "I'm sorry," he said, "I can't let you in without an escort."

They'd already suspected that, but Tom made his voice sound incredulous when he broke in, saying, "You can't let *us* in?"

The guard looked more apologetic than ever, but still just as firm. "I'm sorry, officer," he said, "but that's my instructions."

Movement on one of the TV screens down at the end of the counter attracted everybody's attention then, and they all turned their heads and watched a man crossing a room from left to right. He looked to be in his middle fifties, slightly heavy-set, thick gray hair, jowly face, very expensive well-tailored suit, narrow dark tie, white shirt. He had a long stride, moving as though he was a man who got

144

annoyed easily and was used to getting his own way. He'd get waiters fired in restaurants.

"He's coming now," the guard said. You could see he didn't like the position he was in; cops in front of him, and a tough boss behind him. He said, "Mr. Eastpoole's one of the partners here. He'll take care of you."

Tom always had a habit of empathizing with the working stiff. Now, trying to make conversation and put the guard at his ease a little, he said, "Not much doing around here today."

"Not with the parade," the guard said. He grinned and shrugged, saying, "They might as well close up, days like this."

Joe was suddenly feeling cute. "Good time for a robbery," he said.

Tom gave him a fast angry look, but the thing had already been said. The guard didn't see the look, and apparently Joe didn't either.

The guard was shaking his head. "They'd never get away," he said, "not with that crowd out there."

Joe nodded, as though he was thinking it over. "That's right, too," he said.

The guard glanced at the TV screens, and Eastpoole was just crossing another of them. Apparently feeling he had the time to relax, the guard leaned on his elbows on the counter again and said, "Biggest robbery they ever had in the world was right down here in the financial section."

Tom, really interested, said, "Is that right?"

The guard nodded, for emphasis, and said, "That's right. It was in the World Series. Remember the year the Mets won the pennant?"

Joe laughed and said, "Who'll ever forget?"

"That's right," the guard said. "It was in the last game, the ninth inning, everybody in New York City was at their radio. Somebody walked into a vault at one of the firms

145

on the Street, and walked out with thirteen million dollars in bearer bonds."

They looked at one another. Joe turned back to the guard and said, "They ever get him?"

"Nope," said the guard.

At that point, Eastpoole came in from the door on the right. He was being brisk, impatient, slightly hostile. He probably didn't like his employees gawking out of windows instead of getting their work done, and he surely didn't like a couple of cops coming around and telling him there's something wrong going on in his shop. He strode over, efficient, in a hurry to give them the brush-off, and said, "Yes, officer?"

Joe had a natural talent for people like this. He just slowed himself down and became very official and very dense; it drove the hurry-up types right up the wall. Joe gave this one a suspicious look and said, "You Eastpoole?"

Eastpoole made an impatient little hand gesture, brushing a minor annoyance away. "Yes," he said, "I'm Raymond Eastpoole. What can I do for you?"

"We got a complaint," Joe said, taking his time about it. "Items ejected from the windows."

Eastpoole didn't believe it, and made no attempt to hide the fact. Frowning, he said, "From these offices?"

Joe nodded. "That's the report we got," he said. He was showing that nothing would either ruffle him or hurry him up. He said, "We want to check out the northeast corner of the building, all the windows over on that side."

Eastpoole would rather have had nothing to do with them or their complaint or anything else concerned with today. He glanced over at the guard behind the counter, but there was obviously no help there, so finally he gave an angry shrug and said, "Very well. I'll accompany you myself. Come along."

Joe nodded, still taking his time. "Thank you," he said,

146

but not as though anybody had done anybody any favors. His style was that they were all equals in this room. It was a style guaranteed to rub somebody like Raymond Eastpoole the wrong way.

Which it did. Eastpoole turned away, to lead them on their tour of the northeast corner of the building, and then turned back to frown at the guard again and say, "Where's your partner?"

The guard hesitated, showing his embarrassment. And when he lied, he did a lousy job of it, saying, "Uh, he's, uh, he's to the men's room."

Eastpoole couldn't show his anger in the cops' direction, but he could aim it at the guard. His voice taut with fury, he said, "You mean he's leaning out a window somewhere, watching the parade."

The guard was blinking, scared of this bastard. "He'll be right back, Mr. Eastpoole," he said.

Eastpoole thumped a fist onto the counter. "We pay," he said, "for two men at this counter, twenty-four hours a day."

"He just went off a minute ago," the guard said. He was really sweating.

Partly to get the guard off the hook, and partly because they had their own schedule to think about, Joe broke in at that point, saying, "We'd like to check things out, Mr. Eastpoole, before anything else gets dropped."

Eastpoole would clearly have preferred to keep nagging at the guard. He glowered at Joe, glowered at the guard, and then mulishly gave in, turned on his heel and led the way from the room. They followed him, Joe going first and then Tom coming along behind. Passing through the doorway, Tom glanced back and saw the guard hurriedly reaching for the phone; to call his partner to haul ass away from the window, no doubt.

They walked down a fairly long corridor, and then

147

through several large offices, each of them full of desks and filing cabinets, and all of them lined with windows along one wall. The desks were all unoccupied, and people were standing looking out of all the windows.

They hadn't heard the drums or the music from the time they'd gotten into the elevator to come up here, but now the sound was with them again, and they walked automatically to the rhythm of the drums. Tension seemed to shimmer upward from the street outside those windows like heat waves off asphalt paving in the summertime. Both of them were tense again, walking along in Eastpoole's wake, the drums echoing in their bloodstreams.

And yet, they still hadn't reached the point of no return. They could still even at this late date change their minds and not go through with it. They could do an inspection tour of the windows with Eastpoole, find nothing, give him a lecture, and walk out. Return the squad car, drive home, forget the whole thing; it was still possible. But any second now, it would stop being possible for good and all.

Twice, as they walked along, they saw TV cameras mounted high on the wall in the corner of a room. The camera would turn slowly back and forth, like a fan, angled shallowly downward so as to get a good view of the entire room. These two were among the six that showed up on the screens out by the reception area. And on other sets of screens on this floor, as well. One of the big advantages of this brokerage for Tom and Joe was that their check into the security systems showed there wasn't any closed-circuit TV communication to any other floor; it was all confined to this one level.

From the office with the second camera in it, they passed on to a short empty corridor. They entered it, and Joe made the decision that moved them finally over the line, making them criminals in fact as well as in theory. And he did it with two words: "Hold it," he said, and reached out to

148

take Eastpoole by the elbow and stop him from walking on.

Eastpoole stopped, and you could see he was offended at being touched. When he turned around to find out what the problem was, he jerked his elbow free again. "What is it?" he said. He sounded very petulant for a grown man.

Joe looked around the corridor and said, "Is there a camera in here? Can that guard check this area?"

"No," Eastpoole said. "There's no need for it. And there are no windows here, if you'll notice." He half-turned away again, gesturing at the far end of the corridor. "What you want is—"

Joe put an edge in his voice, saying, "We know what we want. Let's go to your office."

"My office?" Eastpoole didn't have the first idea what was going on. Staring at them both, he said, "What for?"

Tom said, "We don't have to show you guns, do we?" He spoke calmly, not wanting Eastpoole to be so upset he'd lose control.

Eastpoole kept staring. He said, "What is this?"

"It's a robbery," Tom said. "What do you think it is?"

"But—" Eastpoole gestured at them, at their uniforms. "You two—"

"You can't tell a book by its cover," Tom said.

Joe poked Eastpoole's arm, prodding him a little. "Come on," he said, "let's move. To your office."

Eastpoole, starting to get over his shock, said, "You can't believe you can get away with—"

Joe gave him a shove that pushed him into the corridor wall. "Stop wasting our time," he said. "I'm feeling very tense right now, and when I'm tense sometimes I hit people."

Eastpoole's skin was turning pale under the eyes and around the mouth. He almost looked as though he might faint, and yet there was still arrogance in him, he might still be stupid enough to talk back. Tom, moving forward

149

between Joe and Eastpoole, being the calm and reasonable one, said, "Come on, Mr. Eastpoole, take it easy. You're insured, and it isn't your job to deal with people like us. Be sensible. Do what we want, and let it go."

Eastpoole was nodding before Tom had finished talking. "That's just what I'll do," he said. "And later, I'll see to it you get the maximum penalty of the law."

"You do that," Joe said.

Tom, turning to Joe, said, "It's all right, now. Mr. Eastpoole's going to be sensible." He looked back. "Aren't you, Mr. Eastpoole?"

Eastpoole was looking sullen, but subdued. Half-gritting his teeth, he looked at Tom and said, "What do you want?"

"To go to your office. You lead the way."

Joe said, "And don't be cute."

"He won't be cute," Tom said. "Go ahead, Mr. Eastpoole."

Eastpoole turned and started walking again, and they both followed him. It's such an old tried-and-true technique, one partner hard and one partner soft, that it's become a cliché in the television police shows. But the fact is, it works. You give a guy one person to be friends with and one person to be scared of, and between the two you'll most of the time get whatever you want.

This time, what they wanted was Eastpoole's office, and that's what they got. They walked there, and the outer office was empty, and they went directly on through. Eastpoole's secretary, who should have been at the desk in the outer office, was in here, looking out a window at the parade. Her own room didn't have any windows in it.

Eastpoole's office looked like half of a living room and half of a rich man's den. It was a corner office, with windows in two walls, and near the juncture of those two walls was the desk, a big free-form mahogany thing with an onyx desk set and two telephones—one white, one red

150

—and only a few neatly stacked pieces of paper. A couple of chairs with upholstered seats and backs in a blue-and-white vertical-stripe cloth were near the desk, and a large antique refectory table was over against the inner wall.

Down at the end of the room opposite the desk there was a white latticework divider that separated off about a third of the floor space. Behind it was a glass and chrome dining-room table, several chrome chairs with white vinyl seats, and a bar with fluorescent lights on each shelf. Some kind of real ivy growing out of pots on the floor had been trained to grow up the latticework, giving the glass-and-chrome section behind it the look of a special private nook, the kind of secret place that shows up in children's stories.

In front of the latticework on this side was a long blue sofa, with an octagonal wooden coffee table in front of it, and a pair of armchairs nearby. There were lamps and end tables and heavy ashtrays. Spotted on the walls around the room were half a dozen paintings, probably original, probably valuable. And amid them, positioned for easy viewing from the desk, was the double rank of six television screens. Tom and Joe looked at those screens the instant they walked into the room, and there was no unusual activity showing on any of them. So far, so good.

They both noticed that there were now two guards showing on the screen for the reception area.

Eastpoole's secretary belonged in this setting. She was a tall, cool, beautiful girl in a beige knit dress. She turned away from the window now and came walking over, saying to her boss, "Mr. Eas—"

Eastpoole, angry, not wanting to hear whatever normal business the secretary had been about to discuss with him, interrupted her, gesturing over his shoulder at the two cops and saying, "These people are—"

Not that way. Tom overrode him, pushing forward and saying, "It's okay, Miss. Nothing to worry about."

151

The secretary, looking from face to face, was beginning to get alarmed, but not yet really frightened. Addressing the question to all of them equally, she said, "What's the matter?"

Bitterly, Eastpoole said, "They aren't really police."

Tom made a kind of joke of it, to keep the girl from going into panic. "We're desperate criminals, mam," he said. "We're engaged in a major robbery."

Whenever Joe was confronted by a woman he wanted to get into bed with and knew it wasn't possible to he got hostile, and showed it in a kind of angry smiling manner. As he did now, coming forward and saying, "They'll ask you questions on TV, just like a stewardess."

With an unconscious automatic gesture, she reached up and patted her hair. At the same time, her eyes were getting more frightened, and there was a tremor in her voice when she said, "Mr. Eastpoole, is this really—"

"Yes, it's really," Tom said. "But you yourself are in absolutely no danger. Mr. Eastpoole, you sit down at your desk."

The secretary stared at everybody. "But—" she said, and then ran down, unable to formulate the question. She moved her hands vaguely, and stared, and looked frightened.

Eastpoole did what he was told. Sitting down behind the desk, he said, "There's no way you can get away with this, you know. You're just endangering people's lives."

"Oh, my God," the secretary said. Her right hand fluttered upward to her throat.

Joe pointed at the guards on the TV screens, and said to Eastpoole, "Any of them gets excited while we're here, you're all through."

Eastpoole tried to give him a scornful stare, but he was blinking too much. "You don't have to threaten me," he said. "I'll let the authorities pick you up later."

Nodding, Tom said, "That's the way to think, all right."

Joe pulled one of the blue-and-white striped chairs around behind Eastpoole's desk, so he could sit beside him. But he didn't sit yet; instead, he stood next to the chair and said to Eastpoole, "You and me are going to wait here. My partner and your lady friend are going to the vault."

The secretary's head jerked back and forth. "I—I can't," she said, in a thin voice. "I'll faint."

Reassuring her, Tom said gently, "No, you won't. You'll do just fine, don't worry about a thing."

Joe told her, "You just do what your boss tells you to do." Then he gave Eastpoole a hard meaningful look.

Eastpoole's response was surly, but defeated. Gazing down at his neat desktop, he said, "We'll do what they want, Miss Emerson. Let the police handle it later."

"Right," Joe said.

Tom, looking at the secretary, gestured toward the door. "Let's go, Miss," he said.

She gave one last appealing look in Eastpoole's direction, but Eastpoole was still brooding at his desktop. Her hands fluttered again, as though in accompaniment to the statement she hadn't quite found the words for; but then she turned and walked obediently to the door, and she and Tom went out together.

• Tom •

UNTIL THE second Joe reached out and grabbed Eastpoole's elbow and said, "Hold it," I still hadn't been one hundred per cent sure we were actually going to go through with this. Maybe it had been necessary that I keep some doubt in my mind, maybe that was what had made it possible for me to go on moving along through all the preparations and then get out of bed today and come to New York and in real life start step by step to do the things we'd decided on. That small uncertainty had been a kind of escape

154

hatch for me, I suppose, to keep me from getting too nervous and frightened of what we had in mind.

Well, now the escape hatch was gone. We were in it now, we'd started. If there was anything we hadn't thought of, it was too late to think of it. If there was any fact that we should know that we hadn't picked up in our studies, it was too late to find it out. If there was any flaw in our plan, anything at all, it was too late now to fix it. It would fix us instead.

The first part, escorting Eastpoole to his office and keeping him calm and tractable, hadn't been too bad. It wasn't that different, really, from dealing with a suspect about whose guilt you weren't really sure, but who could possibly make things very tough if he weren't handled just right. It was like a variation on a part of my job I already knew about, so I could almost let automatic responses do it for me.

Besides, Joe and I had been working together at that point. I don't know if my presence made things easier for him, but his presence definitely made things easier for me. Seeing him in the same position I was in, knowing we were locked into this together, had made it easier to keep moving.

But now I was on my own. Eastpoole's secretary, that he'd called Miss Emerson, was walking with me through offices filled with people. What if she suddenly panicked, started to scream? What if her fright was only an act, and she was just waiting her chance to pull a fast one? What if she fainted, or refused to do what I wanted? What if a thousand different things happened that weren't supposed to happen? I hadn't the first idea how I'd handle it if she didn't obey orders, and I wasn't sure any more what was the best way to treat her to make sure she would obey. Her physical being, walking beside me, terrified me, and all I knew for sure was that I couldn't let her know how nervous I was. It would either throw her into a complete panic or make her start thinking she could outsmart me, and I didn't want either of those things to happen.

There was a sexual element, too, which surprised me; I hadn't expected anything like that. I don't mean my sexual instincts are dead, or that my awareness is limited to Mary. I covet other women as much as any man, and in fact several years ago I had an affair with a woman in the neighborhood. She lived down the block from us, her husband worked for Grumman Aircraft. They're gone now, they left a few years ago and moved out to California. It happened in the fall, early in October, and it was possible because of the funny shifts I work that have me around the house a lot in the daytime. This woman—Nancy, her name was—came around one day setting up a car pool for something with the kids. Mary wasn't home but I was, and Nancy had just the night before had a big fight with her husband, and all of a sudden there we were screwing on the living-room floor. It was amazing.

It was also the only time we made it in my house. From then on, if I was home in the daytime and felt like it, I'd drift on down to her place and we'd have sex in her bedroom, on the bed. She had slightly different preferences and manners from Mary, and newness makes things exciting, and for a while I was really pleased with myself, having two women on the same block. Then the holidays came along, and there was a whole different mental attitude developed in both our minds, where we both grew much more interested in our own families again, and it all sort of faded away. We never had a fight or anything, we never officially broke it off, but by the middle of December I wasn't making any more visits and she wasn't calling up—as she'd done a couple times in October and November—to suggest it was a nice day for a bounce on the bed.

Nevertheless, good-looking women definitely still turn

156

me on, and I can get a real letch for something tall and slender with a good figure and a good walk, all of which is a pretty good summation of Miss Emerson. I'd noticed her in the usual sexual way when I'd first walked into Eastpoole's office, but then my mind had been distracted by the problems of dealing with Eastpoole, and in the normal course of events that would have been the end of it.

Which was why I was so surprised and troubled at the sexual aura that hung between us now. It was a different sort of thing from my usual awareness, it was both stronger and unhealthier, and the most embarrassing thing about it was that I knew what was doing it. She was my prisoner. "Ah, me proud beauty, you are in my power!" It was that number. It wasn't really true that she was my prisoner in the sense that I could do anything I wanted with her, but there was a feeling of that between us, of her actually being in my power and of me being in the role of the villain.

And of course, I *was* in the role of villain, wasn't I? I was there to commit, as I'd told her, a major robbery. Which helped to make the situation different from those rare times when I actually have had good-looking female prisoners in my control, in the course of my working life. In those instances I haven't been the villain, I've been on the good guy's side. Also, I've been limited by the rules of my profession and the laws of the land. None of which applied this time.

Well, I wasn't going to rape her, though God knows she had a body I would have liked to touch. But it was much more important to keep her calm than to satisfy irrelevant bodily urges of my own that I didn't really want to have in the first place. So I wanted to talk to her, to ease her tension a little, but I wasn't sure what to say that wouldn't just increase the sexual discomfort hanging around us, so

157

for too long a time I walked beside her in silence; which couldn't have been very reassuring.

Finally I decided the best thing to do was be brisk and businesslike, so I said, "I'm going to tell you exactly what we want. You'll have to go into the vault alone, so I'll tell you what to get from it."

She didn't look at me. Facing front as she walked along next to me, she nodded and said, "Yes." Her face showed strain, the skin stretched tight over her cheekbones, her eyes open a little too wide.

I said, "We want bearer bonds. You know what I mean?"

"Yes," she said.

Of course she knew what I meant, she worked here. "Right," I said. "Now, we don't want any of them with a face value over a hundred thousand dollars, and nothing under twenty thousand, and we want them all together to add up to ten million."

She gave me a surprised look then, but immediately faced front again and nodded and said, "All right."

I said, "Now, I know you're going to be smart and do things right, but I just want to remind you. My partner's in your boss's office, and he can see the vault on one of the TV screens there, and the vault anteroom with the guard. If you try talking to the guard, or doing anything you shouldn't in the vault, he'll be able to see you."

"I won't do anything," she said. She sounded terrified again, and on the verge of tears.

"I know you won't," I said. "I just thought I should remind you, that's all, but I know you won't do anything."

We'd been passing through one of the big offices with all the empty desks and crowded windows. Thirty or forty people in the room, all with their backs to us, looking out the windows at the parade going by. I was still marching along in time to the drums, whether I liked it or not, but Miss Emerson was walking in an erratic sort of way, quick

158

steps and then an occasional slow step, no consistent rhythm at all. I supposed it was part of her nervousness that made her walk like that, and I did my best to adjust my speed to hers, though I still paced myself to the sound of the parade.

In the doorway, leaving that office and entering a corridor that led away to the right, she suddenly stumbled. I automatically reached out to grab her arm and help her keep her feet, and she pulled away from me, terrified, wide-eyed. Keeping her balance by fear alone, she staggered backwards across the corridor and brought up against the wall on the other side.

I followed her into the corridor, looked down to the right, and saw we were alone. "Take it easy," I said, fast and low. I was afraid there was a scream in her throat just dying to come out. "Take it easy, nobody's going to hurt you."

Her right hand went up to her throat again, as it had in the office. I could see her forcing herself to take long deep breaths, to get control. She was really very good, she got hold of the reins herself and pulled the whole thing back together. I stood there, waiting it out, and finally she said, in a low voice, "I'm all right now."

"Of course you are," I said. "You're doing fine. There's nothing to worry about, I promise you. All we want is money, and none of it is yours, so what's there to be afraid of?" I grinned at her, spreading my hands.

She nodded, and came away from the wall at last, but she wouldn't respond to my grin, and as much as possible she avoided meeting my eye. How much of that was simple fear and how much the sexual overlay I don't know, but there was no point trying to calm her entirely. It wouldn't have been possible anyway, and all I really needed was her functional and rational.

Which she was, again. We walked down the corridor

159

together, and then she gestured at a closed door ahead of us and said, "That's the anteroom."

Where the vault guard would be stationed. The vault itself would be just beyond. "I'll wait out here," I said. "Now, you know what I want."

Not looking at me, she nodded her head, a sudden jerky movement.

I said, "Tell me. Take it easy, don't get upset, just tell me what I said."

She had to clear her throat before she could talk. Then she said, "You want bearer bonds. Nothing over a hundred thousand dollars, nothing less than twenty thousand."

"Adding up to?"

"Ten million dollars," she said.

I nodded. "That's right," I said. "And remember, my partner can watch you."

"I won't do anything," she said. She still didn't look at me. "Should I go in now?"

"Sure."

She opened the door and went inside, and I leaned against the wall to wait; either for ten million dollars or the roof to fall in.

• Joe •

WHEN I PULLED the chair over behind Eastpoole's desk, it was strictly bravado. I didn't plan on using it; the truth is, I was too tense to sit. If I couldn't be up and moving around, I'd bust every blood vessel I had.

Still, the best place to keep an eye both on Eastpoole and the television screens was from back around behind his desk. So I let him go on sitting there, and I stood behind him, leaning my back against the corner of the wall, between windows facing out in two directions, where I could watch what was happening both inside the room and out on the street.

The arrangement of the TV sets was the same as the six out in the reception area. The one on the top right showed the reception area itself, with the two guards behind the counter there. The top middle, top left, and bottom right showed three different offices, two of which we'd gone through when we'd come in here. The bottom middle screen showed the vault, and the bottom left showed the anteroom that led to the vault.

The vault was empty of people, and looked like a deep walk-in closet. You couldn't see a door in any part that showed on the screen, so the door was probably directly under the camera. The three walls visible to the camera were all lined from floor to ceiling with letter-size file drawers. The open space in the middle of the room was only about six feet square, and there wasn't any furniture in there at all.

The anteroom wasn't very big either. Where the camera was positioned, you could see the heavy vault door standing open in the far wall. A desk was to the left where the only guard was sitting, facing toward the camera. He had an ordinary wooden chair, without arms, and he was sitting there reading the *Daily News*. There was nothing on his desk but a telephone and a sign-in sheet with a ballpoint pen. A second wooden chair stood beside the desk, and that was it for the furniture. The same as with the vault, the entrance must have been under the camera.

After Tom and the secretary left, I took up my position behind Eastpoole, checked out the TV screens, and then took a quick gander out the window on my left, the one facing the street with the parade. The bands were still going by, thumping away, like the world's longest halftime show. Way down to the right, blocks away, it looked like it was snowing; in July. That was the ticker tape and paper coming down, marking where the astronauts were. You couldn't see them yet, they were still too far away.

I checked out Eastpoole, then. He was sitting there with his head a little forward and down. His palms were flat on the desk in front of him, and I guess he was studying his fingernails. His shoulders were hunched just a bit, meaning it made him nervous to have me behind him. Which was really tough.

People like this Eastpoole really irritate me. You see them driving Caddies, air-conditioned cars. I love to give them tickets, the bastards, but I know it doesn't do any good. What's twenty-five dollars to people like Eastpoole?

I looked over at the television screens, and Tom and the secretary were just walking through one of the offices; the one on the top left. I watched them walk, and the secretary had a really nice ass. I like that kind of knit dress she was wearing, it shows a lot about a woman's shape, and this one was built very nice indeed.

I wondered if Eastpoole was getting into that. There wasn't any point asking him; whether he was or he wasn't, he'd deny it. And he'd give me a look, as though he couldn't believe there were such animals as me running around loose. Oh, I know that type. He hired her for her shorthand, that's what he did. Sure. Her shorthand, and his short arm.

It was tough to wait here like this, with nothing to do. I had the urge to needle Eastpoole a little, maybe poke him in the shoulder to see if he was as nerved-up as I was. But I knew I shouldn't do it, I shouldn't do anything that might make him forget to be smart and cool and quiet. It wasn't worth twenty years in a federal penitentiary to get a rise out of Eastpoole.

Twenty years. That thought suddenly brought it home to me; we were doing it! The thing we'd been talking about, building up for, kidding around with, we were actually do-

163

ing it, we'd passed the stage of maybe yes, maybe no. There weren't any more maybes now. It's like the first time you ski down a real hill on your own; all the chances for thinking it over are gone, and from here on the only thing you can think about is keeping your balance.

I almost hadn't done it. I came this close to not bracing Eastpoole at all. Coming in with him from the reception area, I kept thinking about just running the whole thing through as though it was a gag. I mean, actually look at the windows on the northeast corner, maybe give the employees a lecture about throwing offensive objects onto the people below—I had this whole thing worked out in my head where I'd give a whole speech about shit without ever quite using the word—and then just turn around and walk out again. Pretend that's all I'd ever meant to do, that the whole robbery thing had never been anything but a gag anyway.

If it hadn't been for Tom there with me, that's probably exactly what I would have done. But I could feel Tom there beside me, waiting for me to make the move, and I just couldn't chicken out. Same as with skiing again; there comes that point, you've done your boasting, everybody's watching you, and it suddenly doesn't matter if you break your neck or not. You've got to do it, because if you don't you've made a fool of yourself, and nothing is worse than that.

Twenty years?

Well, almost nothing.

Movement on one of the television screens. I looked over there, and I was aware of Eastpoole tensing up right in front of me.

The secretary had walked into the anteroom. She had her back to me, I couldn't see the expression on her face. Any other time, honey, I'd love to see your ass, but right now it's your face I want.

164

At least I could see the guard's face. He looked up and gave her a big smile. So far as I could tell, she didn't say anything wrong to him, because the smile didn't flicker for a second. She moved forward, bent over to sign the sheet of paper on his desk, and then walked on into the vault. I kept watching the guard, and he didn't do anything wrong at all. He didn't even bother to look at her signature, just opened his newspaper again the second she was out of the anteroom and into the vault.

Now I could see her on the next screen. She walked into the vault, looked around, and glanced up at the camera. Yeah, honey, I'm watching.

I looked at the screen showing the reception area. The two guards were both leaning on the counter, talking together. Neither of them was looking toward the screens.

Back in the vault, the secretary was opening one of the file drawers. She started to finger through it, and pulled out a sheet of heavy paper like a high school diploma. She opened another drawer and rested the sheet of paper on top of the things in the drawer, then went back to the first one to select some more.

I hoped she was getting the right stuff. I hoped Tom had gotten the point across to her and that she'd understood what it was we wanted. I didn't want to get home later on and find out we'd gone through all this for a lot of paper we couldn't use.

It was taking her a goddam long time. She kept looking at paper after paper, and most of them she just shoved back into the drawer. What was taking so long? Come on, damn it, grab the paper, let's go. We don't want to miss the parade, that's part of our scheme.

I looked out the window again. The astronauts would be the wind-up of the parade, and that's where the stream of ticker tape was coming down. It was closer, but still blocks away. But it wouldn't take forever.

I looked back at the screens again. The girl in the vault was still picking through the file drawer. "Come on," I whispered, too low for Eastpoole to hear me. "Come on, come on."

But she kept doing it. The stack on the other drawer was getting pretty thick now, but she still wasn't finished.

We'd wanted too much, that was all. We should have settled for half of that. Five million, that would get us half a million each. Five hundred thousand dollars, who needs more than that? It's nearly forty years of my salary. We'd been greedy, that's what, and it was taking too long.

Come *on,* bitch, come on!

Movement. I looked at the screen on the top right, the reception area. An elevator door had opened there, and three uniformed patrolmen were coming out of it, moving toward the two guards behind the counter.

I slapped a hand down on Eastpoole's shoulder. He'd seen it, too, he was tensing up like fast-drying concrete. My throat was so dry my voice came out like steel wool. I said, "What's going on?"

The three cops stopped at the counter, one of them talked to the guards. A guard turned toward the telephone.

I squeezed Eastpoole's shoulder, clamping down on it. *"What's going on?"*

"I d-don't know." I could feel him trembling under my hand, the concrete was breaking up. He was frightened for his life, and he had a right to be. "I swear I don't know," he said, and sat there trembling.

The guard was dialing. On the vault screen, that stinking bitch was still picking out papers, one at a time. All the other screens were fine.

The phone rang, on Eastpoole's desk. Eastpoole stared at it. His head was twitching.

So was mine. I fought the goddam holster, I got my pistol into my hand. "By God," I said, "you're a dead man."

166

And I meant it. I thought we were both dead men, and if I was, Eastpoole was.

Eastpoole lifted his hands. He stared at the telephone. He didn't know what to say or what to do. He really and truly didn't know whether to shit or go blind.

I kicked the chair out of the way that I'd dragged around behind the desk before. It went over on its side with a crash, and Eastpoole jumped. I crouched down beside him, so I'd be able to listen on the phone and still watch the television screens. I pushed the pistol barrel against Eastpoole's side. "Answer it," I said. "And be goddam careful."

He had to take a couple of seconds to get some control, so he'd be able to move and talk. I let him have the time he needed, and then he reached out and picked up the phone and said, "Yes?"

I could only make out about half the words the guard said to him. But it didn't seem as though there was any tension in the voice, or any sense of excitement out there in the reception area.

On the other hand, if they were here because they knew what was going on, they'd know we could see them on television, wouldn't they?

But how would they know? There hadn't been any breakdowns, there wasn't any reason for anything to go wrong.

Eastpoole said into the phone, "But do they have to—? Well, one moment. One moment." He put his hand over the mouthpiece, and turned to talk to me. "They're here to check security for the astronauts," he said.

I kept watching the screen. I said, "What do they want?"

"Just to station themselves at windows."

We didn't want cops in here. What the hell was the matter with them, why didn't they pick some other floor? Why didn't they go on the roof, for Christ's sake, that's

167

where your snipers come from. "God damn it," I said. I felt like blowing up into a million pieces. "God *damn* it."

"I'm not responsible," Eastpoole yammered, "I didn't know they—"

"Shut up, shut up." I was trying to think, trying to decide what to do. He couldn't refuse, that wouldn't look right. "Listen," I said. They can do it, but not in this office. Tell them that."

He nodded, fast and nervous. "Yes," he said, and into the phone he said, "Go right ahead, tell them it's all right. One of you escort them in. But I don't want any of them in here. Not in my office."

I could read the guard's lips on that one, see him say, "Yes, sir." Eastpoole hung up, and so did the guard. The guard turned back to the three cops, said something to them, and then walked around the end of the counter to lead them in.

I looked at the vault screen, and the girl was finally finished. Carrying a double armful of papers like a schoolgirl with her books, she pushed the two drawers shut and turned toward the door.

I jabbed Eastpoole with the pistol again. "Call the vault!" I told him. "I want to talk to that girl."

"There's no phone in the—"

"The anteroom! The anteroom! For Christ's sake, call!"

He reached for the phone. The girl was out of sight of the vault camera now. On the anteroom camera, I saw her come through the doorway. The stack of papers in her arms was maybe three inches thick, as thick as two ordinary books, but of course stacked somewhat looser. There were maybe a hundred and fifty sheets of paper there.

Eastpoole was dialing a three-digit number. The guard in the anteroom turned his head when the girl walked in, saw the stack of paper she was carrying, and jumped to his feet to open the hall door for her.

168

I kept jabbing Eastpoole in the side with the gun. "Hurry it up!" I said. "Hurry it up!"

The guard and the girl were both moving toward the camera, they'd be out of sight under it in a second. "Come *on*," I said. I wanted to shoot everything in sight; Eastpoole, the television screens, the astronauts out in the street. The goddam drums were pounding away down there as though I didn't have enough pounding from my heart.

"It's ringing," Eastpoole said, still terrified, still trying to show me he was cooperating. And just before the guard disappeared out of sight, I saw him look back over his shoulder toward the phone on his desk.

But he was polite, he was. Ladies first. He went on, he disappeared. The girl disappeared.

"It's ringing," Eastpoole said again, and from the sound of his voice and the look on his face I thought he was about to cry.

The guard appeared again, alone, moving toward the desk and the telephone. I reached over and slapped my free hand down on the phone cradle, breaking the connection. On the screen, the guard picked up the receiver. He could be seen saying hello into it, being confused.

Eastpoole was jabbering, he was going to shake himself right out of his chair. Staring at me, he was saying, "I tried! I tried! I did everything you said, I tried!"

"Shut up shut up shut *up!*" The other cops were long since gone from the reception area. Tom and the girl would be walking through all those offices, Tom having no idea about the three cops.

Eastpoole was panting like a dog. The six screens were all normal. I stared at them, and bit my upper lip, and finally I said, "A phone on their route." I looked at Eastpoole. "What's their route back?"

He just stared at me.

169

"Damn you, what's their route?"

"I'm trying to think!"

"Anything goes wrong," I told him, shaking the pistol in his face, "God *damn* it, anything goes wrong, you're the first one dead."

Shakily he reached for the phone.

• Tom •

I STOOD in that corridor a long time. I must have figured out fifty different ways for things to go wrong while I waited there, and no ways at all for things to go right.

For instance. It was true that Joe could keep an eye on Miss Emerson through the television screens in Eastpoole's office, but what good would that do me if she decided to blow the thing to the guard in the anteroom after all? Joe would see her do it, he'd know what was going on, but he didn't have any way to get in touch with me to warn me. For all I knew, it had already happened, and Joe was out of the building by now, leaving me to stand here and wait to be picked up.

Or say she didn't do it on purpose, Miss Emerson, but her nervousness made her do or say something that got the guard suspicious. Same result; me standing out here as though I was waiting for the bus.

The bus to Sing Sing.

Would Joe clear out, if that happened? If the roles were reversed, and I was the one in Eastpoole's office and saw it all going wrong on the television screens, what would I do?

I'd come looking for Joe, to warn him. And that's what he'd do, too, I was sure of it.

Aside from anything else, it wouldn't do Joe any good to get away and leave me here. Even if I never said a word, how long would it take the investigating officers to get from me to my next-door neighbor, who was also my best friend and also on the force? They'd have us both booked by nightfall.

Where was she, what was taking so long?

But Joe would come looking for me, I was sure of that.

Which didn't mean he'd find me. He didn't know the route from Eastpoole's office to the vault any more than I had. I'd followed Miss Emerson, that's all.

That would be beautiful. Everything gone to hell, me standing here not knowing about it, and Joe running back and forth all over the seventh floor looking for me. That would be too ridiculous to believe, and if that's the way it went we'd almost deserve to be caught.

What was she *doing* in there?

I looked at my watch, but it didn't tell me anything, because I didn't know what time she'd gone in. Maybe five minutes ago, maybe ten. It seemed like a week.

The parade. If she didn't get a move on, we'd miss the

parade, and that would screw things up all over again.

You spend your life waiting around for women, I swear to God you do. You'll be late for church, late for the movies, late for dinner, late for the parade, late for everything. You sit out in the car and honk the horn, or you stand in the bathroom doorway and say, "Your hair looks all *right*." Or you stand around looking at your watch, in the middle of committing a felony. Nothing ever changes, men just wait for women and that's all there is to it.

A door opened, farther down the hall. A girl came out, carrying a thick manila envelope. She was short and dumpy, in a plaid skirt and a white blouse, and she looked like the kind of girl who would go on working when everybody else in lower Manhattan was watching the parade. I stood there, clenching my teeth, watching her walk toward me. She gave me a neutral smile on the way by, walked on, and went through another doorway and out of sight. I exhaled, and looked at my watch again, and another minute had gone by.

I'd looked at my watch twice more before the anteroom door opened. I was standing back against the wall to one side, so I couldn't be seen from inside the room, and it's a good thing I was, because apparently the guard had come over to open the door for her. "See you again," I heard him say, with that smile in his voice that men have when talking to a good-looking woman.

"Thank you," she said. Her voice seemed to me too obviously frightened, but he didn't make any connections from it; at least, not that I could tell.

He probably thought it was her period. Any time a woman acts upset or nervous or weepy or anything at all out of the ordinary, everybody always takes it for granted it's her period, and pretends not to notice.

She came out to the corridor and gave me a haggard look, and the guard closed the door behind her. I heard his phone ring as the door was closing. Let it be nothing, I thought.

She had a stack of documents in her arms, held against her chest. I nodded at them and said, "All set?"

"Yes." Her voice was very small, as though she were talking from a different room.

"Let's go, then."

We headed back for Eastpoole's office, retracing the same route as before. Parade noises still thumped in through the open windows, employees were still jammed at all the windows with their backs to us, everything moved along exactly as before.

At the end of one corridor there was a closed door. I'd opened it for her the last time, coming through, and now that her hands were full there was even more reason to do so. I did, and we stepped through into the next office, and I'd gone another pace or two when I suddenly thought about fingerprints.

Now, that would be smart. The most basic thing in police procedure is fingerprints, every six-year-old boy in the country knows about fingerprints, and I was about to go off and leave prints all over two doorknobs; the one going, and the one coming.

"Hold it a second," I said.

She stopped, giving me an uncomprehending look. I went back to the door and smeared my palm all around the knob, then pulled it open and leaned out to do the same thing on the other side. I rubbed it good, and was about to shut the door again when movement attracted my attention. I looked down at the far end of the corridor, and one of the guards from the reception area was coming in, followed by three uniformed cops.

I ducked back into the room and shut the door. I was sure they hadn't seen me. I rubbed the inner knob again,

174

then turned back to Miss Emerson, took her by the arm, and started walking fast. She was startled, mouth open, but before she could speak I said, low and fast, "Don't do anything, don't say anything. Just walk."

The windows were on the right, lined with employees. Band music was loud, making our own movements silent. Nobody saw or heard us.

There was an alcove on the left, full of duplicating equipment; a row of filing cabinets partly shielded it from the main area of the room. I turned that way, steered Miss Emerson in there. "We're going to wait here a second," I said. "Crouch down. I don't want you seen over the tops of the cabinets."

She crouched a bit, but apparently found that too uncomfortable because a second later she shifted position and knelt instead. She knelt in a prim way, back straight, like an early Christian martyr about to get it. She watched me, wide-eyed, but didn't say anything.

I hunkered down, and peeked around the edge of the last filing cabinet. I'd let them go past me, and then follow. That way, if they were headed for Eastpoole's office I'd at least be behind them, where I might be able to do some good.

Did Joe know about the cops being here? He'd have to, he would have seen them come in.

What was he doing now? Had my worst fears come true, was Joe wandering around these offices somewhere looking for me?

God damn it, what a mess.

I could smell the secretary. Fear was making her perspire, and the perspiration was mixing with whatever perfume or cologne or something she had on, and the result was a half-musky, half-sweet scent that brought back the whole sexual thing all over again.

I didn't have time to think about that. I was doing some sweating myself right now.

The guard and three policemen appeared. Past them, a phone rang on one of the desks. The cops all stopped, right in front of me, to talk things over.

On the second ring of the telephone, a girl at one of the windows turned around reluctantly, gave an exaggerated sigh, looked long-suffering, and strolled over to answer it.

The cops had decided one of them would stay in this room. While the others walked on, he went over and forced a place for himself at one of the windows, looking out.

Meanwhile, the girl had answered the phone. "Hello?" She paused, then looked more alert and on-the-job. "Mr. Eastpoole? Yes, sir." Another pause. She looked around, and shook her head. "No, sir, Mr. Eastpoole, she hasn't been through yet." Another pause. "Yes, sir, I certainly will." She hung up, and hurried back to the window.

Now what? How the hell was Eastpoole making phone calls? Where was Joe? What was going on?

And I didn't need that cop at the window, I really didn't.

Well, I had him. Straightening up to look over the top of the filing cabinet, I saw him standing there, having taken a window for himself, and he was looking out, his back squarely to me. If he'd only stay like that, there was still a chance.

I hunkered again, and turned to Miss Emerson. "Listen," I said. "I don't want a lot of shooting."

"Neither do I," she said. She was so sincere it was almost comic.

"We're just going to get up and walk," I told her. "No trouble, no fuss, no attracting anybody's attention."

"No, sir," she said.

"Okay. Let's do it."

I helped her up from her knees, and she gave me a quick nervous smile of thanks. We were developing a human relationship. We came out from behind the filing cabinets and walked down the length of the office, and out, without being seen.

· 12 ·

THE NEXT time they saw one another, they both started talking at the same time. Tom opened the door and ushered the secretary into Eastpoole's office, and Joe snapped around from where he was glaring at the television screens, trying to find out where everybody was.

Tom said, "There's cops out—"

Joe said, "Where the hell—"

They both stopped. There was so much tension in the air they could both have thrown themselves on the floor

178

and started screaming and kicking and thrashing around.

Joe gestured at the phone on Eastpoole's desk. "I tried to call you," he said, "I saw them come in."

Tom had shut the door behind him. Now he walked across toward Joe and the desk and Eastpoole, saying, "I almost walked right into them. What are they doing?"

"Security for the astronauts."

Tom made a face. "Christ," he said. Then, suddenly remembering, he said, "The astronauts! We don't want to miss the end of the parade!"

Joe turned and hurried to the window and looked out. The paper snow was about two blocks away, approaching slowly. He turned back to the room, saying, "We're all right."

"Good," Tom said. He took a blue plastic laundry bag out of his left rear trouser pocket. It was all folded up small, into something about the size and shape of a pack of cigarettes. He shook it open, and it opened out into a good-size laundry bag; big enough to put a couple of sheets in, plus a regular wash.

Meantime Joe had walked over to the other area of the room, behind the white latticework. There was a door there, next to the bar. He pushed it open, reached in to switch on the light, and found a small but complete bathroom in there. Just as it had shown on the blueprints filed downtown. Sink, toilet, shower stall. It all looked very expensive, including the fact that the hot-and-cold-water faucets were in the shape of golden geese; the water would come out of their open mouths, and you'd turn their flared-back wings.

Tom turned to the secretary, holding open the laundry bag. "Dump them in here," he said.

As she dumped the bonds into the bag, Joe came back from his inspection of the bathroom and said to Eastpoole, "Okay, you. Get up from there."

179

Eastpoole knew enough now to be obedient right away, but he was still terrified. Rising, he said, "Where are you—?"

"Don't worry," Joe told him. "You were a good boy, you'll be okay. We just got to lock you up while we get out of here."

Tom threw the bag over his shoulder. He looked like a thin blue Santa Claus with a blue bag over his shoulder.

Joe wiggled his finger at the secretary. "You, too, honey," he said. "Come along."

Joe led them to the bathroom, then had them precede him into the room. He took handcuffs out of his left hip pocket and said to Eastpoole, "Give me your right hand."

Tom waited in the main part of the office. He didn't think they could see him now, but he didn't want to take any chances.

Joe put the cuff on Eastpoole's right wrist, then told him, "Kneel down. Right here by the sink." When Eastpoole did it, looking both frightened and confused, Joe turned to the secretary and said, "You too. Kneel right next to him."

After the girl had knelt, Joe crouched down with them and pushed Eastpoole's right arm so he could pass the handcuffs around behind the run-off pipe under the sink. Then he took the secretary's left forearm and held it back to where he could hook the other cuff onto her. The position he had to get to, in order to do it, all their heads were close together, like a football huddle. Their breaths mingled, and Joe found himself squinting as he put the cuffs on, as though there were bright lights on both sides of his face. Eastpoole and the secretary both kept their eyes down, looking toward the floor; kneeling there with eyes lowered, they looked like penitents.

Joe straightened, and nodded in satisfaction. They wouldn't be leaving this room, not without help. "You'll be getting out in a few minutes," he told them. "I'll leave the light on."

They watched him now, neither of them saying anything. Eastpoole didn't even say they wouldn't be getting away with it.

Joe went out the door, and paused with his hand on the knob. "Don't bother yelling," he said. "The only ones that'll hear you is us, and we won't come help."

Tom, across the room, standing near Eastpoole's desk, watched Joe in the bathroom doorway, and waited for him to come out and shut the door. When he finally did, Tom turned the laundry bag upside down, grabbed it by the bottom, and shook the bonds out onto the desk.

Joe came hurrying across the room. "They're closed in," he said.

"I know." Tom was looking at the television screens, and there was nothing unusual showing on any of them.

"There's no keyhole," Joe said, "so they won't be able to see what we're doing."

"They better not," Tom said. "How's the parade?"

"I'll take a look."

This was the part they'd argued about, while planning things. It had been Tom's idea to do it this way, and Joe hadn't liked it for a long while. In fact, it still troubled him now, but he did finally agree with Tom that it was the best way to handle things.

Joe headed for the window to look at the parade, and Tom picked up a thin stack of bonds; about ten of them. The top one was plainly marked "Pay To Bearer," and the amount of it was seventy-five thousand dollars. Tom gave the number a happy smile of welcome, shifted the grip of his two hands on the papers, and ripped them down the middle.

Joe was at the window. He looked out and to the right. He saw the parade, but he also saw a cop at another window on this floor. The cop was glancing in this direction, and when he saw Joe he waved. Joe nodded and waved back, and brought his head back in.

Tom was ripping the bonds into smaller and smaller pieces, working quickly but efficiently. Joe came over to the desk, gave the stack of paper a regretful look, and said, "Less than a block away."

"Help me with this."

"Sure."

Joe picked up a dozen bonds and gazed at them. "This one's for a hundred grand," he said.

"Come on, Joe."

"Right." Smiling sadly, shaking his head, he started to rip up the bonds.

Outside, the parade noises were getting louder; mostly the crowd noises, nearly blotting out the sounds of the bands. Turning his head for a fast look at the windows, Tom saw bits of paper already starting to flutter down. And less than a quarter of the bonds had been ripped up so far.

The two of them stood there, ripping paper. Shouting and yelling from down below. Then, in a different broken rhythm, a foot started thudding against the bathroom door.

They looked at one another. Tom said, "Will it pop open?"

"Christ."

Joe dropped the paper in his hands and ran down to the other end of the office. Eastpoole was kicking steadily and strongly at the door; apparently with the flat bottom of his shoe, sole and heel together. The door itself seemed solid enough to hold against that, but the catch could pop at any time and the door swing open.

What Joe would have liked mostly would have been to open the door and start doing some kicking himself; but there was a chance Eastpoole and the girl would be able to see through the latticework what Tom was doing. And the point of all this was that everybody think the crooks had gotten away with the bonds.

Joe looked around, grabbed one of the chairs away from the dining room table, and propped the back of it under the doorknob. He kicked the rear legs to jam them more firmly into the carpet, then stood back and watched. Inside, Eastpoole was still kicking at the door, but there wasn't even a tremor showing around the knob or the chair.

Tom was still ripping paper, back by Eastpoole's desk. Joe trotted over and said, "Fixed. It won't open now."

"Good."

There was a mound of ripped paper on the desk, all little irregular pieces no more than an inch square. Joe grabbed a double handful, carried it over to the window, and leaned his head out slightly first to see if the other cop was still visible down to the right. He was, but he was turned the other way, watching the roofline across the street.

Down below, through thousands of descending specks of paper, Joe could see the three convertibles in a row, each one with an astronaut sitting up on the back, waving and smiling. The lead car wasn't quite opposite this building yet, and they were all moving very slowly, no more than three miles an hour. The air was full of cheers and paper.

Joe grinned, and tossed his handful of ripped-up bonds out the window. The mass went out like a snowball, and disintegrated at once, all the pieces mixing with the rest of the torrent of paper coming down.

Tom's thumbs and wrists were getting sore. The bonds had been printed on heavy paper, and he'd been tearing them up as quickly as he could, the stacks as thick as he

183

could manage. Now he took a break, grabbing up a handful of shreds and turning toward the window.

Joe was coming back. "Be careful leaning out," he said. "There's a cop down the row to the right. Waved at me."

"I'll be careful."

Tom tossed the paper out without showing himself, or trying to see the cop at the other window. When he turned back, Joe was picking up more paper. Tom hurried over, saying, "No, not that. Smaller pieces, smaller. They aren't ready yet."

Joe nodded at the window. "They're going by, Tom. The cars are going by right now."

"Small, Joe," Tom said. "So nothing shows." He pushed a little stack of paper together. "Take this."

Joe gave an irritable impatient shrug, gathered up the stack Tom had made, and carried it over to the window. Tom went back to ripping, and when Joe came to the desk again he also started shredding the bonds that were still left.

For the next minute or so the two of them stood side by side at the desk, tearing the last of the bonds into tiny remnants. Then they threw them all out, double handfuls fluttering down through the paper-filled air, disappearing. The three convertibles had all gone by, were all in the next block by now, but there was still enough paper coming down from all the buildings in this block so that Tom and Joe's contribution didn't show.

Tom gathered up the last few pieces left on the desk, hurried to the window, and tossed them out. Joe walked slowly around the desk, searching the floor, and found half a dozen pieces that had fallen in their hurry to be done. Tom spent time looking at the floor around the window, and found three more pieces that he picked up.

When Joe came over to the window with the few scraps

he'd just gathered up from the floor, Tom said, "We can't leave any."

"We won't," Joe said. He tossed the last scraps out. "Let's go," he said. "It's time to get out of here."

But Tom kept prowling around, frowning down at the floor. "If we leave even one little piece for them to find," he said, "it blows the whole thing. They'll know what we've done, and that kills it."

"We've got them all," Joe insisted. "Come on, let's go."

"Hah!" Tom pounced on one last bit of paper midway between desk and window. He hurried to the window, where the snowfall of paper was starting to thin, and tossed the final piece out. "Now," he said.

Joe was already opening desk drawers. He found a stack of typewriter paper in one and pulled out a handful. Tom joined him at the desk, opened the blue laundry bag, and Joe dumped the paper into it. Then they both took a quick last look around.

"Okay," Tom said.

Joe was looking at the television screens. All quiet. "Fine," he said. "Let's go."

They walked out of Eastpoole's office together, through the secretary's office, and down the corridor toward the reception area and the elevators. Tom carried the laundry bag over his shoulder. It was very obvious there, but that was the point; they had to be seen carrying the loot out with them.

Walking along, Tom said, "I wish we knew a way out that wouldn't take us past any of those damn cameras."

Joe nodded. "I know. It'd be better if the guards didn't know we were coming."

"We could try," Tom said. They'd come to an office entrance now, but Tom stopped and said, "There's a camera in there. Why don't we go down this other way instead? Maybe we can go around, come at it from the other side."

"Get lost in here? Wander around until we get picked up?"

"It isn't that big," Tom said. "And if we get lost, we just stop somebody and ask."

Joe grinned at him. "You get funny ideas," he said. "Okay, let's try it, what the hell."

So they went off into new territory. They both had a pretty good sense of direction, and they had a general idea of the way things were set up around here. If they kept to the right for a while, then made a left farther on, they should come at the reception area from the opposite side.

It worked, all right, insofar as getting them to the reception area along a different route was concerned. But it didn't do any good when it came to avoiding television cameras. There had been two along the old route, which left a third, and they found that halfway to the reception area.

They didn't notice it until they were already in the room with it, with the damn thing pointing at them. Then Joe said under his breath, "You see what I see?"

"I see it," Tom said.

They walked through that office, casual and unconcerned, then began to move faster once they were away from the camera. They already knew there was a rule around here that visitors didn't travel unescorted, even if the visitors were policemen in uniform. They were traveling unescorted, from Eastpoole's office; the guards on duty in the reception area might not leap to the conclusion they were thieves, but they'd suspect something was wrong, and they'd start right away to look into it.

First they'd try phoning the boss. They wouldn't get any answer, either from Eastpoole or his secretary, and that would upset them even more. But making the phone call would take time, maybe all the time needed for Tom

186

and Joe to cover the rest of the ground and get them under control.

If not, if they didn't get there in time, what would the guards do next? Would they put in an alarm right away? Since the visitors were supposed to be cops, they might be a little more careful, a little more cautious. They might get in touch with the guard in the vault anteroom. They might send somebody to alert the other three cops up here, the ones assigned to the security detail for the astronauts. They might get in touch with somebody Tom and Joe didn't know about, down at the street level. There were a thousand different things they might do, and Tom and Joe could be pretty sure they wouldn't like any of them.

They hurried, but it still took a while to travel the rest of the way to the reception area, and when they got there only one guard was behind the counter. It was the same one who'd been here when they'd first come up. He looked at them now, and he was very nervous and trying not to show it. They angled across toward the elevators, and he called over, "Where's Mr. Eastpoole?"

Tom gave him a smile and wave of the hand. "In his office," he said. "Everything's okay."

Joe pressed the down button for the elevator.

The guard couldn't keep the nervousness from affecting his voice. He pointed at the laundry bag Tom was carrying and said, "I'll have to inspect that bag."

Tom smiled at him and said, "Sure. Why not?"

Joe stayed behind, by the elevator doors, while Tom walked over to the counter and set the laundry bag atop it. The guard, losing some of his nervousness because they were acting as though nothing was wrong, came down the counter to look into the bag. As he was reaching for it, Tom nodded toward the screens down on the far wall. He said, "The guy in the vault anteroom. Does he have a set of screens like that?"

187

The guard looked over at the screens. "Sure," he said. "He can see us?"

The guard gave Tom a warning look. "Yes, he can," he said.

Joe, back by the elevators, was watching the screens very carefully; all of them. The guard in the anteroom was still reading his *Daily News*. On one of the office screens, the other guard from out here suddenly appeared, moving fast. He wasn't quite running, and he was apparently headed for Eastpoole's office.

Tom, still talking in a conversational tone of voice, said, "Well, if he can see us, I guess you don't want me to show a gun."

The guard stared. "What?"

"If I show a gun," Tom told him, "he'll know something's wrong. Then I'll have to kill you so we can take off out of here."

From his position by the elevators, Joe called to the guard, "Take it easy, pal. Don't get anybody upset."

The guard was scared, but he was a professional. He didn't make any large moves that the anteroom guard might see on his screen. Holding himself in tight control, he said, "You'll never get out of the building. You'll never make it."

Joe said, casually, "It isn't your money, pal, but it is your life."

"Come around the counter," Tom said. "You're going out with us."

The guard didn't move. He licked his lips and blinked, but he had guts. He said, "Give it up. Just leave that bag on the counter and take off. Nobody'll chase you if you don't have the goods on you."

An elevator arrived. Its door sliding open prompted Joe's next remark. "Come on, pal," he said. "Don't waste

188

time. We'd rather do it the easy way, but we don't have to."

Reluctantly, the guard moved, going down to the flap at the end of the counter, lifting it, stepping through. On the anteroom screen, the guard could be seen still reading his paper. He hadn't noticed yet that the reception area was about to be left undefended. When he did, he'd know something was wrong, but it would still take him a minute or two to figure out the right procedure to deal with the situation. He'd try to call Eastpoole, he'd try to call the reception area. He wouldn't want to leave the vault, just in case the whole thing was a stunt to lure him out. His indecision would give them time.

The elevator was empty. Joe was holding the door open and watching the television screens. Tom was carrying the laundry bag again, and watching the guard.

"If you take a hostage," the guard said, coming out from behind the counter, "you run the risk you'll have to shoot somebody."

He meant himself, and all things considered he delivered the sentence very calmly. Joe said to him, "Just get in the elevator."

The three of them stepped into the elevator, and Joe pushed the button for the first floor. The door closed, they started down, and the guard said, "You can still get out of this. Go down to one, leave the bag with me, take off; by the time I get back upstairs you'll be gone. And you won't have taken anything, so who'll be looking for you?"

They already knew the answer to that, far more than he could guess, but neither of them said anything. Tom was watching the guard, and Joe was watching the numbers showing which floor they were passing.

You couldn't hear the parade in the elevator at all. It had Muzak in it, playing some melody they both recognized but neither of them knew the name of.

189

The guard said, "Listen. With a hostage, you're risking a shoot-out. Plus kidnapping, it's technically kidnapping."

The elevator was passing the fourth floor. Joe reached out and pressed the button marked 2. The guard looked at that and frowned. He didn't know what they were doing, and his bewilderment shut him up. He didn't have anything else to say at all.

The elevator stopped on the second floor. Joe reached over, plucked the guard's pistol out of his holster, and said, "Move."

"You aren't going to—"

"No, we're not," Joe said. He was snappish and in a hurry. "Just move."

The guard stepped out. They made as if to follow him, but when the door started to slide shut they stepped back again. The guard was turning, open-mouthed, as the door finished closing and the elevator descended to the first floor.

"Christ," Joe said. He took off his hat, showing big beads of perspiration high on his forehead. He used the hat to smear his prints from the guard's pistol, then put the pistol on the floor in the rear corner of the elevator. As he straightened, the elevator stopped, the door opened, and the lobby floor was in front of them.

Clear. They were ahead of pursuit, and if they just kept moving briskly along they'd stay ahead of it.

They walked out across the lobby, Tom carrying the laundry bag. They pushed through the doors and went out to the street, and the parade crowd was beginning to break up. Some paper was still floating down from windows in the upper stories, but not much.

It was tougher to get through the crowd this time; the convenient empty lane between crowd and building fronts had gone, swallowed up by the generalized movement of the crowd away from here.

The pursuit would be slowed just as much, they had to keep reminding themselves of that.

They reached the arcade, and it too was full of people now, though not quite as bad as the street; they moved through at a good pace.

The squad car was right where they'd left it, just as it was supposed to be. A lot of people were milling around, but none of them were interested in two cops. Tom paused by a wire trash can at the curb. He held the laundry bag by a bottom corner, and quietly upended it into the trash can. The typewriter paper fell out, and the weight of it all together in a pack drove it down through the crumpled newspapers and cigarette packages and paper cups, halfway out of sight.

They moved on toward the squad car. Tom squashed the laundry bag into a ball and stuffed it into his pocket. They got into the car, Joe behind the wheel, and drove away.

Two blocks later, they had to stop at an intersection to let two other patrol cars rush by, sirens screaming and lights flashing. Then they drove on.

· 13 ·

ONCE AGAIN they changed the license plates and the identifying numbers on the squad car, this time switching everything back to the original way. Their actions were shielded by the highway stanchion and the parked trailer. Joe made the transfer on the rear plate and Tom the front, and then they met at the back of Tom's Chevvy. Tom opened the trunk lid, and they tossed the plates and numbers and the two screwdrivers in with the canvas bag containing Tom's civilian clothing.

Neither of them said anything. They were both feeling very down, very deflated. It was the letdown after all the excitement, and they knew it, but knowing what the trouble was didn't change it.

Tom was making some attempt to shake the feeling off. Pulling the blue plastic laundry bag out of his pocket, he shook it out to its full length and then held it up in front of himself like a doctor holding up a newborn baby. His hand was trembling as he held the bag, and he gave it a shaky, uncertain grin. "Well, there it is," he said.

Joe gave the bag a sour look. He wasn't fighting against his depression at all. "Yeah, there it is, all right," he said.

"Two million dollars," Tom said.

Joe shook his head. "Air," he corrected.

Tom gave him a grin that was supposed to be brave and sure of itself. "We'll see," he said.

Joe shrugged. The gesture meant that he was skeptical, and that he was too weary to give a damn. "Yeah, we will," he said.

Suddenly feeling defensive, Tom told him, "We talked it over, Joe. We agreed this was the way to do it."

Joe shrugged again, and gave an exhausted nod. "I know, I know." Then, seeing Tom's expression, he tried to act more friendly, and to explain himself. "I just wish we had something to show for it," he said.

Tom said, "But that's just what we didn't want. Nothing we had to carry away from the scene, nothing we had to hide, nothing to get caught with, nothing to be used as evidence against us."

"Nothing," Joe said. Then he spread his hands and said, "What the hell, you're right. We did talk it over, we did agree. Come on, let's go. I need a drink."

Tom was going to argue some more, but Joe had turned away, walking back toward the squad car. And Tom thought, what's the point in arguing? We've already done it, and we did it this way, and it was the right way. He dropped the plastic bag into the trunk, and shut the lid.

They got into the two cars, and Joe led the way back uptown to the police garage. The parking space he'd taken the car from was gone now, but there was another one near it. Joe left the car there without doing anything under the hood; tomorrow morning, a mechanic would find the car had mysteriously fixed itself. If he was a normal mechanic, he'd first take it for granted there'd never been anything wrong with the car other than a stupid driver, and second take credit for having fixed it.

Tom was waiting around the corner in the Chevvy. Joe walked around and got in, and they drove back over to the Port Authority. While Joe stayed outside in the car, Tom went in and changed back to civvies. When he came out, Joe said, "I wasn't kidding about that drink. My nerves could use one."

Tom was agreeable; the idea of a drink was a good one to him, too. "Where do you want to go?"

"Nowhere we're known."

"I'll find a place over in Queens."

"Good."

Tom drove across town and up to the 59th Street Bridge and over to Queens. They found a bar on Queensboro Boulevard with nobody in it except the bartender and an old fellow dressed in striped railroad coveralls. The railroad man was sitting at the bar, watching an afternoon game show on the television set mounted at the end of the room. They ordered a couple of beers, and sat in a booth to drink them.

They were both in the mood for a drink, but they had different reasons. Tom was hoping liquor would make him feel happier, more like celebrating their success, and Joe was in the kind of a bad mood that requires a bad-mood drunk. So they sat in a booth and socked it away for a while and did very little talking.

It was about two-thirty when they first went in there. About an hour later, which was five or six rounds later, Tom roused himself and looked around and said, "Hey."

Joe turned his head and stared at him. He was already feeling pretty bleary. He said, "What?"

"We're making a mistake," Tom told him. "We're making one of the basic mistakes of the whole world."

Joe frowned, not following the meaning. He closed one eye and said, "Which mistake is that?"

"That's the mistake," Tom said carefully, "where a fella pulls a job and then goes right out and gets drunk, and while he's drunk he talks about it. Happens all the time."

"Not to us," Joe said. He was a little indignant.

"Happens all the time," Tom insisted. "You know that yourself. You've picked them up your own self, I know you have. And so have I. My own self, I've picked them up."

"We're smarter than that," Joe said. He drained his glass.

"Well, look at us," Tom said. "What are we doing, if we're smarter than that?"

Joe looked around. There were only the four of them in the bar; railroad man, bartender, Tom, Joe. "Who am I gonna talk to?"

"The night's young," Tom told him. Looking out at the daylight past the front windows, he said, "In fact, the day's still young."

"I'm not gonna talk," Joe said. He sounded a bit belligerent.

"You said that pretty loud," Tom told him. "Also, you're in uniform."

Joe looked down at himself. He wasn't wearing the hat or the badge or the gunbelt, all of which were locked up in the trunk of Tom's Chevvy, but his shirt and pants were

195

identifiably those of a police officer. "Son of a bitch," he said.

"I've got a better idea," Tom said.

Joe looked at him, interested. "I could use one," he said.

"We'll go home."

"Shit, no!"

"No, wait, listen to me. We'll go home, and we'll go down into my bar. I got my own bar, remember?"

Joe frowned, thinking about it. "You mean the basement?"

"It's *in* the basement," Tom said, with dignity, "but it's the bar. It isn't the basement."

Joe studied that one. "It's in the basement," he said thoughtfully.

"That may be true," Tom said. "But it's the bar."

"If you say so."

"It isn't the basement."

Joe nodded, judiciously. "I get the idea," he said.

"So that's where we'll go," Tom said.

"To the bar," Joe said. "*In* the basement."

"In the basement."

"And drink there."

"And drink there," Tom agreed.

"That's not a terrible idea," Joe said.

So that's what they did.

· 14 ·

THEIR HANGOVERS were beyond belief, and they both had morning duty the next day. They rode in together in Joe's car, both of them stunned by last night's drinking, and by too little sleep, and by this morning's heat; it was going to be a hell of a day, they could see that already.

They had the radio on in the car, and it was full of yesterday's robbery. The first they heard of it was when the news announcer said, "Two men, disguised as police officers and apparently driving a New York City Police Depart-

197

ment car, made off yesterday with nearly twelve million dollars in negotiable securities in what police term one of the largest robberies in Wall Street history."

Tom said, "Twelve million? That's good."

"It's bullshit," Joe said. "They're padding it for the insurance company, just like anybody else."

"You think so?"

"I guarantee it."

Grinning, Tom said, "I'll tell you what we'll do. Ten million or twelve million, we'll still let Vigano have it for the two million we said to begin with."

Joe laughed, then winced and took one hand off the steering wheel to clutch his forehead. Still holding it, but still laughing, he said, "We're a couple of sports, we are."

"Quiet a second," Tom said, and patted the air.

On the radio, they were still talking about the robbery. The announcer had been replaced by somebody interviewing a Deputy Police Commissioner. The interviewer was saying, "Is there any chance at all that these actually were police officers?"

The Commissioner had a deep voice, and a slow dignified manner of speech, like a fat man walking. He said, "We don't at this time believe so. We do not believe that this was a crime such as police officers would have committed. The police force is not perfect, but armed robbery is not in the pattern of police crime."

The interviewer asked, "Is it possible they really did use a Police Department squad car to make their getaway?"

The Commissioner said, "You mean stolen?"

"Well—" said the interviewer. "Stolen, or borrowed."

The Commissioner said, "That possibility is being investigated. The investigation is not yet complete, but so far we have no evidence of any stolen police vehicle."

"Or borrowed," said the interviewer.

198

The Commissioner, sounding a little irritated, said, "Or borrowed, yes."

"But that possibility is being investigated?"

Heavily, sounding like a man having trouble holding onto his temper, the Commissioner said, "All possibilities are being investigated."

Joe said, "That wise-ass reporter could lay off on the borrowed for a while."

"We're safe on that," Tom said. "You know we are. We worked it out, and there's no way anybody can figure out what car was used."

Joe said, "We're safe on *that?* What do you mean, we're safe on that? Where aren't we safe?"

"We're safe all over," Tom said. "You were talking about the car, that's all. I'm saying they can't get to us through the car, there's no way."

"I already knew that," Joe said. Squinting out at the traffic, he said, "I should have worn sunglasses."

They both had sunglasses on. Tom looked over at Joe and said, "You are wearing sunglasses."

"What?" Joe touched his face and felt the glasses. "Jesus Christ, it must be bright out there." He lowered the glasses slightly, looked at the glare, and shoved them back into place. "I should have worn two pair," he said.

"Wait," Tom said. "They're still talking about it."

A different interviewer was on now, asking questions of the Inspector from the downtown precinct who was in charge of the investigation. The interviewer was asking him, "Do you have any leads or suspects so far?"

That's the question they always ask, and it's the one question that can never be answered while an investigation is still going on. But they always ask it, and the spokesman has to deal with it somehow. What the Inspector said was, "So far, the best we can say is, it looks like an inside job.

They knew exactly what to take, negotiable instruments as good as money."

The interviewer said, "All bearer bonds, is that it?"

"That's right," the Inspector said. "They were very explicit with the girl they sent into the vault to get the stuff for them. They wanted all bearer bonds, no bond worth less than twenty thousand or more than a hundred thousand."

"And that's what they got," said the interviewer.

"Exactly," said the Inspector. "To the tune of almost twelve million dollars."

"And the fact that the robbers wore police uniforms?"

"Definitely a disguise," the Inspector said.

The interviewer said, "Then you're confident the robbers have no connection with the Police Department."

"Absolutely," said the Inspector.

"And that's more bullshit," Joe said. "We'll be lucky they don't run the whole force through the line-up, give East-poole a look at us all."

"I'd rather not," Tom said.

"If they do," Joe said, "I hope it's this morning. I don't even recognize myself right now."

"We drank too much last night," Tom said. "We shouldn't do that."

"Not when we got to work."

"Not anyway," Tom said. "That's the way you get fat."

Joe gave him a look, then faced the highway again. "Talk about yourself, pal," he said.

Tom didn't have the strength to be insulted. "Anyway," he said, "a year from now, we won't have to go to work at all any more. Not ever."

"I want to talk to you about that," Joe said.

"About what?"

"About how long we stick around."

Tom roused himself toward anger. "Are you going to start that again?"

Joe, being low and intense even though it made his head hurt more, said, "A year is too long, that's all, too much shit happens. You do what you want, I'm giving it six months."

"We agreed—"

"Sue me," Joe said, and glowered at the traffic.

Tom stared at him, and for a few seconds he was boiling mad. But then the rage suddenly drained out of him, like water out of a sink, and all he felt was tired again. Looking away, he shrugged and said, "Do what you want, I don't care."

They were both silent for a couple minutes. Then Joe said, "Besides, we've still got Vigano to think about."

Tom kept looking out the side window. He wasn't mad about the six months any more; in fact he agreed with it, though he'd never admit that. But the Vigano thing was something else. "Yeah, that's right," he said.

"We'll want to give him a call," Joe said. "You call him, right? You know him."

"Yeah, sure," Tom said. "I'm the one he's got the arrangement with, how I'm supposed to call and everything."

"When will you do it? This afternoon?"

"No, not today," Tom said. "It's not a good idea to do it today."

"Why not?"

"Well, in the first place, I've got too much of a headache to think straight. In the second place, we ought to let a couple days go by, maybe a week. Let things quiet down a little after the robbery before we do anything else."

Joe shrugged. "I don't get the point," he said.

"Listen," Tom said, "what's the hurry?" He was getting annoyed again, and that was making the headache worse, and that was making him more annoyed. "We're going to be here six months no matter when I call Vigano."

"Okay," Joe said. "Do it any way you want."

201

"So there's no reason to rush. He'll keep."

"Fine with me," Joe said.

"Just let me do it at my own pace."

"That's what I'll do," Joe said. "Forget I brought it up."

"All right," Tom said. He was breathing hard. "All right," he said.

· Vigano ·

VIGANO SLOWLY turned the pages of the book. He was sitting at a wooden table in the library of his own home, turning the pages, looking at the faces on each page. Marty was also at the table, looking through a second book. The other books were being studied over at a second table by everyone who'd had a look at the guy who'd come here a month ago to ask what he should steal that Vigano would pay two million dollars for.

The messenger who'd brought the books down from New

York was waiting in a car in the driveway. It had cost a lot of money to get the loan of these books for the night, and the messenger had to get them back no later than six tomorrow morning. The books contained the official photo of every policeman currently on active duty with the New York Police Department.

During the day, these same books were being looked at by the employees and guards of the stock brokerage that had been robbed. So far, according to Vigano's information, they hadn't come up with anything.

Neither had Vigano. The faces all began to blend together after a while, all those eyebrows, hairlines, noses. Vigano was tired and irritable, his eyes were burning, and what he really wanted to do was kick these goddam books across the room.

If only Marty hadn't lost the son of a bitch the night he was here. Afterwards, it was easy to see the thing had been a set-up, the cop at the head of the stairs in Penn Station had to have been the first guy's partner, but at the time there hadn't been any way for Marty to guess that. He hadn't been present for the conversation, he hadn't known there was a possibility the guy he was following was a cop, nor that he'd spoken about having a partner. Later on, when they'd compared notes back here at the house, it had been easy to see what had been done.

It had been simple and clever, like the robbery. Whether the two of them were really cops or not, they were fast and shrewd, and they shouldn't be underestimated.

Whether they were cops or not. That was the worst of looking through these lousy books, there was still a good chance the guy wasn't really a cop at all. At what point was he disguised as a cop and at what point was he a real cop? He and his partner had been disguised in police uniforms when they'd pulled off the robbery; had his claiming to be a

204

police officer while he was here in this house been simply the same disguise?

All the faces in the books looked alike. Vigano knew he wasn't going to get anywhere, but he believed in being thorough. He would look through all the books, every one. And so would Marty, and so would the others. It wouldn't do any good, but they'd do it.

One way and another, Vigano was determined to find those two. Cops or no cops.

· Tom ·

SOMETIMES ON the night shift Ed and I go out and do a turn around the precinct in our Ford, rather than sit in the Detective Division squadroom and wait for the calls to come in. The night shift is when you get most of your street crime, and it sometimes helps to be out there and in movement; often, when a squeal comes in, we're already in the neighborhood, and can get to it faster with instructions from the dispatcher than if we'd actually taken the phone call from the complainant ourselves.

206

So that's what Ed and I were doing that night, around one in the morning. This was nearly a week after the robbery. Joe and I hadn't talked about the robbery at all since the morning after in the car, and I hadn't yet made my phone call to Vigano. I hadn't worked out in my own head any reasons for not calling Vigano, I just hadn't seemed to get around to it.

The robbery itself had stayed hot news for three or four days. It was linked up with some department-store holdups in Detroit from a couple of years ago that had also involved guys wearing police uniforms, but that seemed to be about the only lead the authorities had. An interdepartmental memo had come through, asking everybody to think back to the day of the robbery and try to remember anything unusual they might have noticed in connection with any patrol car on that day, or with any other member of the force. That was about the extent of the investigation within the Police Department, but even that was too much for the PBA. The Patrolmen's Benevolent Association, which I must admit is very rarely benevolent about much of anything, raised such a stink about that memo, and the implication it contained that police officers might actually have been involved in the crime, that the Commissioner himself called a press conference to apologize and say the memo had been "ill-judged." And that had been about the last newsworthy item in connection with the robbery; for the last day or two, there'd been nothing about it on television at all.

It was beginning to look as though we hadn't made any mistakes in planning the job or pulling it off. Now all we had to do was not make any of the normal post-crime mistakes, such as getting drunk in public and talking about what a sharp operator you are, or hiding the loot some place where it could be found by the wrong person, or spending the money right away in a big spree, or quitting

207

our jobs and taking off to live a completely different life. We knew all the mistakes, we'd seen them all from the other side. So far, we seemed to have done all right for ourselves.

Before the robbery, I'd thought it would be very tough to come back to work after it, that I'd have a hard time going through the regular grind knowing I had a million dollars salted away. But the fact was, I seemed to enjoy the job more than I had in years. The robbery had been like a vacation. It was true I didn't actually have Vigano's million dollars yet, but I took it for granted I was going to get it, and I didn't care. Except for that morning with the hangover, I'd been actually happy to go to work every day I'd had duty since the robbery.

Partly I suppose it was the vacation idea; committing the robbery had been such a total break in the routine that it gave the routine a kind of fresh lease on life. But also, for the first time in my life I could look forward to an end of the routine. I mean, an end other than death or retirement, neither of which prospect had ever cheered me very much. But now the routine was going to end at a time when I'd still be young enough to enjoy it. And rich enough to enjoy it, too; a hell of a lot richer than I'd ever thought I was going to be.

Who wouldn't be happy working six months for a salary of one million dollars?

Then there was another thing. Weather affects crime, believe it or not. If it's too hot or too cold, too rainy or too snowy, a lot of crimes just don't get committed; the people who would have committed them stay at home and watch television. This last week had been very hot, and my tours had been quiet and peaceable. I'd caught up with a lot of my back paperwork, I'd relaxed, I'd taken it easy. Even if I weren't being paid a million dollars for it, I wouldn't have minded very much working this last week.

Which changed, all of a sudden. And it was a very small thing that made it change, small and stupid. I never really entirely understood why it made such a big difference inside my head.

It was the night Ed and I were on the night shift, and out driving around in the Ford. Things had been quiet for about an hour until a little after one o'clock a call came in that somebody had been attacked over in Central Park. We were pretty close to the park at the time, so Ed, who was driving, said, "Shall we head on over there?"

The squeal hadn't been directed to us, though we'd heard it on the radio. "Sure," I said. "Let's see what's going on."

"Fine," he said.

There was no urgency, since we weren't the primary team responding to the squeal, so we drove over without siren or red light, and stopped near the park entrance at West 87th Street. We got out of the car, unlimbered the pistols in our hip holsters, left the guns holstered, and walked into the park.

We could see the group ahead of us, down the black-top path and under one of the old-fashioned street lights they have in there. One guy was sitting on the black-top, and three others were standing around him. One of the standing men was in uniform, all the others were in civvies.

When we got a little closer, I could make out the faces. I didn't know the patrolman, but the other two standing men were detectives from my precinct; one was named Bert and the other Walter. They were talking to the guy sitting on the ground.

I recognized him, too. Not individually; I mean I recognized his type. He was a homosexual, young and slender and delicate, wearing tight pale-blue chinos and white sandals and a white fishnet shirt. He was pretty obviously what's called a cruiser, a faggot who hangs around one of

209

the gay areas of the city looking to get picked up. They very frequently get beat up, too, and sometimes they get killed. They also have a higher incidence of VD than any other group in the city. I won't say it's a kind of life I understand.

At the moment, this one was scared out of his mind, terrified, trembling all over. He was so fragile-looking, he looked as though he might break his own bones with all that shivering he was doing.

When we got close enough to hear voices, it was the boy on the ground who was talking. He could hardly speak; his voice was trembling and his throat apparently kept closing up on him. All the time he struggled to talk, his hands kept fluttering around. I hate to say they fluttered like butter-flies, but that's what they reminded me of.

He was saying, "I don't know why he'd do it. There wasn't any reason, there was just— There wasn't any rea-son. Everything was fine, and then—" He stopped talking, and let the fluttering of his hands finish the story.

Walter, one of the plainclothesmen, preferred words to hands. Not sounding at all sympathetic, he said, "Yeah? Then what?"

The hands fluttered to his throat. "He started to choke me." The street-light glare was in his face as he looked up at us, bleaching out whatever color was left in it, reducing his face to little more than a twisting mouth and staring eyes. With that face, and the gracefully twitching hands, he suddenly also reminded me of pantomimists I've seen on television. You've seen them; they cover their faces with white make-up, and wear dark clothing and white gloves, and they pretend to be in love, or to be an airplane, or to be mixing a martini. This one seemed to be doing a panto-mime impression of terror.

Except that he was talking. Hands still at his throat, he said again, "He choked me. He was screaming awful

210

things, terrible, and just choking me." His hands trembled at his throat.

Walter, still not sympathetic, said, "What was he saying?"

The expressive hands came down, flattening out. "Oh, please," he said. "Oh, just terrible things. I don't even want to remember them."

Walter's partner Bert was grinning a little as he watched and listened, and now he said, "What did you say you were doing just before the attack?"

Evasiveness cut through the young man's agitation. Suddenly nervous as much for his present situation as for what had happened to him in the past, he gestured vaguely with both hands, looked away from us all, blinked, and said, "Well—" He stopped, ducked his head, twisted his shoulders around. "We were just talking, just—" He looked up at us again, looking like the heroine of a silent movie melodrama, and said, "Everything was fine, there wasn't any reason at all."

"Talking," Bert said. He jerked his head to the right and said, "Over there in the bushes at two in the morning."

He clasped his hands together. "But there wasn't any reason to *choke* me," he said.

I wondered why he kept reminding me of silent things—pantomimists and silent movies—when he was steadily talking. Of course, as much as anybody was really listening to him, he might as well have been silent. He'd thought he'd found a friend, and he'd been betrayed, and that was most of the pain he was showing us. But we'd all seen it before, and we had other ways to describe it. All Walter and Bert were hearing—and all I'd be hearing, if I was the one who'd have to fill out the report on this—were the facts. Like that old police show on television used to say, all we want are the facts, ma'am.

211

Walter was saying now, "Can you give us any identification on him?"

"Well . . ." He thought about it, sitting there in the middle of us, and said, "He, uh, he had a tattoo." He said it as though he were proud of having remembered, and expected a gold star.

Ed said, "A tattoo?" The incredulity in his voice was almost comic.

I looked at Ed beside me, and saw he was grinning. Looking down at that poor jerk and grinning. I thought, Ed's a nice guy, he's really a very nice guy, decent and straight. What the hell was he doing grinning down at some poor bastard who's been betrayed and choked and humiliated by some other son of a bitch?

And me, too. I was in the ring around the guy, one of the five cops standing around him, brought out to do our duty to protect him from bodily harm.

I took a step backward, as though to get out of the circle. I really didn't understand it myself, it was just a feeling I had, that I didn't want to be a part of this any more.

The guy on the ground was explaining about the tattoo. "On his forearm," he said. "His, uh, his left forearm." He pointed to his own left forearm. "It was in the shape of a torpedo," he said.

Walter laughed, and the guy pouted at him. He was getting over his fear now, and his normal mincing mannerisms were returning to him.

That wasn't the way God had made him. And none of us were the way God had made us, either.

I remembered again that hippie talking about what the city does to people, and that none of us had started this way.

Bert was saying, "What about a name? He give you any kind of name before you went off in the bushes with him?"

He raised his eyes again, and clasped his hands in his

lap. Christ, he looked like Lillian Gish. Wistfully, remembering having liked the bastard, he told us, "He said his name was Jim."

I took another step backward and looked up at the sky. It was one of those rare nights in New York when you can see a few stars.

· Joe ·

I'D BEEN in a bad mood ever since we pulled it off. Tom
didn't feel that way, he was going around happy and chip-
per and easy in his mind, but as for me, most of the time
I felt like punching somebody in the head.

It would have been a different thing if we had the money
in our hands. Even if we had the bonds, something we
could sell, something we could touch and hold and know
that this was the result of our labors. But what did we
have? A blue plastic laundry bag full of air.

I'm not arguing. I know the case for doing it that way, and we did it that way, and I agree with it. As Tom said, the Mafia is not going to give away two million dollars if it doesn't absolutely have to, so we can take it for granted when the time comes to make the switch they'll try to double-cross us. And, since they already know this is a one-shot operation, we're never going to be useful to them again, they'd be smart not only to cheat us but also to kill us.

Why not? We're the only connection between the bond robbery and the mob, the only ones that know the whole story. Kill us, and they not only save two million dollars, they protect themselves from getting implicated just in case we should ever get picked up by the law later on.

So they'll try to double-cross us, and they'll try to kill us. We knew that before we went ahead and did the job. Because the next step is, we're the ones who decide the method of transfer. And to bring us to the transfer point, they have to produce the cash, the two million for us to look at and touch. We can make it a part of the arrangement, that we see the cash before we give them the bonds.

They'd expect that. They'd expect us to be careful with them, because they'd expect us to be afraid of them.

What they *wouldn't* expect is a double cross right back.

As Tom said, money isn't just green pieces of paper in your wallet, it's credit cards and charge accounts and all kinds of things. It's bonds. It's anything you *think* is money.

You know what we stole from Parker, Tobin, Eastpoole & Company? The *idea* of ten million dollars. And that's what we figured to sell Vigano. His newspaper and television set would tell him we did the job. He'd have no reason to think we didn't have the bonds any more. So when the time for the switch came around, they'd have to have real cash, and all we'd have to have was a good plan and a lot of luck.

215

But the point is, we'd be needing that anyway. Double-crossing them on the bonds wouldn't make any difference, they were going to try to cheat us and kill us whether we showed up with ten million dollars' worth of bonds or two dollars' worth of ripped-up newspapers. It made no difference whether we conned them or not. And in pulling the robbery, it had been easier not to carry the bonds away with us, to destroy them. So that's what we did.

You see, I understand the argument and I agree with it. But that still didn't change the fact I would have liked something in my hand afterward to show me I'd accomplished something. And not having anything meant I was spending my time in a really lousy mood.

For instance. When I was on duty now, I was becoming a real hard-ass with the tickets. I was giving them out left and right, citing store owners for dirty sidewalks, hitting delivery trucks for driving down streets where commercial traffic was prohibited, even going after jaywalkers. I'm telling you, I was mean.

Paul was out of the hospital now, so that was good, but he wasn't back on duty yet. He'd have a couple months at home for rest and recuperation, the lucky bastard. In the meantime, I still had Lou to contend with.

He wasn't bad, but his attitude needed work. He was over-eager, that was his problem. For instance, Paul would have known how to calm me down when I was out there ticketing the entire population of the Upper West Side, but so far as Lou was concerned I was tough but good. It got so he was becoming pretty nearly as mean as I was, though nobody is ever going to top the time I ticketed the pregnant woman for obstructing the sidewalk with her baby carriage. That's one of those records where you retire the trophy.

As an example, though, of where Lou's attitude went overboard, there was the night about a week and a half

216

after the robbery when we really did lose our car for repairs. Which I already considered ironic.

What happened, late at night we caught sight of these two guys coming out of a jewelry store on Broadway. We yelled at them to stop, and they jumped into a four-door Buick parked in front of the shop and took off southbound. I was driving, and I could keep on their tail but I couldn't catch up with them, not with the piece of crap I was driving. I'd been putting in requests for a new car for eight months, and never even got a response.

Meanwhile, Lou was on the radio. But shit, that time of night, everybody's either already got problems of their own or they're off some place cooping. You know, having a doze.

The Buick headed straight down Broadway, with me a full block back. I had the siren and flasher going, mostly to make other traffic stop up ahead and keep the clown in the Buick from killing somebody while running a red light. Of course, at that time of night, nearly four in the morning, there's practically never any traffic anyway.

He was a good driver, I'll say that much for him. His brake lights didn't go on until less than half a block before he made his right turn onto a cross-street in the Fifties. His inside wheels left the ground as he shot around the corner, but he made it without losing control, and by the time I came screeching around the intersection after him he'd leveled himself out and was tear-assing away, the other side of Eighth Avenue already, heading due west along a narrow side street with cars parked along both curbs and just barely room for two cars next to one another in the middle.

"Jesus!" Lou yelled. "We're losing him!"

Boy, are you hot to trot, I thought, but I was too busy driving to say anything out loud.

The light was with us both on Ninth Avenue, though it

217

wouldn't have made any difference. We both shot through, him not getting away but me not gaining any ground. What we needed was another car in front of us, to head him off before somebody got hurt.

The block between Ninth and Tenth is mostly red-brick tenement buildings, half of them with shops in the ground floor, but the block between Tenth and Eleventh is warehouses, and there's trucks parked along both sides instead of passenger vehicles. The same thing is true between Eleventh and Twelfth, and after that you can't go any farther west without a boat. That's the Hudson River out there, and you have to turn either north or south.

He wasn't quite as sure as I was on this narrow street, with the parked cars crowding in on both sides, and that was doubly true after we crossed Tenth and he was traveling down between two walls of trucks. The trucks take up more room than cars do, leaving less space down the middle for driving, and I could tell the guy in the Buick didn't care for that. Given another two or three miles of the same kind of street and I probably could have caught up with him. But what actually happened was, he almost creamed a cab on Eleventh Avenue.

The light was red down there. Big-sided trucks were parked along both curbs right down to the corner, restricting everybody's vision, making a kind of tunnel out of the street. The trucks and the warehouses also probably contained my siren too much, so that it couldn't be heard by somebody out on Eleventh Avenue.

And there was somebody out there; a cab, going north, traveling empty. He was probably on his way to check in at one of the garages farther uptown on the West Side, having been out for eight or ten hours hacking around the city. In other words, tired. And alone in the area, so far as he knew. And with the light in his favor.

Well, he entered the intersection just as the Buick did.

218

And he was damn lucky God had given him fast reflexes, because he just about stood on his brake with both feet and threw an anchor out back besides. The Buick swerved to its right, just nicked the front bumper of the cab on the way by, swerved to the left again, and kept going toward Twelfth Avenue.

And here was I, half a block away. The cabby had to figure the first guy through was a nut, but with me he could see the flashing red light even if he had all his windows closed and maybe air-conditioning on and couldn't hear the siren. So he had to know I was a cop. And twice in a row he did exactly the right thing.

Because he hadn't managed to completely stop before the Buick went by. In fact, the nose of the cab was still down like a pig looking for truffles, and the vehicle was still in motion. Which put it right directly in front of me.

"Stop!" yelled Lou. As though I could have stopped by then, any more than the cab could. It takes a long distance to stop, hundreds and hundreds of feet—the only time you can stop on a dime is when you're walking.

Besides, the cabby was doing his second right thing in a row. The instant the Buick was past him, he hauled in that anchor, switched both feet away from the brake and over to the accelerator, tromped down hard, and yanked that yellow mother out of the intersection.

I had to swerve left to miss his ass, just as the Buick had had to swerve right to miss his nose. But I did miss, and I never took my foot off the accelerator, and I entered the next block in fine shape.

In a lot better shape than the Buick. The near miss with the cab had loused him up for good. He shot into that next block angled wrong, coming in from the right because of having gone around the cab, and didn't get straightened out in time. He sideswiped a truck on his left, scraping along the body, and then careened off that and headed down the block at an angle to the right, and damn if he didn't hit another truck over on that side. He was like a drunk running down a hallway, bouncing from one wall to the other.

All the sideswiping, and all the struggling to get his car under control, were slowing him down. He did it a third time, over on the left again, and this time his front bumper or fender or something must have got hooked for a second on a truck cab, because all at once the Buick swerved around and jolted to a stop crossways in the street, the front bumper inches from the side of one truck and rear bumper inches from a truck across the way. The driver's side was toward us, and I could see his white face in there in my headlights.

I stood on the brakes myself the second I saw what the Buick was doing, and the squad car dug its nose in and screamed, me fighting a skid to the left every inch of the way.

The passenger door of the Buick, the one on the far side, had popped open the second the Buick came to a stop, and somebody jumped out and laid what looked like a black stick across the roof of the car, pointing at us. That is, it looked like a black stick until the end of it blew up in red and yellow, and the windshield got peppered with a dozen sudden new holes.

Lou yelled, "What the fuck is *that?*"

"Shotgun!" I was still fighting that leftward skid, the squad car was still in motion, I was still praying for it to quit so I could get my head down out of the way of that shotgun. And finally we did shudder to a stop, no more than twenty feet from the Buick.

I hit the switch that turned off the siren, and shoved my door open. The driver's face was no longer showing in the window of the Buick, and the black stick was no longer pointing at us over the top of the car. I leaned my head out to the side, and heard them running into the darkness in the opposite direction.

As I was getting out of the car, I saw Lou jumping out on his side and making a dash for the Buick. "Hey!" I yelled. "Where the hell are *you* going?"

He looked back and saw me standing behind the open door, which would give me some protection if they opened up with that goddam shotgun again. He stopped running forward and crouched there, pistol pointing straight ahead but head still turned around facing me. Looking baffled, he said, "After them. Don't we—?"

I said, "In that darkness? With a shotgun? They'll blow your ass off."

He straightened out of his crouch, all momentum gone, but he still didn't come back. "But we'll lose them," he said.

"We lost them," I told him. I would never have had to explain that to Paul. "Get back here," I said, "and call in."

The footsteps had faded away. Those two were gone for good, and just as well. I came out from behind the door and walked around to look at the front of the car. Very little of the shotgun blast had reached the windshield, so where had the rest of it gone?

Into the radiator, as I'd thought. Red cooling fluid was oozing out of a thousand holes. The headlights had also been smashed. A little higher, I thought, and my face would look like that.

It was in that instant that I knew Tom had to stop fucking around on this Vigano deal. He had to call him, we had to make the arrangements and get the money, and we had to do it and get it over with. I was still willing to hang around the six months before I'd pack up my family and go off to Saskatchewan, but God damn it, I wanted to *see* what I'd accomplished. I wanted that money in my hand, where I could touch it.

221

Lou was walking by me, heading for his side of the car. I told him, "They shot the shit out of our radiator. When you call in, tell them we need wheels."

"Okay," he said.

I stood there looking at the radiator, thinking about what I was going to say to Tom.

And another thing. After this, they'd *have* to give us a new car.

• 15 •

IT WAS A hot day. It would be really muggy and bad in the city, but fortunately they both had the day off and they could sit around on lawn chairs in Tom's backyard, near the barbecue, and drink beer and work on their tans and watch the ballgame on the Sony portable Mary had given Tom for last Christmas.

Tom hadn't been thinking about anything, except how hot it was and how glad he was he wasn't working and how maybe he'd cut out the beer and start losing weight when the hot weather broke, but Joe had been thinking for the last few days, ever since the shotgun incident, how to approach Tom on this Vigano question, and he was beginning to think the only way to do it was straight out, no beating around the bush, dead ahead.

It was a very dull game. Cincinnati had got six runs in the first inning, and nobody had done a damn thing since. In the bottom of the fourth, with a deliberate walk coming up, Joe said, "Tom, listen."

Tom gave him a half-awake look. "What?"

"When do we call your Mafia man?"

Tom looked back at the deliberate walk. "Pretty soon," he said.

"It's been two weeks," Joe told him. "We've already passed pretty soon, we're catching up on later, and I see never dead ahead."

Tom frowned, staring at the television set, and didn't say anything.

Joe said, "What's the story, Tom?"

Tom made a face, shook his head, frowned, shrugged, gestured with his beer can; did everything but talk, or meet Joe's eye.

Joe said, "Come on. We're in this together, remember? What's the problem, what's the delay?"

Tom turned his head and frowned at the barbecue grill. He looked as though he had a toothache. He said in a low voice Joe could barely hear, "Day before yesterday I went into a phone booth."

"Fantastic," Joe said. "Three days from now you drop the dime?"

Tom grinned, despite himself. He looked at Joe, and he surprised himself by being relieved that he was getting this off his chest. He said, "Yeah, I guess so."

Joe said, "So what's the matter?"

"I don't know, it's like—" Tom clenched his teeth, trying

224

to find the way to put it into words. He said, "It's like we already got away with it, you know? Like we shouldn't push our luck."

"Got away with what? So far all we got is air."

Tom shook his head violently back and forth. He was angry at himself, and he let it show. "The goddam truth is," he said, "I'm afraid of that son of a bitch Vigano."

Joe said, "Tom, I was afraid of the robbery. I was scared shitless when we went in there to do that thing, but we did it. It worked, just like we thought it would."

"Vigano's tougher."

Joe lifted an eyebrow. "Than us?"

"Than a stock brokerage. Joe, we're talking about beating them out of two million dollars. You think it's going to be easy with those people?"

"No, I don't," Joe said. "But the other part wasn't easy either. I say we can do it."

"I don't have a way," Tom said. "It's as simple as that. It's easy to say we'll work out a system where they have to bring the money and show it to us and all that stuff, but when it comes right down to it, where the hell's the system?"

"There is one," Joe said. "There has to be. Look; did we steal ten million dollars? We aren't stupid. If we can figure that we can figure this."

"How?"

Joe frowned, trying to think. He looked at the television set and the inning was over, and some actor made up to look like a cowboy was peddling razor blades. Joe shrugged and said, "Disguised as cops."

"We already did that."

Joe grinned at him. "We can't do it again? Treat it the same way, use the equipment and everything just like last time."

"Like how? Doing what?"

225

Joe nodded, feeling very pleased with himself. "We'll think of it," he said. "I know we will. If we just keep talking about it, we'll work it out."

And a little later that afternoon, they did.

· 16 ·

THEY'D GOTTEN off duty together at four in the afternoon. Joe had his Plymouth today, and they drove across town, through the park at 86th Street, and over into Yorkville where they stopped at a corner with a pay phone. Tom called the number Vigano had given him, and asked for Arthur, and said his name was Mr. Kopp. A gravelly voice said Arthur wasn't in, but was expected, and could he call Mr. Kopp back? Tom read off the number of the pay phone, and the gravelly voice hung up.

227

Then twenty minutes went by. It had been a hot day, and it was gradually becoming a hot evening. They both wanted to go home and take their clothes off and stand in the shower for a while. Tom leaned against the side of the phone booth and Joe sat on the fender of the Plymouth, and they waited, and twenty minutes went by with the speed of grass growing.

Finally Tom looked at his watch for the fifteenth time and said, "It's been twenty minutes."

Reluctantly Joe said, "Maybe we should—"

"No," Tom said. "He told me if he didn't call back in fifteen minutes, we should try again later. We've waited twenty minutes, and that's enough." Joe was still reluctant, because he didn't want to have to nerve Tom up to this all over again, but he gave in without any more argument, saying, "Okay, you're right. Let's go."

Even though they now had a plan, Tom hadn't been all that eager to talk to Vigano again. "Fine," he said, and started toward the passenger side of the Plymouth, and the phone rang.

They looked at each other. They both tensed up right away, which Tom had expected but which surprised Joe. He'd had the idea he was under better control than that. "Go on," he said.

Tom had just been standing there. "Right," he said, and turned back, and went into the phone booth. The phone was just starting to ring for the second time when he lifted the receiver and said, "Hello?"

"Is that Mr. Kopp?" Tom recognized Vigano's voice.

"Sure. Is that Mister—"

Overriding him, Vigano said, "This is Arthur."

"Right," Tom said. "Arthur, right."

"I expected to hear from you a couple weeks ago."

Tom could feel Joe's eyes on him through the glass walls

228

of the booth. With a sheepish grin, he said, "Well, we had to get things set up."

Vigano said, "You want me to tell you where to bring the stuff?"

"Not a chance," Tom said. "We'll tell *you* where."

"Doesn't matter to me," Vigano said. "Give me your setup."

Tom took a deep breath. This was another of those moments of no return. He said, "Macy's has a wicker picnic basket. It costs around eighteen bucks, with the tax. It's the only one they've got at that price."

"Okay."

"Next Tuesday afternoon," Tom said, "at three o'clock, no more than four people, two of them female, can carry one of those baskets into Central Park from the west at the Eighty-fifth Street entrance to the park roadway. They should turn right, go down near the traffic light, and sit down on the grass there. No later than four o'clock, either I or my partner will show up to make the exchange. We'll be in uniform."

Vigano said, "With another basket?"

"Right."

"Isn't that kind of public?"

Tom grinned at the phone. "That's what we want," he said.

"It's up to you," Vigano said.

"The stuff in your basket," Tom said, "should not have traceable numbers and should not be homemade."

Vigano laughed. "You think we'd palm off counterfeit on you?"

"No, but you might try."

Serious again, almost sounding as though he'd been insulted, Vigano said, "We'll examine each other's property before we make the switch."

"Fine," Tom said.

"You're a pleasure to do business with," Vigano said.

Tom nodded at the phone. "I hope you are, too," he said, but Vigano had already hung up.

• Vigano •

VIGANO SLEPT for most of the trip. He was lucky that way, he could sleep on planes, and for that reason he tried to do as much of his traveling as possible late at night. Otherwise, too much time was wasted going from place to place.

He was riding in a Lear jet, a private company plane owned and operated by a corporation called K-L Inc. K-L's function was to own and care for and run the fleet of six planes that were available around the country to Vigano

231

and some of his associates. The company also leased hangar space in Miami and Las Vegas and two other places, and in addition owned some real estate in the Caribbean. It had been financed by a private stock offering a few years ago, most of which had been bought by various union pension funds. Its assets were the planes and the island real estate, but its expenses were very high and it had never shown a profit, and so had never paid taxes or dividends.

The interior of the plane was comfortable, but not lush, in a kind of motel-lobby style. There was seating for eight, large soft chairs similar to first-class accommodations on a scheduled airliner, except that the front pairs of seats faced backwards and there was an unusual amount of leg room. Aft of the seats was a partition, followed by a dining area; a long oval table that would also seat eight, around three sides, leaving one of the long sides open for passage. A lavatory and galley came next, and farthest back was a bedroom containing two single beds. That was where Vigano traveled, sleeping on one of the beds while his two bodyguards sat up front, joking with the hostess, a girl who used to be a dancer until she'd had to have an operation on her hip. She was a beautiful girl, and her former bosses had done right by her.

The hostess came back finally and knocked on the bedroom door, calling, "Mr. Vigano?"

He woke up right away. His eyes opened, but he didn't move. He was lying on his right side, and he looked around, shifting only his eyes, until he'd oriented himself. He'd left one small light on, over the door, and it showed him the other bed, the curving plastic wall of the plane, the two oval windows looking out on nothing but blackness.

On the plane. Going to see Bandell about the stock market robbery. Right.

Vigano sat up. "All right," he called.

232

"We'll be landing in five minutes." She said that through the door, not opening it.

Of course they'd be landing in five minutes, otherwise she wouldn't be waking him. "Thank you," he said, and reached for his trousers on the other bed.

He'd stripped to his underwear for the flight, and now he quickly dressed, then opened his attaché case and out of the small separate compartment in it took his toothbrush and toothpaste. Carrying them in one hand and his tie in the other, he left the bedroom for the lavatory.

The hostess was in the galley, doing this and that. She smiled at him and said, "Coffee, Mr. Vigano?"

"Definitely."

He didn't take long in the lavatory, and then he carried his attaché case up front to the regular seats to have his coffee and watch the landing. His bodyguards were sitting facing one another on the right, so he took the forward-facing window seat on the left. The bodyguards were named Andy and Mike, and Vigano never called them bodyguards. He didn't even think the word; they were just the young guys he traveled with. They both carried their own attaché cases, and they were presentable in a tough kind of way, and he simply traveled with them because that's what he did.

Vigano sipped at his coffee and looked out the window at the lights of the city. You could always tell a resort town, it ran much heavier to neon. A place like Cleveland, now, you could hardly see any neon from the air at all.

Andy, grinning, said, "Mr. Vigano, it's a waste of time to come here in the summer. We ought to come for the winter."

Vigano smiled back. "Maybe I'll work something out," he said. He liked these two boys.

It was a smooth landing. They taxied away from the normal passenger terminals and over to the private area.

When they rolled to a stop a black limousine drove out to meet them. Vigano and the two young men he traveled with picked up their attaché cases, thanked the hostess, congratulated the pilot on his landing, and stepped out into incredible heat. "Christ," Andy said. "What's it like in the daytime?"

"Worse," Vigano said. The heat lay on his skin like a wool blanket. It made New Jersey seem cool.

They crossed quickly to the limousine, and slid inside, where the air was a cool, dry seventy degrees. The chauffeur shut the door after them, slid behind the wheel, and drove them smoothly to the hotel. It was nearly four in the morning, and the streets were deserted; even a resort city goes to sleep sooner or later.

They had another blast of heat between the car and side entrance of the hotel. They were also put on film, though it didn't matter, by a team of federal agents concealed in a bakery truck parked on a side road just off the hotel property. It was infra-red film and the faces were blurred, but they already knew who it was they were filming, so there wasn't any problem about identification. This strip of film would eventually join the strip that had been taken earlier tonight outside Vigano's home in New Jersey, and the two strips would establish the fact that on this date Anthony Vigano had gone to a meeting with Joseph Bandell. The fact would never mean anything to anybody, but it would have been established and placed on film and filed away, at a cost to the government of forty-two thousand dollars.

Vigano and his bodyguards rode up in the elevator to the twelfth floor, and walked down the corridor to Bandell's suite, at the end. They went in and Bandell was there with his advisers. "Hello, Tony," he said.

"Hello, Joe."

They spent a few minutes in civilities, taking drink

234

orders and asking after one another's wives and making the couple of introductions necessary; one of Bandell's assistants was a new man freshly in from Los Angeles, named Stello. There were handshakes and general chitchat.

Bandell was stocky and short and gray-haired, a man in his sixties, wearing a dark suit and a conservative tie. The three men with him were in their thirties or forties, tanned, all dressed casually in the style of a resort town. Everybody deferred to Bandell, who sat alone on a sofa with his back to a picture window. Vigano was the only one present who called him Joe instead of Mr. Bandell, but he too deferred to the older man, in smaller ways.

After three or four minutes, Bandell said, "Well, it's nice to see you again. I'm glad you phoned. I'm glad you could take the time to come visit."

He meant the chitchat was done, and he wanted to know the purpose of the trip. Vigano hadn't attempted to explain anything on the phone, had only suggested he make the trip. (The phone conversation was also in a government file now, at a cost of twenty-three hundred dollars.) Now, in guaranteed privacy, Vigano set aside the drink he'd been given and explained the story of the two possible cops and the twelve-million-dollar stock-market heist.

Bandell interrupted once, saying, "It's usable paper?"

"They took exactly what I said, Joe. Bearer bonds, in amounts between twenty and a hundred grand."

Bandell nodded. "All right."

Vigano went on, explaining the payoff terms he'd agreed to. When he was finished, Bandell pursed his lips and looked across the room and said, "I don't know. Two million dollars is heavy cash."

Vigano said, "It'll be back in the bank within two hours." Because that was the point of this meeting; he couldn't draw two million cash on his own say-so, he needed Bandell's approval.

235

Bandell said, "Why take it out at all? Use a bag full of newspapers."

"They aren't that dumb," Vigano told him. "The caper they pulled shows how cute they are."

"Then use a dressed roll," Bandell said. "Take out a hundred thousand or so."

Vigano shook his head. "It won't work, Joe. They're very cute and very cautious. They'll have to see the two million before they relax. They'll reach in and see what's in the bottom of the basket."

Bandell said, "How about wallpaper?"

"They already talked about that," Vigano said. "They're ready for it."

Stello, the new man, said, "If they're that good, how do you know they won't figure out a way to keep the money?"

"We've got the manpower," Vigano said. "We can smother them."

Another of Bandell's assistants said, "Why not leave them alive? If they did this first job so good they can do more."

"We don't have anything on them," Vigano pointed out. "We don't know who they are, we don't have any handle on them, and they don't want to do any more. They were only interested in the one job. They're amateurs, they said so from the beginning and they acted like it."

"Smart amateurs," suggested Stello.

"Granted," Vigano said. "But still amateurs. Which means they could still make a mistake and get picked up by the law, and that leads right directly from them to me."

Bandell said, "Are they cops or aren't they?"

"I don't know," Vigano said. "We tried to find them in the force, we asked around with our tame cops, nobody knows anything. I myself personally looked at mug shots on twenty-six thousand New York City cops, and I didn't

236

come up with them, but that doesn't mean anything because the guy came to me in a wig and moustache and eyeglasses, and who knows what he looks like with his normal face?"

Bandell's other assistant said, "Why didn't you take the disguise off him when you had him?"

"That was before he pulled the job," Vigano pointed out. "If I broke his security ahead of time, he never would have gone through with it."

Bandell said, "What do you think, Tony? You yourself, personally. Are they cops or not cops?"

"I just don't know," Vigano told him. "The guy who came to me said he was on the force. They pulled the job in uniform and used a police car for their getaway. But I'll tell you, I don't know for sure what the hell they are."

Stello said, "If they're cops, maybe it's not such a good idea to have them hit."

"If they're cops especially I want them hit," Vigano said. "One of them visited me in my own home, remember."

Bandell said, "If you do it, you do it quietly."

"Quietly," Vigano agreed. "But to relax them so I can do it, I need to be able to show them cash."

Bandell considered, pursing his lips again and staring at a spot in midair. Then he said, "What's your setup for the changeover?"

Vigano clicked his fingers at Andy, who immediately got to his feet, opened his attaché case, and brought out a map of Manhattan. He opened the map and stood there being a human easel, holding the map so everybody could see it, while Vigano pointed at it to explain the situation.

"I told you they're cute," Vigano said, and went over to stand next to the map. "Their idea is," he said, "that we'll switch picnic baskets in Central Park next Tuesday at three o'clock in the afternoon. Do you know where the snapper is in that?"

237

Bandell didn't want to guess; he was strictly business. "Tell us," he said.

Vigano said, "Every Tuesday afternoon, Central Park in New York is closed to automobiles." Gesturing at the map, he said, "There's nothing allowed in there but bicycles."

Bandell nodded. "How do you counter?"

"We can't use cars, but neither can they." Vigano started touching the map with his finger, explaining it all. "We'll put a car at every exit from the park. All the way around, here and here and here. Inside, we'll have our own men on bicycles, all over the place. They'll be in touch with one another by walkie-talkie, back and forth." He turned away from the map, held his hand out in front of himself, palm up, and slowly closed his fingers into a fist. "We'll have the whole park bottled up," he said.

Stello said, "You'll have a thousand witnesses."

"We can smother them," Vigano said. "When we have them at the spot where we make the switch, we can just surround them with our own people. There won't be anybody to see a thing, and we carry them the hell out of there afterwards, and nobody going by on bicycles is going to know a thing about it."

Bandell was frowning at the map. "You have this clear in your mind, Tony? You're sure of yourself?"

"You know me, Joe," Vigano said. "I'm a careful man. I wouldn't get involved in this if I wasn't sure of myself."

"And it's twelve million. In bearer bonds."

"Just under." Vigano looked around at them all and said, "It's a good big pie to slice up."

Bandell nodded slowly. He said, "You want to take the cash out of our accounts in New York, put it together to make two million, show it to them, and then put the cash right back again."

"Right."

238

"What's the chance of losing the two million to somebody else?"

Vigano gestured at his young men. "Andy and Mike will be with it all the way. And the other soldiers in the operation don't have to know what's in the basket at all."

Bandell shifted position on the sofa, half-turning so he could look out the picture window behind him. The seconds went by, and he continued to show the room only the back of his head. Vigano gestured to Mike, who quietly folded the map again and put it away. Still Bandell looked out at the city.

Finally he turned back. He gave Vigano a level look and said, "It's your responsibility."

Vigano smiled. "Done," he said.

· Tom ·

JOE LET me off at Columbus Avenue and 85th Street, and I walked the one block over to Central Park West. I crossed with the light, and the park was now directly in front of me, the grass separated from the sidewalk by a knee-high stone wall.

There are benches along this part of Central Park West with their backs against that low wall, so that if you sit in one of them you're looking at the apartment buildings across the way. I've never understood why anybody would

240

want to sit on a park bench facing away from the park, but there are always plenty of people sitting on them in the warm weather, so there must be an attraction to it that I don't understand. Maybe they like to count the cabs.

Today, I joined them. I sat on an unoccupied bench and counted cabs, and found nothing exciting in it.

I spent nearly an hour sitting there, with a newspaper in my lap and a moustache on my face, waiting for the mob to show up. It was a humid day and the moustache tickled like crazy, but I was afraid to scratch it for fear it would fall off. Every once in a while when it got to be more than I could stand I'd twitch my upper lip around like a beaver, but I tried to limit that relief to moments of true emergency, since for all I knew that too would make the damn thing break loose, and I didn't want a moustache in my lap when Vigano's people arrived.

The reason I was thinking about the moustache and park benches so much is that I was afraid to think about Vigano and his mobsters, and what we were here to do.

This one was worse than the robbery, a hundred times worse. That other time, we'd been operating against decent civilized human beings, who at the very worst would arrest us and try us and put us in jail. This time, we were operating against thugs who were going to try to kill us no matter what we did. Last time, we were pitting our one-shot plan against a normal company's normal routine. This time, we were pitting our lives against the experience and manpower and malevolence of the mob.

When I did think about it, I simply thought we were crazy. If I'd worked it all out back in the beginning, say when I'd been on the train going to talk to Vigano, if I'd figured it out then that sooner or later we would be making ourselves murder targets for the Mafia, I never would have gone through with it. And Joe the same, I'm sure of it. But all we could concentrate on in the beginning was stealing

241

the bonds, and not what would happen afterwards. And when it did occur to me what Vigano's natural reaction would have to be, I was still so caught up in the other thing that all I thought about was how much easier that would make things for us, since we didn't really have to steal the bonds, just make it look as though we had.

It was the morning after the robbery, while suffering that hangover in Joe's car on the way to work, that I'd first looked the thing full in the face. We had done part one, and we'd done it pretty well. But part two was the crunch. Part two was where death waited for us if we weren't very smart and very careful and very lucky.

But if we didn't do part two, there was no point in our having done part one.

I was in a real funk for a while after that. I couldn't even think about the problem, couldn't concentrate on it. It just seemed more than I could deal with, reaching into the trap and pulling out the two-million-dollar piece of cheese without getting the spring across the back of my neck.

I'd been coming out of it anyway, spurred on by the scene with the homosexual in the park—very near here, in fact—but it was Joe who finally goosed me back into action again. I think Joe probably has less imagination than I do, but that's a good part of his strength. If you can't imagine the things that might go wrong, you won't be afraid of them.

I don't mean that Joe wasn't scared of the mob. Any sane man would be, particularly if he meant to sell them a lot of old newspapers for two million dollars. It's just that Joe was never paralyzed by his fear the way I'd been paralyzed by mine. Joe dealt more with specific things that he could touch and taste. What made me the most nervous was the mob, but what made him the most nervous was that we'd done part one and didn't have anything to show

242

for it. It really pained him when we ripped up those bonds, I know it did.

Well, we'd committed ourselves again. We could still turn around, of course, we could still cop out, but I didn't think we would. We were at the stage now equivalent to when, in the robbery, we'd met Eastpoole but Joe hadn't grabbed his arm yet. We'd set things up with Vigano, we were both in position, but we hadn't yet made contact, we could still change our minds at the last second.

Joe made his first pass twenty minutes after I'd sat down, but I didn't give him the signal because Vigano's people hadn't showed up yet. I watched him drive by, and then I counted cabs some more, and fifteen minutes later he went by again, and still they hadn't showed up.

Weren't they going to? If after all this, after nerving ourselves up to it and working out the best scheme we could think of, the mob didn't show up this time for the transfer, I didn't know what I'd do. I wouldn't be able to stand it, that's all. To have to start all over again, phone Vigano again, set up another meeting, I'd have an ulcer before it was over. Or a nervous breakdown.

But what if they weren't coming at all? What if they'd decided the hell with it, they didn't want to buy the bonds?

Christ, that would be something. Then Joe would really be sore, and at me. Because if we actually had the bonds, and the mob reneged on us, we could maybe go fence them to somebody else. But Vigano was the only person on earth to whom we could sell the *idea* of the bonds. It was him, or nobody.

The arrangement Joe and I had was that he would come by every fifteen minutes until I gave him the signal. Then our second timing sequence would begin, with me making the first move. We hadn't made a contingency plan for what we'd do if the mob never showed up, but I figured if Joe was still circling the neighborhood an hour from now

243

we might as well throw in the towel and go away and see what we could do next.

Get drunk, most likely.

Five minutes before he was due to come by for the third time, the mob arrived. A black limousine came up Central Park West and pulled to a stop in the entrance to the roadway. Gray police sawhorses blocked the road to automobiles this afternoon, and the limousine stopped broadside to the sawhorses, out of the way of northbound Central Park West traffic. Nothing happened for a few seconds, and then the rear door opened and four people got out; two men and two women. None of them looked like the kind of people who normally travel around in limousines. Also, the general practice with limousines is that the chauffeur gets out and opens the door for the passengers, but this time the chauffeur stayed behind the wheel.

A man came out first. He was stocky and tough-looking, and despite the heat of the day he was wearing a light zippered jacket closed about halfway up. He looked around warily and cautiously, and then motioned for the other people to come out.

The two women appeared. They were both in their twenties, both a little too full in hip and breast, both wearing plaid slacks and ordinary blouses, both in full night-style make-up, and both with big bouffant hairdos. One of them was chewing gum. They stood around like collies waiting their turn to appear at a dog show, and the other man came out of the car after them.

He was the one. He looked like the first guy, and he too wore a half-zippered jacket, but the important part was that he was carrying the picnic basket. From the way he held it, the thing was heavier than hell.

Let it be full of the real thing, I thought. Let them not try that kind of fast one, I don't want to have to go through this twice.

The four of them made very unlikely picnickers. There didn't seem to be any coherent connection among them; the men didn't hold the women's hands or elbows, and there wasn't any conversation back and forth. Nor could you figure out which woman was supposed to be with which man. The four of them seemed as arbitrarily joined together as four strangers in an elevator.

They walked off in a group into the park, the second man struggling with the heavy picnic basket. They disappeared from sight, but the limousine stayed where it was. Thin exhaust showed from the tailpipe.

I took the newspaper off my lap and tossed it down to the other end of the bench. In less than a minute a thin old fellow came along and picked it up and walked off with it, reading the stock reports.

Joe came by right on schedule. I didn't look directly at him, but I knew he would see that I didn't have the paper in my lap any more. That was the signal. He would dope out for himself what the limousine meant, parked sideways in the entrance.

After Joe passed, I got to my feet and walked on into the park. Strolling down the asphalt path, I saw the four picnickers sitting in a bunch down near the traffic light on the interior road, where I'd said they should be. They had the picnic basket on the ground and they were sitting in a tight circle around it. They weren't talking among themselves, they were all facing and concentrating outward, not even pretending to have a picnic together. They looked like Conestoga wagons waiting for Indians.

Vigano would have other people in the area, to guard the basket and try to keep us from going away with it. Walking around, I spotted four of them, guys sitting or standing at strategic locations where they could watch the picnickers. There'd be more of them, I was sure of that, but four was all I'd seen so far.

245

I'd probably see more later, whether I wanted to or not.

I kept an eye on my watch. It would take Joe a while to get into position. At the right time, I walked forward across the grass and down a gentle slope toward the picnickers.

They watched me coming. The one who'd first gotten out of the car put his hand inside his half-open jacket.

I walked up to them. I had a smile tacked to my face, as phony as the moustache. I hunkered down in front of the first man and said, quietly, "I'm Mr. Kopp."

He had the eyes of a dead fish. He studied me with them and said, "Where's your stuff?"

"Coming," I said. "But first I'm going to reach into the basket and take some bills out."

His expression didn't change. He said, "Who says?" Both women and the other man kept looking away from us, outward; watching for Indians.

I said, "I have to check them out. Just a few."

He was thinking it over. I glanced away to my left and saw one of the guys I'd spotted earlier, and he was closer now. He wasn't moving at the moment, but he was closer.

"Why?"

I looked back at him. The question had been asked in a flat tone, as though he were a computer instead of a man, and his face was still expressionless. I said, "You know I'm not going to make the deal until I know for sure what you've got in that basket."

"We have what you want."

"I'll have to check it out for myself."

The other man turned his head and looked at me. Then he faced outward again and said, "Let him."

The first man nodded. His fish eyes kept watching me. He said, "Go ahead. A few."

"Fine," I said. As I leaned forward to reach into the basket, I looked down the road. Joe was due about now.

246

• Joe •

I LET Tom off at Columbus Avenue and 85th Street, went on up to 90th, made a right turn, and headed over to Central Park West. Then I turned south, and drove slowly down alongside the park to consider the situation.

Everything looked normal, as far as I could see. I didn't believe it, but that was the way it looked. There's a long oval road called the Drive that goes all the way around inside the park, and every entrance to it that I saw was blocked with gray Police Department sawhorses; the usual

247

thing for a Tuesday afternoon. People with bicycles were going in past the sawhorses, and wherever I could catch a glimpse of the Drive inside the park it was full of bicycles sailing by. Nobody I saw had a sign on his back that read *Mafia.*

It took twenty minutes to go down to 61st Street and then come back up again, and when I went past 85th Street it was fine by me that Tom was still sitting there with the newspaper in his lap. I wasn't ready to leap into action just yet. To tell the truth, I was getting a late case of cold feet.

Maybe it was because everything looked so peaceful. When we'd gone up against the brokerage, there had been people around with uniforms and guns, there'd been closed-circuit television and locked doors to go through and all kinds of things to pit ourselves against. But here there was nothing, just a peaceful afternoon in the park, summer sunshine everywhere, people riding bicycles or pushing baby carriages or just lying on the grass with a paperback book. And yet this was a much tougher situation; the people we were up against were meaner, and we were pretty sure they were out to kill us, and they knew we were coming.

So where were they?

Around; that much I could be sure of. Since I'm on the uniformed force I haven't had much to do with stakeouts, but I know from Tom that it's possible to flood an area with plainsclothesmen and not have anything look out of the ordinary at all. And if the Police Department could do it, the mob could do it.

I was supposed to check with Tom every fifteen minutes, so after I saw him I headed over to Broadway and farted around there for a little while. Ran my beat, in fact. I was on duty at the moment, which was the simple straightforward way I'd gotten hold of a car this time. It had turned out Lou had a girl friend that went to Columbia and lived up near the campus and didn't have any classes on Tuesday afternoons. So for the last three weeks I'd been giving him a couple hours to shack up with her; drop him off at her place, pick him up later. It was an established pattern now, nothing out of the ordinary, and it gave me a couple of hours alone with the car; with the numbers changed again.

Fifteen minutes. I went back over to the park, passed by Tom again, and he still had the newspaper in his lap.

This time, I didn't like it. I was still nervous, I still had cold feet, but my reaction when I'm scared of something is that I want to get it done and over with. No stalling around, building it up, making myself even more nervous than I was already.

Come on, Vigano. Make your play, let's do something.

Because of my nerves, my driving was getting bad. A couple times, if I'd been in a civilian car I would have racked it up for sure; but people pay more attention to police cars, so they saw me in time to get out of the way. But that's all I needed, was to be involved in some fender-bumping argument over on Columbus Avenue while Tom was making contact in the park; so after the second trip past him I didn't do much driving at all, just pulled in next to a hydrant on 86th to wait the fifteen minutes out.

I had the radio on, listening to the dispatcher, though I don't know why. I sure wasn't going to respond to any squeals, not now. Maybe I was listening for something to tell me the whole thing was off, we'd blown it and could go home and forget the whole thing.

In the back seat, directly behind me, was the picnic basket. It was half full of old copies of the *Daily News*. On top we'd scattered some fake diplomas and gag stock certificates we'd picked up in a novelty shop on Times Square. They ought to look good enough for a fast peek, which is all we meant to give the other side before we made our play. If things worked out right.

Fifteen minutes. I pulled away from the hydrant, made a loop around, and passed Tom again, and he didn't have the newspaper on his lap any more.

All of a sudden I had a balled-up wet wool overcoat in my stomach. I was blinking like a hophead, I could barely make out the numbers and the hands on my watch when I raised my arm in front of my face to check the time. Three thirty-five. All right. All right.

I drove up to 96th Street, the next entrance to the Drive. I stopped with the nose of the car against one of the sawhorses blocking the road, and stumbled and almost fell on my face getting out from behind the wheel. I walked around to the front of the car, lifted one end of the sawhorse, and swung it out of the way. Then I drove through, put the sawhorse back, and angled the car slowly down the entrance road to the Drive.

I was in the only kind of vehicle that could come into the park on a Tuesday afternoon. That was the edge we had; we could drive, and the mob had to walk.

I stopped by the Drive and checked my watch again, and I had three minutes before I should start to move. Tom needed time to make contact.

Bicycles streamed by me, heading south, the same direction I would go. There's no law about it, but most people who ride bicycles in the park treat the Drive as a counterclockwise one-way street, the way it is the rest of the week for cars. Every once in a while somebody would come up in the other direction like a salmon going upstream—usually it was a teen-ager—but most of the traffic was southbound. Even the women pushing baby carriages were all heading south.

250

I didn't want any shooting in here today. Aside from what would happen to Tom and me, they could really rack up a score on women and children.

Time. I shifted into drive and joined the stream of bicycles and matched their pace on down toward Tom.

· 17 ·

THEY HAD rehearsed this, they'd gone through it over and over again, they both knew their parts; and still, when Tom looked up from the picnic basket and saw the police car threading its way toward him through the bicycles, he was amazed at the relief he felt. Now that Joe was actually here, Tom could admit to himself the fear he'd been carrying in the back of his mind that for one reason or another Joe would fail to show up.

Joe hadn't had that worry about Tom. The only unacknowledged fear he'd been ignoring was that Tom would already be dead before the patrol car got there. Seeing Tom alive relieved Joe's mind a little, but not much; they were still just at the beginning of this ride.

Joe eased the car to a stop near the picnickers. Tom had half a dozen bills from the basket clenched in his right fist, taken from the top and the middle and the bottom—they didn't want the fakery with old newspapers done right back at them—and now he said to the picnickers, "Take it easy. I'll be right back."

They didn't like it. They were looking at the patrol car and at each other and up the hill toward their friends. They obviously hadn't figured on the patrol car, and it was making them upset. The first man, with his hand still inside his jacket, said, "You better move very slow."

"Oh, I will," Tom said. "And when your hand comes out from under there, it better move slow, too. My friend sometimes gets nervous."

"He's got reason," the picnicker said.

Tom got to his feet and walked slowly over to the patrol car, coming up to it on the right side. The passenger window was open. He bent to put his elbows on the sill, hands and forearms inside the car. A nervous grin flickering on his face, he said, "Welcome to the party."

Joe was looking past him at the picnickers, watching their tense faces. He looked tense himself, the muscles bunched like a lumpy mattress along the sides of his jaw. He said, "How we doing?"

Tom dropped the handful of bills onto the seat. "I spotted five guys so far," he said. "There's probably more."

Reaching for the microphone, Joe said, "They really don't want us to get paid."

"If there's enough of them," Tom said, "we're fucked."

Into the microphone Joe said, "Six six." To Tom he said, "That's the chance we took. We worked it out."

253

"I know," Tom said. He rubbed perspiration from his forehead onto the back of his hand, and from there to his trouser leg. Half-turning, staying bent, keeping one elbow on the windowsill, he looked around at the sunny day and said, "Christ, I wish it was over."

"Me, too." Joe was blinking again, having trouble seeing things. Into the microphone, he said, "Six six."

The radio suddenly said, "Yeah, six six, go ahead."

Picking up the money from the seat, Joe said, "I got some bills for you to check out."

"Okay, go ahead."

Joe held one of the bills close to his face, and squinted so he could read the serial number. "This one's a twenty," he said. "B-five-five-eight-seven-five-three-five-A."

The radio read the number back again.

"Check," Joe said. "Another twenty." He read off the number, listened to it repeated, and then did the same thing with a third bill, a fifty.

"Give me a minute," the radio said.

Tom muttered, "If we have a minute."

Joe put the microphone away under the dashboard and held one of the bills up by the open window to study it with the light behind it. Squinting at it, focusing with difficulty, he said, "Looks okay to me. What do you think?"

The grin twitched on Tom's face again. "I was too nervous to look," he said, and reached into the car to pick up one of the bills from the seat. He studied it, felt the paper between thumb and first finger, tried to remember the signs of a phony bill. Over on his side of the car, Joe was checking another of the bills, seeing this one a little more easily; he was beginning to settle down, now that something was happening.

"I guess it's all right," Tom said. Irritably he tossed the bill back on the seat. "What's taking him so long?"

254

Joe dropped the bill and rubbed his eyes, then said, "Go talk to the people."

Tom frowned at him. "Are you really as cool as all that, or is it bullshit?"

"It's bullshit," Joe said. "But it'll do."

Tom's grin turned a little sickly. "I'll be back," he said, and left the car, and walked over again to the picnickers, who were watching him with great suspicion. He hunkered down where he'd been before, and talked directly to the first man, who seemed to be the leader of the group. He said, "I'll be going back over by the car. When I give a signal, one of you carry the basket over there."

The first man said, "Where's the trade?"

"The other basket's in the car," Tom said. "We'll do the switch there. But only one of you come over, the rest stay right here."

The first man said, "We've got to look it over."

"Sure," Tom said. "You bring the basket, you get in the car, you check the other one, you get out again."

The second man spoke up, saying, "In the car?" He frowned at his friend, not liking that.

Tom said, "Let's not make it any more public than we have to." Which was an argument they should appreciate.

They did. The first man said to the second, "It's all right. It's better inside."

"Sure," Tom said. "You stick tight, I'll let you know when." He got to his feet, trying to look nonchalant and sure of himself, and walked back over to the car. Leaning in again, he said, "Anything yet?"

Joe was twitching like a wind-up doll. Waiting was the worst thing in the world for him. "No," he said. "How's it going?"

"I don't know," Tom said. "Their friends haven't come down from the hills yet, so I guess we're still ahead."

255

"Maybe," Joe said, as the radio suddenly said, "Six six."

They both started; as though they hadn't been expecting that sound. Joe grabbed the microphone and said, "Yeah, six six."

"On those bills," the radio said. "They're clean."

Joe's face suddenly opened into a big wide smile. It was going to be all right, he all at once knew that as a positive certainty. "Okay," he said into the microphone. "Thanks." Putting the microphone away, he turned and gave Tom the big smile and said, "We go."

Tom hadn't been affected the same way. The fact that the money was real just confirmed for him the knowledge that the mob was out to kill them. Counterfeit money or stolen money with traceable numbers might have meant the mob would be content merely to cheat them, but real money meant their lives were definitely at stake. Having trouble breathing, Tom responded to Joe's big smile with a small nervous grimace, and then turned away to make a little waving gesture toward the picnickers.

The women over there were looking a little green, as though the situation had become trickier than they'd been led to believe. They were sitting staring outward, waiting for disaster to strike or relief to come at last. The two men looked at one another, and the first man nodded. The second one got reluctantly to his feet, picked up the basket, and carried it toward the car.

It took him forever to make the trip. Joe kept staring across the car and out the open side window at him, willing him to move faster. Tom watched the slope up toward Central Park West; three of the guys he'd spotted before were clustered together up there now, talking things over. They seemed excited. Was that a small walkie-talkie one of them had in his hand?

"They've got an army," Tom said. All at once, he saw

256

how hopeless it was; the two of them against an army, with army equipment and an army disregard for life.

Joe ducked his head, trying to see Tom's face. "What?"

The guy with the picnic basket was too close. Tom said, "Nothing. Here he comes."

"I see him."

Nervousness could have made both of them irritable right then. If it hadn't been for the pressure of what else they were doing, they could have turned on each other instead, bickering and snarling like a couple of dogs in a vacant lot.

The guy with the basket reached the car. Tom opened the rear door, and saw the guy's face register that he'd seen the other basket in there. But he didn't make a move to enter.

"Get in," Tom said. Up the slope, one of the trio was using the walkie-talkie.

"Tell your friend to open the basket. Lift the lid."

"For Christ's sake," Tom said, and called in to Joe, "Did you hear him?"

Joe was already twisting around in the seat, reaching over the back of it for the basket. "I heard him," he said, and lifted the lid. The gag certificates with their fancy designs showed indistinctly in the shadows.

The men up the hill were moving this way; casually, not hurrying yet. Some other men were also strolling this way from other directions. Tom, trying to keep his voice calm and assured, said, "You satisfied now?"

For answer, the guy shoved his basket ahead of himself onto the back seat, and immediately slid in after it, reaching across it toward the other basket to get a closer look at the papers in there.

Tom slapped the door shut, pulled the front door open, and slid in. "They're coming," he said.

Joe already knew that; there were more of them coming up from the other side of the road, he could see them through the bicycle riders. He had the car in gear already, and at once they rolled forward.

The guy in the back seat yelled, "Hey!"

Tom's hand patted the seat between himself and Joe, found the .32 there where it was supposed to be, and came up with it. Turning in his seat, seeing the guy back there reaching into his jacket, Tom laid the pistol atop the seat-back, aiming at the guy's head. "Take it easy," he said.

• Vigano •

VIGANO SAT in an office on Madison Avenue with an absolutely clean phone; guaranteed. He had an open line to a pay phone on the corner of 86th Street and Central Park West, across the street from the park. He had a man in the booth, pumping change in, keeping the line open. A second man, outside the booth with a small walkie-talkie no bigger than a pack of cigarettes, was the relay between Vigano and the one hundred and eleven men he had scattered in and around the park. From the phone to the walkie-talkie, he could get an order to any man in the park in less than half a minute.

Aside from the transverse roads, the ones that simply cross the park and don't connect with the interior road, there are twenty-six entrances to and exits from the Drive. Every one of them was covered, with either one or two cars, and a minimum of three men; including the one-way entrances that no vehicle was supposed to use in leaving the park, such as the one at Sixth Avenue and 59th Street and the one at Seventh Avenue and West 110th. His people with the two million dollars in the picnic basket were completely surrounded by Vigano's men, and six others roamed the general vicinity on bicycles. If the two amateurs with the bearer bonds tried to get away by bicycle they'd be stopped at a park exit. If they tried to cut across the park on foot they wouldn't get twenty yards.

Vigano had the interior people all in position before the basket was delivered, but he held off blocking the park exits until after contact was made with the amateurs; no point scaring them off. He had a conference call hook-up on the phone, so that it broadcast into the room and he could reply without holding the speaker to his mouth, and he sat back in the desk chair, his hands up behind his head, and smiled at the thought that he was the spider, and his web was out, and the flies were on their way.

"One man," the speaker-phone said.

Vigano frowned and sat forward in the chair, bringing his hands down to rest on the empty desk. Over on the sofa, Andy and Mike looked alert. Vigano said, "What's that?"

"One man, civilian clothing, has approached our people."

Just one? Move the cars into position now, or wait for the other one? "What's happening?"

Silence for nearly a minute. Vigano frowned at the phone, feeling tense even though he knew everything had to be all right. But he didn't want anything unexpected now; if he lost that two million, it would be his head.

He wouldn't lose it.

"Mr. Vigano?"

Vigano gave the phone an angry look. Who else would it be? He said, "What's going on?"

"It's one of them all right. He's taken some of the money out of the—Hold on a second."

"Took some money? What the hell are you talking about?"

Nothing. Andy and Mike were both looking as though they wanted to find something cheerful to say, but they'd damn well better keep their mouths shut.

"Mr. Vigano?"

"Just talk, I'm not going anywhere."

"Yes, sir. The other one showed up, in a police car."

"A what? In the park?"

"Yes, sir. In uniform, in a police car."

"Son of a bitch," Vigano said. Now that he knew what was going on, he felt better. Giving Andy and Mike a tight grin, he said, "I told you they were cute." He turned back to the phone: "Move the cars in. Don't change anything, do it all like we figured."

"Yes, sir."

Andy got to his feet in a sudden motion, betraying the nervousness he'd been covering up. He said, "They must really be cops."

"Probably." Vigano felt grim, but confident.

"How do we stop cops?" Andy spread his hands, looking bewildered. "What if they just drive out of the park, order our people to move over?"

Mike said, "We can follow them, take care of them some place quieter."

"No," Vigano said. "There's too many ways to lose them outside. We finish it in the park."

261

Mike said, "Against cops?"

"They're just men," Vigano said. "They wipe themselves like anybody else. And they can't call their brother cops to come help them, not with two million bucks in the car."

"So what do we do?" Mike said, and at the same instant the phone said, "Everybody's set, Mr. Vigano."

"Listen," Vigano told Mike. He said to the phone, "Spread the word. They stay in the park. If they try to get out, we can force them to stop at our cars. When they do, kill them, take our goods, clear out."

"Yes, sir."

"Hold on, there's more. If they don't try to leave the park, we just keep them bottled up until the park is opened to cars. Then we drive in, surround them, finish it the same way."

"Yes, sir."

"The main point is, they don't leave the park."

"Yes, sir."

Vigano leaned back again, smiled at Andy and Mike, and said, "See? They're cute, but we've got everything covered."

Andy and Mike both grinned, and Andy said, "They've got a surprise coming."

"That's just what they have," Vigano said.

Nobody said anything after that for a minute or two, until the phone suddenly said, in an excited voice, "Mr. Vigano!"

"What?"

"They're crossing us! They took off with our goods and didn't leave anything! And they've got Bristol with them in the car."

"He's gone over to them?" That didn't sound right; the people to carry the money had been very carefully selected.

"No, sir. They must have pulled a gun on him."

"They're headed south?"

262

"Yes, sir."

Vigano squinted, visualizing the park. If they'd come in to try a double cross, they had to have some method for getting away again. Where would it be? Vigano said, "Cover the transverse roads. They might decide to cut across the grass and out that way."

"Yes, sir."

"Pass that one on."

While the man was gone from the phone, Vigano kept thinking. How fast would a car move, surrounded by bicycles? It was no good settling for holding them in the park now; they had to be stopped, as quick as possible.

"Mr. Vigano?"

"All spare men," Vigano said, "get over to the section of the Drive on the east side, just south of the bridge over the first transverse road. Block the road there. Don't let them through, finish them off."

"Yes, sir."

"Move!"

Andy and Mike were both leaning on the desk, giving him worried looks. Andy said, "What's going on?"

"They're starting from 85th Street," Vigano said, "going south. The Drive takes them down to 59th, and then across the bottom of the park. They can't move fast, not with all those bikes. Our people get over to the east side of the park first, block the road there. If they try to get out before then, they're stopped. If they last that long, they're stopped."

"Good," Andy said. "That's good."

"They've been cute for the last time," Vigano said.

· 18 ·

THEY WERE in motion. Joe faced front, steering the patrol car southward along the Drive, while Tom faced the rear, holding the .32 aimed at the guy in the back seat.

Joe tapped over and over on the horn, and ahead of him the bicyclists reluctantly got out of the way, their front wheels waggling back and forth as they glared at the automobile immorally in here during their special time.

From left and right, as they started away, they could see men running after them. There weren't any guns in plain

264

sight yet, but there might be any second. The other male picnicker was running along in their wake, leaving the two women sitting on the grass behind him, looking stunned.

They'd only been moving ten seconds or so. To both of them, every instant now seemed a distinct and separate thing, as though they were working in slow motion.

Tom said to the guy in the back seat, "You've got a gun under there. Take it out slowly, by the butt, with your thumb and first finger, and hold it up in the air in front of you."

The guy said, "What's the point in all this? We're making the payoff."

"That's right," Tom said. "And all your friends were here because they like fresh air. Take the gun out the way I said and hold it up in the air."

The guy shrugged. "You're making a big thing over nothing," he said. But he pulled a Firearms International .38 automatic from under his jacket and held it up in front of himself like a dead fish.

Tom switched his own pistol to his left hand, and took the automatic away with his right. He dropped that on the seat, switched the pistol back to his right hand again and, still watching his prisoner, said to Joe, "How we doing?"

"Beautiful," Joe said grimly. By keeping up almost a steady honking, he was managing to get bicycles and baby carriages out of his path without running over anybody, and was up to maybe twenty miles an hour; twice as fast as the general flow of bicycle traffic, and four times as fast as the men chasing them on foot.

The 77th Street exit was a little ways ahead. They couldn't afford to stop and unload their passenger until they got out and away from the park, but that shouldn't be long now.

Joe started the turn, seeing the sawhorses down at the other end of the feeder road, and just in the nick of time

265

he saw the green Chevvy and the pale blue Pontiac across the road, just beyond the sawhorses. Three men were standing in front of the Chevvy, looking this way.

Joe hit the brakes. Tom, startled but not looking away from the guy in the back seat, said, "What's the matter?"

"They got us blocked."

Tom snapped his head forward and back, taking a quick look out the windshield. The patrol car was stopped, cyclists were streaming by on both sides of it. They couldn't stay here. "Try another one," Tom said. "We can't get through there."

"I know, I know." Joe was twisting the wheel, tapping the accelerator, leaning on the horn. They slid away from that exit and headed south again, hurrying through the cyclists.

Both of them—Tom by looking out the back window and Joe by looking at the rear-view mirror—saw the three men who'd been standing by the Chevvy suddenly run around the end of the sawhorses and come trotting after the patrol car. They couldn't catch up, obviously, but that didn't mean much; they acted as though they knew what they were doing. Tom remembered the walkie-talkie one of them had carried back by the picnickers, and the army imagery seemed stronger than ever all of a sudden; they must have a central-command post somewhere, with men reporting in from all around the park.

If there'd been a way to call the whole thing off, Tom would have done it right then and there. Just give it up, forget it, make believe none of it had ever happened. As far as he was concerned, they'd had it, they were defeated already, and only going on because there wasn't anything else to do.

But not Joe. His sense of combat had been aroused, he was feeling nothing but the warring instinct. As a little kid, his comic-book hero had been Captain America; shield and fist against entire swarming armies of the enemy, and

266

he won out every time. Joe hunched over the steering wheel, weaving the car through all the people with small taps on the accelerator, tiny shifts of the wheel, steady pushing at the horn, feeling himself the master of his machine in a slow-motion Indy 500.

It was almost no time at all to the next exit at 72nd Street, even at these slow speeds. Joe felt no surprise, only a sense of grim determination, when he saw the two cars parked broadside beyond the sawhorses. "That one, too," he said, and swung away, still heading south.

Tom turned his head to the left and saw the blocked exit. Grimacing, staring at the guy in the back seat again, he said to Joe, "Then they're all blocked."

"I know," Joe said.

The guy in the back seat grinned a little, nodding. "That's right," he said. "Give it up. What's the point?"

Tom's mind was scrambling. He was sure they were going down in defeat, but he'd keep bobbing and weaving all the way to the bottom. "We can't just drive around," he said. "We've got to get out of here."

Frustration was making Joe angry; things were supposed to work differently from this. Thumping a fist against the steering wheel, he said, "What the hell do we do now?"

The guy in the back seat finally reached into the other basket, and pulled out a handful of phony stock certificates and pieces of newspaper. He looked surprised for just a second, then held the papers up, gave Tom a pitying grin, and said, "You two are really stupid. I just can't believe how stupid you are."

"You shut your face," Tom said.

Joe abruptly slammed on the brakes. "Get him out," he said. "Get him out or shoot him."

Tom gestured with the gun. "Out."

The guy pushed open the door, making a passing cyclist wobble onto the grass to avoid an accident. "You're all through," the guy told them, and slid out of the car, and Joe hit the accelerator while he was still departing. The door, snapping shut, nicked him on the left elbow, and Tom saw him wince and grab the elbow and trot away toward Central Park West.

Tom faced front. Fifty-ninth Street was just ahead of them, with the spur road angling off toward Columbus Circle. Cars there, too.

"There's got to be a way out," Joe said. He was clutching the steering wheel hard enough to bend it. He was enraged and bewildered because he was the hero of his life, and the hero always has a way out.

"Keep rolling," Tom said. He expected nothing any more, but as long as they were moving it hadn't ended yet.

They swept around the curve at the southern tip of the park, the car moving through the cyclists like a whale through trout. They passed the Seventh Avenue turnoff and there were cars out there, too, but they expected that by now.

The Sixth Avenue entrance was ahead of them, on the right. Sixth Avenue is one-way, leading uptown toward the park, so there's no automobile exit there, just an entrance. It was blocked anyway, with two cars parked across it.

The Drive was curving again, leftward, starting up the other side of the park. The Sixth Avenue entrance angled in ahead of them on the right. Farther along, up by the bridge, they both suddenly saw maybe fifteen or twenty men, standing around in the roadway.

Just standing around. Some with bicycles, some not. Talking together, in little groups. Leaving enough room between them for bicycles to get through, but not enough for a car.

"God damn it," Joe said.

"They blocked—" Tom stopped, and just stared.

It wasn't any good. Run those people down and it

wouldn't be the mob they had to worry about any more, it would be their own kind that would get them. The park would fill up with law in nothing flat.

But they couldn't stop.

Joe hunched lower over the wheel. "Hold tight," he said.

Tom stared at him. He wasn't going to plow through those guys anyway, was he? "What are you going to do?"

"Just hold tight."

The Sixth Avenue entrance was right there, the long approach road curving back southward to the edge of the park. Suddenly Joe yanked the wheel hard right; they climbed a curb, cut across grass, bounced down over another curb, and were headed toward Sixth Avenue, due south, with Joe's foot flat on the accelerator.

Tom yelled, "Jesus Christ!"

"Siren," Joe shouted. "Siren and light."

Pop-eyed, staring out the windshield, Tom felt on the dashboard for the familiar switches, hit them, and heard the growl of the siren start to build.

The patrol car lunged at the sawhorses, and at the two cars parked sideways beyond them. They blocked the road from curb to curb.

But they didn't block the sidewalk. Siren howling, red light flashing, the car raced at the roadblock, and at the last second Joe spun the wheel leftward and they vaulted over the curb, slicing through between the blockage and the stone park wall.

"Move!" Joe yelled at the people running every which way on the sidewalk. Even Tom couldn't hear him, with the siren screaming, but the people moved, diving left and right, yanking themselves out of the way by their own shirt collars. Traffic going east and west on 59th Street abruptly jammed up as though they'd hit a wall, opening a line across like the path through the Red Sea. The hoods

269

at the roadblock were clambering into their cars to give chase, and the patrol car wasn't even past them yet.

Lamp post. They shot across the sidewalk, Joe nudged the wheel a bit to the right, and they flicked by between the post and one of the parked cars. They both felt the jolt when the right rear of their car kissed off the bumper of the other; and then they were through.

And Joe headed straight south. Tom threw his hands up in the air and screamed at the top of his voice, *"Holy jumping Jesus!"*

Sixth Avenue is one-way north, and five lanes wide. The patrol car was heading south, and three blocks ahead was a phalanx of traffic spread completely across the avenue, coming this way, moving along at about twenty-five miles an hour, following the sequence of the staggered green lights. They covered the road from left to right, they were coming in a tight mass like a cattle drive, and Tom and Joe were tearing toward them at about sixty, and accelerating every second.

Joe was driving one-handed, waving the other hand at the oncoming traffic, yelling at them under the siren, while Tom pressed against the seatback and braced the heels of his hands against the dashboard, and just stared.

Cabs and cars and trucks down there veered left and right as though an atomic bomb had just gone off in Central Park. Cars climbed the sidewalks, they practically climbed each other's shoulders, they went tearing away down side-streets, and hid behind parked buses, and jaywalkers ran for their lives. A lane opened up down the middle of the street, and the patrol car went down it like a bullet through a rifle barrel. Open-mouthed drivers flashed by in cars on both sides. Joe wriggled and squiggled the wheel and tight-roped past taxi bumpers and the jutting tails of trucks.

Elation suddenly grabbed Tom and lifted him up into

270

the sky. Still bracing himself with one hand, he pounded his other fist on top of the dashboard and yelled, "Yeah!! Yeah! Yeah!"

Joe was grinning so hard he looked as though he was imitating all those automobile grilles out front. He was practically lying on top of the steering wheel, hunched around it so tight he was driving as much with his shoulders as with his hands. He was concentrating like a pinball player on a streak, goosing the ball past all the dangers toward the big winner.

Three blocks, four blocks, and they were out of that swarm, with the next bunch half a dozen blocks ahead, coming up with the next traffic-light sequence. "Siren and light off!" Joe yelled. He couldn't be heard, so he pounded Tom's leg, and jammed a finger toward the switches, simultaneously making a screaming two-wheel left turn onto West 54th Street.

Tom hit the switches as they shot around the turn, and then braced himself again, because Joe was standing on the brake with both feet. He brought them down to about twenty, and they rolled the rest of the way to the traffic waiting for the light at Fifth Avenue, and came to a gentle stop behind a garment delivery truck.

They grinned at one another. They were both shaking like a leaf. Tom said, with both admiration and terror, "You're a madman. You're a complete madman."

"And that," Joe said, "is how you don't get followed."

· 19 ·

THEY BOTH had day shift, so they were with the rush-hour
traffic again on the Long Island Expressway, heading toward the city. Joe was driving, and Tom was beside him,
reading the *News*.

This was about a week after the business in the park.
When they'd gotten the picnic basket home that night,
they'd found it had the full two million dollars in it, to
the penny. They'd split it down the middle, and each of
them had taken his share for safekeeping. Tom put his in

a canvas bag he'd once kept gym equipment in, and locked it away in a cabinet behind the bar in his basement. Joe put his in the blue plastic laundry bag they'd used during the bond robbery, moved his pool filter (which was on the fritz once more), dug a hole under it, put the bag in the hole, filled it up again, and put the filter back on top.

The main result of the activity in the park was a notice on the bulletin boards in all the Manhattan precinct houses, a couple days later, urging caution if anybody ever had to travel the wrong way on a one-way street. The Department surely would have liked to find out who had done that stuntman number on Sixth Avenue, but there was no way they were going to do it, and they probably didn't even try.

They'd been sitting there in Joe's Plymouth in silence for a pretty long while, inching along in stop-and-go traffic, when Tom suddenly sat up and said, "Hey, look at this."

Joe glanced at him. "What?"

Tom was staring at the newspaper. "Vigano's dead," he said.

Joe glanced at him. "What?"

Tom was staring at the newspaper. "Vigano's dead," he said.

"No shit." Joe faced front again, and moved the Plymouth forward a little bit. "Read it to me."

"Uhh. Crime kingpin Anthony Vigano, long reputed to be an important member of the Joseph Scaracci Mafia family in New Jersey, was shot to death at ten forty-five yesterday evening as he emerged from Jimmy's Home Italian Restaurant in Bayonne. The killing, which Bayonne police say bears all the earmarks of a gang-type slaying, was done by an unidentified man who stepped from an automobile parked in front of the restaurant, shot Vigano twice in the head, and left in the automobile. Police are also seeking the two men who had been with Vigano in the

273

restaurant and who left with him but who had disappeared before police reached the scene. Vigano, who was still alive when the first police officers responded to a call from the restaurant owner, Salvatore "Jimmy" Iacocca, died in the ambulance en route to Bayonne Memorial Hospital. Vigano, fifty-seven, first attracted the attention of the police in nineteen—uhh, the rest is all biography."

"Is there a picture?"

"Just of the restaurant. A white X where he got it."

Joe nodded. A small smile of satisfaction was on his face. "You know what that means, don't you?"

"He lost the mob's two million dollars," Tom said, "and they didn't like it."

"Besides that."

"What else?"

"They can't find us," Joe said. "They've tried, and they can't do it, and they gave up."

"The mob doesn't give up," Tom said.

"Bullshit. Everybody gives up, if there's nothing left to do. If they thought they could still find us and get the money back, they wouldn't kill Vigano. They'd let him keep looking." Joe gave Tom a big smile and said, "We're free and clear, buddy, that's what that thing in the paper means."

Tom frowned at the newspaper report, thinking it over, and gradually he too began to smile. "I guess so," he said. "I guess we are."

"Fucking A well told," said Joe.

They rode along in silence again for a while, both of them thinking about the future. A little later, Joe glanced toward Tom, and beyond him he saw the next car over, stopped like they were, and it was a gray Jaguar sedan, one of the big ones. The windows were rolled up, and the middle-aged guy inside there was neat and cool in his suit and tie. As Joe looked at him, the guy in the Jaguar turned

274

his own head, met Joe's eye, and gave him that quick meaningless smile that people invariably flash when they cross glances with somebody in another car. Then he faced front again.

Joe smiled back at him, but with something savage in it. "That's right, you bastard, smile," he said to the Jaguar driver's profile. "Six months from now you're going to be six months closer to your coronary, and I'm going to be in Saskatchewan."

Tom looked at Joe while he was talking, puzzled; then turned and saw the Jaguar driver and understood. The surf on a beach in Trinidad crashed lazily in his mind, and he smiled.

It was going to be a hot day. They sat there in the car, their elbows out the open windows, reaching for a little breeze. Endless stalled traffic stretched away into the hazy distance, and far away they could just make out the scum-covered smoky island of Manhattan, squatting there like that portion of Hell zoned industrial.

The car in front of them moved a little.